MILO'S
BRAIN
AND 9 OTHER COMPELLING
SHORT STORIES

RAY GERRING

All names in this book are fictional. Similarities to actual persons are purely coincidental.

Publisher: Ray Gee Books
rjgerring@yahoo.com
ISBN 1979943761

Cover design by the author.

DEDICATION

*I dedicate this book to the best man
I know, my son, Dale Gerring.*

ACKNOWLEDGEMENTS

I owe a heartfelt acknowledgement to my wife June, for her enormous help without which this book would never have been completed. Thank you, sweetheart!

My profound thanks to Liz Martini for her wonderful assistance in creating this book.

Also, my sincere appreciation to Arlene Preskitt for her professional assistance.

Thanks also to Bill Odgers for his support.

CONTENTS

MILO'S BRAIN

Milo Meeker was nervous and couldn't settle down. He didn't know why. He also couldn't figure out what brought him to Magnolia Park where he paced back and forth along the picturesque pathways that ran between giant rhododendron shrubs and the great madrona trees. Located on a high bluff overlooking the imposing Port of Seattle and Elliott Bay, the park afforded a magnificent sweeping view of one of the world's great saltwater harbors. A short (5'-7") man in his mid-fifties, Milo Meeker was dressed for the light drizzle of a typical October afternoon in the Emerald city. A sparse mop of gray hair still survived, a bit of which poked out from under his 1950's style wide brimmed fedora. A look of bewilderment, somewhat modified by a shy smile and a perpetual look of innocence prevailed in his pale blue eyes. His uneasy feelings seemed to cause the beginning of some anxiousness in his stomach as well as a vague nausea. Looking out on the huge bay below, Milo Meeker peered at the water traffic, which included the usual ferries plowing their way across the waterways, connecting the Kitsap peninsula to the

1

west, the islands dotting Elliott Bay and the adjacent Puget Sound commuter destinations. At that moment it happened. A stupendous blast shattered the air. A resounding incredibly loud boom was heard by a startled population in the city and for miles beyond.

Milo stood transfixed in total shock. A state ferry destroyed in a fiery blast? It couldn't happen. It was a dream. It wasn't reality. It was only an absurd illusion. All this raced through Milo's mind. At the same time he imagined a voice calmly telling him that he had foreseen the incident even though he wasn't entirely aware of his premonition. "I must be going off the deep end," he thought as he hurried to his car, anxious to get home.

* * *

"Tragedy on Elliott Bay! The Bainbridge Island ferry Haida destroyed in blast. Over one hundred killed or injured. Terrorism suspected!" The headlines screamed across the local and national media to the horror of Seattle and Washington State residents.

"You've heard the news?" yelled Milo as he threw open his front door. His wife, Veena, materialized at the entrance to the living room.

Standing stiffly with her arms at her sides, she stared teary eyed at her husband and cried, "How could this happen? Has everyone gone completely mad?"

"It's some kind of madness for sure, dear," said Milo, opening his arms to embrace his wife. "Let's sit and try to calm down."

2

Milo and Veena Meeker had enjoyed a happy marriage for a period of ten years after each had endured a few lonely years of young widowhood.

Veena, who worked as an elementary school teacher, came to the US at the age of twelve when her parents emigrated from Lebanon. Milo grew up in West Seattle, a middle-class neighborhood offering spectacular views of Puget Sound and the incomparable sight of the stunning Seattle cityscape across Elliot Bay. Milo grew up to become a hard-working CPA.

Milo had first met Veena at a bridge club a few years after the death of her first husband. On the occasions when she and Milo were teamed as bridge partners, they admired each other's abilities at the card table which resulted in a quiet friendship. Some weeks after first meeting, their friendship had evolved into mutual feelings of respect and genuine affection. Both in their late forties, they understood their good fortune in meeting another person who was compatible, considerate and affectionate. At first, Milo seemed strangely shy, but Veena sensed that he ran deeper intellectually than other men she had known.

After becoming comfortable with Veena, Milo overcame his natural shyness and invited her to accompany him to a stage play of *Death of a Salesman*. At dinner afterward, their analysis and interpretation of the play's commentary on American culture was similar. They both admired the playwright's commentary on the values, ironies and hypocrisy of society. After that first date there were visits to the ballet, the opera, movies, musicals and walks through the park. The attraction between Milo and Veena became even more serious when they became aware of their mutual appreciation for subtle humor.

From her teenage days, men had considered Veena Bizazza, with her dark complexion, even features, large brown eyes and lustrous black hair, to be strikingly pretty. Despite his small stature and quiet nature, Veena developed great respect for Milo's elegant manners, his pleasant disposition, his devotion to his work and his care and concern for her happiness and well-being. Thinking back on their ten years of marriage, they would both agree that it had been an excellent match, filled with a loving regard for each other and happy times.

Now, seated in their conservatively furnished living room, Veena watched nervously as Milo paced back and forth, occasionally glancing out the living room window. A movement outside caught his attention.

"I think I saw Gabe," he said, as he ran out the front door.

Police Captain Gabriel Friedman stood near their mutual property line peering at Milo's rhododendrons. "Your rhodies are coming along nicely, Milo," said his neighbor.

"Gabe," called Milo, "I thought you would be called to duty after what has happened!"

"The department is in a bit of chaos right now. We are calling reserves and rotating assignments to get a handle on things. I'm reporting for a watch command in about an hour. Things are bad right now, Milo."

"I understand, Gabe, it's horrible. Please listen to me; I have something important to tell you."

"You look like you're upset, Milo, what's it about?"

"I was there! I saw the ferry explode. I watched it from the top of the bluff at the park at the very moment it blew up. Not only that, but I knew last night that it was going to happen!"

"What do you mean you knew it would happen?"

"I don't expect you to believe me, Gabe. I'll try to explain it to you later, but right now I think I know where the guys are who did it."

"Milo, are you telling me that you are one of those psychics?"

"No, oh, I don't know," squealed Milo, "but what I'm pretty sure of – is that I am almost positive – that I know where the guys are who bombed the ferry earlier today."

Gabe resisted his inclination to roll his eyes back in his head. "Okay, where exactly are they?"

"They're in a car headed north on I-5, headed for the boat moorage in Bellingham," said Milo. "That's my strong impression. I think there are two men." Milo looked at the ground as he squinted and blinked through his oversized horn-rimmed glasses, then raised his head and murmured, "I think they are driving a beat-up blue pickup truck."

"What else?" asked Gabe grimly.

"I know you are skeptical," said Milo in a meek voice, "but I want you to know that I am not a *putz*, no matter what you are thinking."

Gabe registered astonishment, "How do you know

what I am thinking?"

"It's enough to know that you think of me as a *schlemiel*. That's what's in your mind right now, right? I've always thought of you as a *mensch*, Gabe, a 'good man.'"

"Milo, I apologize for my thoughts. I'm amazed at what you are telling me, but I wouldn't dare rely on this information without some facts to back it up. If I did, I wouldn't be a good cop."

"I would think that in a disastrous situation like this, a good cop would give the benefit of doubt to following every possible lead." Milo kept stern eye contact with the big cop.

His reputation possibly at stake, Gabe glared at Milo, "I'll take your hunch under advisement. Right now I have to get down to headquarters and get to work."

*   *   *

That night Milo slept fitfully. His dreams of late had been memorable, sometimes symbolic and full of familiar characters exhibiting dramatic action such as running, hiding, falling and disappearing for no apparent reason, frequently enveloped in fire or smoke. His dreams tonight were even more intense – frightful nightmares with confusing violent struggles between unidentifiable entities.

*   *   *

After rising early, Milo prepared an omelet for Veena and himself. Arriving at the breakfast table, Veena insisted on watching TV as they ate. The local damage and death toll was even worse than the previous day's reports had indicated. Sipping his coffee, Milo was surprised to hear the phone ring. The clock struck precisely at seven a.m. as Milo, still chewing his toast, choked his hello.

"Mr. Meeker, this is Doctor Claybo. I'm sorry to call so early, but something regarding your brain surgery of last year has come to my attention."

"I'm surprised to hear from you, Doctor," said Milo. "I thought my brain cancer operation was successful."

"Successful is correct, Mr. Meeker, and there is no cause for worry. Recent research has revealed some unsuspected scientific aspects that pertain to your case for which an exam is recommended in the near future. I assure you that there is no need for worry."

"When do you suggest that I come in? How long will it take?"

"Let's say about two hours. Can you come in today?"

"Well, I really don't like to take time off work, maybe later this afternoon...", Milo dithered. "Oh, now that I think about it I can probably get there by three p.m."

"That would be excellent, Milo," said Doctor Claybo, "no charge of course. This time I'm asking for an appointment with you."

After hanging up the phone, Milo could not help feeling a slight twinge of concern about his upcoming appointment. What could the exam this afternoon be about?

* * *

Following his arrival promptly at three p.m., Dr. Claybo's receptionist ushered Milo directly into the doctor's consulting office. Milo was surprised to see, in addition to the doctor, two unfamiliar men who looked to Milo like official types. *What are those two suits doing here?* he wondered.

"So good to see you again, Mr. Meeker," said Dr. Claybo, with apparent sincerity. "I want you to meet Dr. Herman Stanhope, Director of Neurological Research at the University of Washington and Gary Cartright, Assistant Director from the Regional Office of the FBI."

Hiding his surprise, Milo reminded himself to squeeze a little harder on the handshakes than he normally did. As the four men seated themselves at the small conference table, Milo couldn't help noticing that the others had armed themselves with official looking file folders which they carefully placed on the table in front of themselves.

Dr. Claybo spoke, "Mr. Meeker, there are apparently some important things now occurring in which you are involved. Do you know what I am talking about?"

Somewhat bewildered, Milo stared at the three men in turn. Looking intently into Dr. Claybo's eyes, in a low submissive voice, he answered, "I may have an inkling."

Agent Cartright, the FBI man spoke, "I'm sure you recall your conversation yesterday with Captain Friedman, your next-door neighbor."

"Yes, of course," stammered Milo.

"Your description of the pickup truck and the destination of the suspects, resulted in the arrest of two men last night. I must tell you Mr. Meeker that the FBI considers you a person of interest in the matter of the Skoocum ferry bombing yesterday afternoon."

"Good heavens, how could you possibly suspect me? That's preposterous!"

"Then how did you come to have all that information?" Cartright glared accusingly at Milo.

"I honestly don't know how I sensed all that I did. All that stuff just seemed to come to me out of my subconscious mind or somewhere."

"Are you a Muslim?" demanded Cartright.

"Of course not!" replied Milo, indignantly.

"Your wife Veena is from Lebanon. That's an Arab country, right, Milo? May I call you Milo?" Cartright maintained a hard stare.

"Veena's family are Christians," stammered Milo, "There are many Christians who have immigrated from Lebanon and are loyal hardworking Americans. What are you getting at? You guys must be nuts. Go do your job and catch some terrorists."

Milo's defiant words surprised him as much as they did Dr. Claybo, who raised his hand slightly and spoke in an authoritative tone, "Since it was I who arranged this meeting, I must ask that you all listen to me. This meeting is not intended to be an official FBI interrogation. Our intent is to share information for the purpose of unraveling what I believe may be a medical mystery. Mr. Cartright, if you feel that a serious

9

interrogation is called for, you have the authority, I am sure, to drag Mr. Meeker down to FBI headquarters and talk to him there. If so, I will advise him to immediately hire a good attorney. Until then, I strongly suggest that Milo refuse to answer your questions. If you promise not to ask, I will allow you to stay. It is important that you are privy to the medical circumstances that pertain to this situation. I need the cooperation of each one of you. This may be more important than you think."

"Please tell me what is going on," pleaded Milo.

"Listen, all of you," scolded Dr. Claybo. "Last February, I and my surgical team operated on Milo's brain to remove a cancerous growth in an area of the cerebral cortex. For some years before, we had been involved in a brain research project which had to do with extra sensory perception. Scientists have long suspected that modern humans possess latent abilities in such areas as mental communication, so-called second sight and psychic perceptions of some nature. There are those researchers who are certain that primitive man survived because of those abilities which have been lost as a result of behavioral and physical mutations and evolutionary processes that are little understood. The recent acceleration of brain research has encouraged great interest in pursuing more intensive research.

"That's where Dr. Stanhope here comes in. You may not be aware of the fact that he is Chief Administrator of one of the nation's most important brain research centers at the University of Washington, designed to reveal the mysteries of how the brain functions. Because of the rapid progress in magnetic imagery, digital electronics and computer technology, our insight into brain function is rapidly progressing. For example, it is anticipated that in the near future humans will actually be physically and wirelessly connected via computer chips embedded under the skin, directly to the brain. Superior physical and intellectual powers along with self-healing and longer life spans may be on the horizon. Brain research still has quite a ways to go. Dr. Stanhope and his staff of researchers are working very hard at the University and he has recruited some of us brain surgeons to conduct research with our patients to add to his store of knowledge. Milo," said Dr. Claybo, "your involvement in this situation may very possibly be of vital importance."

"Importance for whom?" asked Milo in a voice pitched higher than before.

"Importance to our research," said Dr. Stanhope.

"It also could be very important to the FBI, the United States and to the world," stated agent Cartright, in the unmistakably serious tone of a federal authority figure, a G-Man, no less.

Milo was sure his undersized body was shrinking so much that he might actually disappear.

Dr. Claybo peered intently at Milo, "Have you forgotten our signed agreement regarding last year's surgery in which you gave us permission to open some of the neural pathways to hopefully allow some slight modifications? This might provide some advanced study opportunities into certain aspects of brain research."

Milo blinked, "Research on my brain?"

"From this point on, Milo, you must get used to the idea of working with us, since we think you may have acquired some extrasensory mental abilities which we need to utilize."

"Utilize?" cried Milo. "Have you done something to my brain?"

"As I explained prior to the surgery last year, Milo, our examination of your brain tumor revealed some unique characteristics of great interest to me and the other specialists on my surgical team."

"Unique characteristics?" gurgled Milo.

A silence ensued for a few moments. Dr. Claybo considered his words carefully. "In layman's terms, your brain may be predisposed to accomplishments beyond our ability to explain scientifically. Have you heard of something called 'mental telepathy'? We believe that this sort of ability is developing inside your brain and is manifesting itself in your mental acuity. Think of it as a new gift, Milo, a gift which could be a giant step for science."

"It is also your patriotic duty," interrupted agent Cartright.

"As an invaluable contribution to humanity," added Dr. Stanhope.

Milo sat with his head in his hands. "Can we count on your cooperation, Milo?" asked Dr. Claybo.

*   *   *

At home that evening, Milo struggled to describe his stressful meeting with the three men at Dr. Claybo's office. He was very much aware of his wife's profound interest, as she fixed an intense stare at Milo's face.

"Wait a minute," Veena exclaimed, "those guys are telling you that when they had you on the operating table last year they did some additional surgery?"

"They said I signed a paper agreeing to it. They said my brain had special characteristics that lent itself to some important research that might be of benefit to humanity."

Veena's jaw tightened, "We are going to contact a lawyer tomorrow morning and sue those guys!" Veena's outburst caused Milo to twinge.

He felt a strong urge to urinate, but continued to explain, "Let me tell you the rest. They have contacted my supervisor at Boeing. I'm excused from going to work for the next few days. I'm supposed to work with the FBI."

Veena sucked in her breath, "What for?" she rasped.

"They want me to see the bombing suspects, the terrorists, to try to read their minds or something," stammered Milo.

"Oh my God, Milo, what are they doing to you? What are they doing to us?"

*   *   *

Promptly at seven a.m., Milo climbed into the back seat of the FBI's shiny black Crown Victoria and was transported to the Federal building downtown. Greeted courteously by agent Cartright, he was escorted to a small room featuring a conference table and several chairs lined against the wall. Milo was surprised to see a comfortable lounge chair at one end of the room. Two other men, dressed in the obligatory suit and tie, entered and shook hands with Milo. Their serious demeanor was modified a bit by what seemed to be a genuinely friendly greeting. Cartright introduced Agent Dennis Flood and a University of Washington psychologist, Louis Shah. The men sat as Cartright described the interrogation procedure that would occur in the next hour or so. "Milo, did you remember to bring your sunglasses?" asked Cartright.

"Yes," answered Milo. The two agents left the room leaving Milo alone in the room with the psychologist.

"May I call you Milo?" asked Dr. Shah.

"You may," said Milo, wondering if Dr. Shah, obviously an East Indian, was privy to any special insight or knowledge of mind-brain psychology.

"Are you familiar with meditation?" asked Dr. Shah.

"I know nothing about it," squeaked Milo.

Dr. Shah spoke slowly, "For the next forty-five minutes I want you to follow my instructions. We will be doing some simple relaxation and breathing exercises to calm your mind and sharpen your thinking at the same time. This is to prepare you for the meeting with the two alleged terrorists."

"Okay, I'll do what you say," sighed Milo

Deep breathing instructions ensued followed by a

restful period of relaxation lying on the Barcalounger. Eyes closed, Milo tried his best to calmly connect his conscious mind with what he imagined could be his subconscious, whatever that was. *Was everything in neutral as instructed?* he asked himself.

The two agents entered the room and allowed Milo to stretch and walk around a bit before they escorted him down a hallway to the interrogation room.

Waiting for him were agents Cartright, Flood, Dr. Shah and a young woman in her twenties whom Milo could not help noticing was attractive with her russet hair and erect posture.

Agent Cartright spoke, "Mr. Meeker, please put your sunglasses on. This is Miss Tinkem. She is here to provide you with a bit of a disguise. We think it is necessary for security reasons. We very much appreciate your going along with all this, sir."

Milo tried his best to endure the discomfort of being disguised by means of a black wig and a generous mustache.

Cartright gestured toward the table, "The two suspects will be seated here at this side of the table. You, agent Flood and I will sit here on the opposite side. The two of us will ask the questions, Milo. Your job is to merely listen and recall any impressions you have after the two suspects are taken away. Do you understand?"

The two suspects suddenly appeared, closely escorted by some very capable looking Marine guards. The two dark complexioned, defiant-looking young men were assigned chairs at the interrogation table facing Milo and the agents. Four Marines stood at attention closely behind the two surly-looking men. Since their capture, they had undergone endless questioning about their families, their personal backgrounds and their political and religious affiliations. This interrogation was to be about their connections with terrorist organizations and individuals. The questioning was to consist of very abrupt and fiercely phrased accusations, questions and threats. This went on for two hours, including a ten-minute break, during which the two agents and Milo were provided with coffee and the Marine guards were relieved by another team of four stern-faced young warriors.

During the questioning, Milo tried to focus as Dr. Shah had instructed and to listen intently but without trying too hard. Some trick. *Is this the recommended procedure for psychics?* Milo wondered. About halfway through the first hour Milo had a breakthrough. When questioned about their whereabouts in recent years, one said he had been living in Saudi Arabia while the other swore he was from Jordan.

"You have been trained in Gaza!" blurted Milo. The two suspects glared daggers at Milo.

"Exactly where have you been living here in the city?" demanded Agent Flood. No answer. "Where do you keep your weapons? We know there are others in on this. Where can we find them?"

The two terrorists stared defiantly into space as Milo studied them intently.

How is it possible to keep both mind and body relaxed while at the same time allowing your brain to receive

16

impressions from peering into the faces of these two murderers? Milo asked himself.

After the two hours of questioning, the captives were led back to their cells. The agents looked at Milo.

"What other impressions did you get, Milo?" asked Cartright.

Milo answered in a low, hesitant voice, "I got a feeling and a kind of blurry image that they have been staying at a house near the south end of Beacon Hill. Let me think... It's a run-down little place with a beat-up little house in the backyard, half-hidden by an apple tree and some blackberry bushes."

"Can you give us an address?" asked agent Flood.

"It's vague in my mind," said Milo. "Somewhere near two cross streets. Just a minute..." Milo tried a deeper level of concentration. "Othello Street, is that it? Beacon Avenue. I'm not absolutely sure, but that's all I can get for now."

"Well done, Milo" said Dr. Shah.

*　*　*

"Don't you like my lamb stew?" Veena asked.

Quietly sitting at the dinner table, Milo seemed even more subdued than usual. "You know it's my favorite, Veena, but I just don't have much appetite."

"You must have had a rough day," murmured Veena, sympathetically. "Why don't you tell me more about it?"

"I was very nervous," murmured Milo, as he related the details of the morning's interrogation. "It was

17

stressful; it left me exhausted."

"Let's hope that's the last of it," said Veena, unable to hide a worried expression.

"Yeah, but it won't be," said Milo. "They want to use me even more. In the morning they are picking me up at seven and driving me out to a South End location. They think I'm going to be able to tell them where some of the other suspects are hiding out."

Veena looked distressed, "Will you be able to do it?"

"Your guess is as good as mine," he murmured.

*   *   *

The five-year-old Impala was unwashed and featured a prominent dent in the left rear fender, as unlikely a police vehicle as one could imagine. Milo sat in the backseat as three plainclothes FBI agents occupied the other spaces in the car. Conversation was at a minimum as they rode south on Beacon Avenue toward the area Milo had seen in his mind's eye the previous day.

An agent named Tony sat next to Milo in the backseat and asked, "Mr. Meeker, do you have any specific directions for our driver? His name is Don."

Don turned and looked at Milo, "Which way now, Mr. Meeker?"

Milo put his finger to his temple in a gesture of concentration. "Pull over here and stop," he directed. Milo rolled his window down and ran his gaze across the neighborhood's streets and houses. "Keep going slowly for a block or two. Okay, turn left down this street and go slow. Stop. Go to the end of the street and make a U-turn. Go right at this next corner. Just creep ahead slowly so I can get my bearings." Milo placed both hands on his temples, "Let me think a minute. There!" he said as his eyes popped open.

Pointing ahead, he exclaimed, "A half block that way in back of that green house. I'm quite sure that's the place we're looking for. It's the small house in the backyard." Everything stopped. The house looked unoccupied.

"Are you absolutely sure, Mr. Meeker?" asked the driver.

"I'm pretty sure," murmured Milo.

The other agent in the front seat snatched an iPhone from his jacket pocket and began speaking rapidly to his counterpart back in the office, "They're on their way," he announced.

"Here's what's going to happen," said Tony the agent sitting next to Milo. "A city fire truck will be pulling up to that green house in about five minutes. A big fire department van will arrive at the same time. Firemen will swarm all over the place as their loudspeaker will announce an emergency evacuation due to a gas leak in the neighborhood and imminent explosion. The firemen are all the real thing but the van will unload twelve armed agents who will arrest the people coming out of the green house and the little house in back. They are all terrorist suspects and will be taken to the Federal building for incarceration and questioning."

As Milo watched, the scene soon exploded with the precise scenario described by the agent in the Impala.

19

Milo was greatly relieved as his insights about the little house were confirmed. He was impressed at the efficiency displayed by the firefighters and the agents which had resulted in the suspects emerging from their houses peacefully. Two swarthy young men were immediately disarmed of a surprising number of handguns. The three residents of the green house were of similar descriptions. All were fitted with handcuffs and leg-irons before being hustled into individual FBI vehicles.

* * *

A quiet discussion ensued that evening at the Meeker household. "Did things work out today as planned?" Veena gently asked.

"Yeah, as far as I know, it came out as planned. I led those agents to the place they wanted and surprised everybody including myself."

"It sounds like you did well, dear. What's next?"

"There will be some very minor surgery; the doctors are going to install some wireless computer chips under my skin connected to my brain. The Feds want me to have more competence as a spy."

"They probably know you're the champion at your chess club," Veena chuckled.

Milo couldn't suppress a modest grin.

"And a winning bridge player," Veena added, "but just being smart doesn't mean you are cut out to be a spy or some kind of mentalist with mysterious psychic powers. That's not you, Milo. You're not cut out for that kind of thing. It's ridiculous and it has me worried."

"I know I'm not the type, Veena, but I have to tell you something. I've known many friends and acquaintances who have been in the military. Some were killed, some wounded, some of their lives ruined. I've never served. I've always hidden some guilt. Those other guys had the guts to do something for their country. Sometimes I've felt ashamed. I hate feeling like some kind of a pipsqueak, a worthless little nerd. Maybe this is my chance to do something I can take pride in. It sounds corny I know, but these government people are asking me to do something for my country. I don't want to think of myself as a coward, so I am going to do as they ask and do my duty. I need to see it through. Could you please try to understand?"

Veena took pride in always maintaining the poise she associated with sensitivity and strength appropriate to her role as a middle-aged woman, an accomplished teacher and loyal wife. Looking deeply into Milo's eyes, she was inclined to break into tears, but she managed to hold it back, "I've been thinking, dear, about avoiding the consequences of pressure and stress in what you might be about to do. Now that I know how you feel, I have to say, I'm so very proud of you." Tears began to flow from her lovely brown eyes.

*   *   *

The surgical procedures completed, Milo was advised by Dr. Claybo to rest, read, exercise moderately and think

21

consciously about achieving a balance between body and mind. His counseling sessions with Dr. Shah would occur three times per week. Milo was relieved to hear that he would be receiving full pay from his employer, although he was quite sure his salary was subsidized by the FBI or some other government entity. For the time being he would not be required to report to the Boeing Company for work. *So I guess that's it,* he thought, *they own me.*

Milo seemed not to suffer any noticeable or bothersome after-effects from the computer chip implants except for a slight itching at the back of his neck and upper arms. *That must be where those little electronic gizmos are stuck under the skin. I wonder how they will affect me. Will I change into somebody else?* Milo wondered. With all his doubts about his new schedule and his new life, Milo tried to keep an open mind at his next appointment with Dr. Shah.

"Are you feeling different in any way since the implant operation?" Dr. Shah peered intently into Milo's eyes.

"Well, I've been having strange dreams just about every night. During the day I seem to be aware of a kind of soft static in my head or inner ears. Sometimes it lasts for a half hour or less and at times, off and on. I didn't know if those things were a result of what the doctors did to me or not."

"Can you describe the dreams?"

Milo thought a moment, "I know that dreams are often symbolic, but I can't make much out of them. My dreams are mostly violent and noisy with lots of movement, volcanos erupting, earthquakes, floods with people being swept away. Maybe they are just memories from the TV disasters we have seen recently."

"These dreams," said Shah, "are probably part of a response to the procedure you have recently undergone. Right now I want to coach you a bit on meditation technique. You must do meditation twice a day for at least twenty minutes. Do you remember what I said about altered states of consciousness? You seem to be okay with *alpha*, but as your technique evolves you will be getting deeper into *beta* and from there into *theta*. It won't take more than a week or so with your natural ability. I should caution you, that when you enter the first stages of *beta*, it is so blissful you may not wish to come out of it, but of course you will. As I have told you, in your altered state you may seat yourself, in your mind that is, in front of a big movie screen where you will see images, pictures of all kinds of things, events and happenings mostly of content or scenes which are unfamiliar to you. Your subconscious will show these things to you, providing you with special insight and information not normally within your conscious ability to perceive or understand. There are also altered states called *gamma* and *delta*, but more about those later. These revelations are from your mind, not your brain. The two have different functions. You will be learning more as we go along. A lot of information will be generated not from me but from within yourself. Your body is composed of billions of tiny cells, each loaded with a special intelligence. Your body, including your magnificent brain and incredible mind is loaded with a super intelligence, abounding creativity and ageless wisdom. The trick is to get yourself in the proper mode or zone in order to take advantage of what you already know." A long pause ensued as Milo attempted to digest Dr. Shah's comments and pull his own thoughts together. "Do you have any questions for now?" asked the psychologist.

Milo responded, "Where does the soul come in?"

Dr. Shah smiled, "Many aspects of the brain are measureable with scientific method, but not so with the mind or the soul. Most laypeople believe in the idea of the mind, but as you know, the belief in a soul is somewhat controversial, probably because the definitions vary from religion-to-religion and culture-to-culture. Many Eastern philosophers, holy men if you will, believe that soul, mind and brain are three separate entities, that human motivation starts in the soul, proceeds to the mind and then to the brain which sends orders for action, energy and fulfillment of the original creative idea. Try tuning in on that one, Milo!"

Milo's hand touched his brow, "I think I have started to visualize things as pictures. Up until now I thought mostly in numbers, equations and diagrams. I just seem to feel it happening just since I've been here this morning. Is that of any significance do you think, doctor?"

Dr. Shah's fingers were busy on the small hand held computer, "It is," he replied. "Are you seeing pictures right now?"

Milo looked into the doctor's dark eyes, "I hope your son recovers and feels better very soon." Louis Shah's mouth dropped open. "I see him in bed with a broken leg in traction," said Milo. "I'm so sorry."

Dr. Shah allowed himself to gulp as he said, "I think we are progressing, Milo, let's keep doing what we're doing and I'll see you at our next appointment the day after tomorrow. Thank you for your concern."

*   *   *

At dinner that evening, Veena encouraged Milo to discuss his meeting with the psychologist. "And another thing, after the session with Dr. Shah," said Milo, "they sent me to another office down the hall to see a technology person, a young fellow with round glasses, long hair and pimples."

"A techie," Veena grinned. "What did he want of you?"

Milo looked thoughtful, "He showed me how to operate an audio reading machine. It's very small, about the size of a cigarette pack. A digital chip fits inside and holds any number of digital books. You can also dictate hours of information and play it back."

"Why did they issue you an audio book player?" asked Veena.

"They don't think I've had enough education," giggled Milo. "There are about twenty books recorded on the chip along with instruction on speed reading using this little device. If I practice properly I should be able to read a three-hundred-page book in less than two hours and mow the lawn at the same time. How does that sound?"

Veena allowed herself a smile, "You will become a champion multitasker, along with your other talents."

"Other talents," Milo repeated thoughtfully. "You should know some of the audio books they have assigned me to read," he said. "Just a few for starters: current government books on terrorists and terrorism, the US Constitution, a comprehensive book on American history, Aristotelian Logic, Bertrand Russell's Logic System, The Koran and Muslim Law. In a week or so they will test my new brain to see if anything stuck. If so, they will assign more books. I kind of like the challenge. I am interested to see if the speed reading experiment works."

Milo dutifully continued his reading assignments, at times feeling exhilarated over his progress and delighted that his audio speed reading was gradually coming to full realization. He was quite fascinated with his new ability to recall virtually everything that he heard from the audio books. Among the newest books assigned included: Machiavelli, Plato, the Talmud, the Jefferson Bible and the histories of World Wars I and II.

In addition to the required reading and the thrice-weekly appointments with Dr. Shah, Milo was required to participate in physical workouts on Monday, Wednesday and Friday at the Seattle Police department gym, a few blocks from the downtown Federal building. Dr. Claybo had arranged for one of the police department trainers to provide one-on-one coaching for Milo to assure the proper form. *A keen mind in a sound body* was an old cliché, but important when creating a super intellect. For the government, every resource was important in the ongoing battle against terrorism.

*   *   *

It seemed to Milo that time was moving at a fast pace as he completed his first two months of supervised activities. The sessions with Dr. Shah had opened Milo's eyes to new worlds of thought, conjecture and amazement as Milo explored new revelations by means of the meditation process he was encouraged to pursue daily. His thoughts seemed to process more quickly than before he began meditating. The quietness, while in the zone, had a calming effect on his actions and his thinking. What was to Milo almost frightening was the information that seemed to emerge from each session, mostly imaginative or creative thoughts unlike any he had experienced before. His feeling of well-being seemed to be at an all-time high, perhaps because of his workouts at the police department gym. He knew he was becoming much stronger physically and it felt great.

About this time, Milo received an evening phone call from a man identifying himself as Special Agent Edward Sharman from the regional office of the FBI. Agent Sharman was notifying Milo that he was instructed to go on a mission for the FBI the following Tuesday morning. Sharman was to pick him up at 0600 and drive to the airport. Milo said he would be ready.

*   *   *

The next Tuesday morning found Milo, accompanied by Agent Sharman, on a flight to San Francisco followed by a ride to the downtown FBI office. That very morning, Milo was directed by agent Flood to serve as an observer at an interrogation of another terrorist suspect. As an observer three months previously in Seattle, Milo was required to simply sit through the interrogation and report his impressions. Milo was informed that he was to participate in two more interrogations: another one today and a second tomorrow.

By this time his training had prepared him to easily slip into a trance-like state upon confronting his subject, the terrorist suspect. His psychic sensitivity had developed to a much higher degree than before, such that his impressions were much stronger. After the questioning session, Milo related his impressions into a recorder as two agents looked on and asked questions about his comments. Sitting across a table from the two FBI interrogators, their skepticism was so obvious to Milo that it was almost laughable. *Typical of most cops*, he thought. Milo looked the agents straight in the eye and said, "The suspect lied with almost every word. I guess we all know that. No surprise. What he is really thinking about is their plan to smuggle an atomic explosive device into the US."

The bald agent's eyes widened, "An atomic bomb?"

"How big? What kind? Smuggled from where?" asked the skinny agent.

Milo half-closed his eyes as he answered, "A small bomb to fit into a suitcase or flight bag, powerful enough to blow up most of San Francisco. It's not clear as to where they plan to smuggle it into the country. I feel it might come from Mexico, but I'm not sure."

The two agents stared at Milo for a long moment, and then looked at each other. The bald one said, "In an hour we question another suspect. Be back here in fifty minutes. There's a small snack bar down the hall."

The next suspect was a small swarthy semi-bearded man with furtive eyes. Milo found it difficult to get a decipherable impression from the suspect. His thoughts were a confusing mix of worry about his family in the Middle East. He seemed to be under a great deal of stress and on the verge of a nervous breakdown. Milo was becoming competent at reading auras. This man's aura was very dark, suggesting that he would not survive much longer in a prison environment. A bit frightened by these thoughts, Milo wondered how much his new extra sensory abilities included predictions of future events.

The interrogation the next day however, provided Milo with some strong impressions which suggested that the terrorist team, of which the suspect was a part, planned to smuggle a suitcase bomb inside some cruise ship's tourist luggage transported from Ensenada, Mexico into the US. Milo expected that this revelation would be of enormous interest to the agent interrogators, but the two men maintained what appeared to Milo to be a kind of aloof skepticism. Agent Bald and Agent Skinny seemed to dutifully prepare the paperwork relevant to Milo's input and send it on to their higher authorities. Milo had a strong feeling that this was not going to happen.

If these two agents are not going to send my impressions to their superiors, what am I doing here?

*   *   *

The next morning Milo was flown back to Seattle. Veena regarded her husband intently as they sat across from each other at the dining room table. "How do you think it went?" she asked.

Milo seemed only half awake, as he enjoyed his bacon and eggs. His mood abruptly switched into gear as he took a deep breath and straightened his position in his chair. His eyes closed halfway as he framed his answer, "I think it went well enough. I felt confident that I was able to reveal some important information to the agents I was supposed to be working with, but those fellows acted like they didn't believe me or didn't understand what I was telling them. They obviously had little respect for the facts I related to them."

"What did you tell them? I'm sure your impressions were accurate. They have been so far."

"I'm not supposed to talk about it even to you dear, as you know, but it has to do with something that the American public has been warned about many times in the recent past. Thank God those terrorists, whoever they are, haven't succeeded in exploding an atomic device in this country. At least not yet."

"Those dreams you have, Milo, are they like predictions of future events?"

"I'm not to talk about that stuff either, Veena, but

30

I'll tell you anyway. I think the answer is yes, but my ability to do so accurately seems to be developing rather intermittently. I confess it scares me." Abruptly changing the subject, Milo's eyes widened as he spoke in a low voice, "Please don't be fearful as I tell you this, dear, but I want you to be especially careful today. It's just a feeling, but be careful when driving and in everything else that you do. Be cautious and you'll be okay. Will you promise me?"

Veena reacted calmly, "Yes, I'll be careful, just as you suggest. I trust you when you assure me there is no real danger. Now I have to hustle off to work. You have a non-appointment day, right?"

"The usual Tuesday, dear," said Milo. "Meditation, a jog in the park, speed reading and homework in the afternoon."

* * *

The green running suit felt good against his skin as Milo began his morning jog, his one ear bud firmly in place. The volume on his digital reader adjusted to his liking, his running shoes snugly tied and his light weight stocking cap snugly in place. The sky was overcast and the air crisply cool, just right for a stimulating jog on a weekday, with nobody around to distract. I think I'll pick up the pace this morning, he thought. Four blocks north on the deserted sidewalk, then onto the nice pathways inside Magnolia Park for a half hour or so, then back home for a shower and lunch. *How lucky I am to be able to enjoy this new phase in my life. But don't get too smug. It may not last long,* he told himself.

It had rained a bit the night before, leaving some mud puddles here and there, but Milo enjoyed slogging right through them, symbolic movements, perhaps demonstrating a kind of recklessness or carelessness that comes with the fun of a free spirit. The free spirit was thoroughly enjoying his nearness to the giant fir and madrona trees, the smell of the rhododendrons and the other lovely plants and wild bushes.

Milo did not notice the sizeable mud puddle a few feet in front of him on the path. As he jogged through the slippery spot, Milo was thrown off balance and that's when it happened. Lurching forward, his head and upper body was abruptly thrown off the line of movement, simultaneous with the sound of a gunshot and a whirring sensation next to his right ear. Milo quickly dove off the trail in a frightened attempt to find cover in the brush growing next to the trail. Another shot rang out sending a bullet tearing through the jacket of his running suit and skimming the surface of the skin on his right shoulder. Although startled, his newfound sensitivity enabled him to maintain a controlled awareness. Continuing to scramble quickly into the thicket, he immediately reached the edge of a brushy ravine into which he plowed headlong. Hearing no more gunfire, he ran in a crouch as rapidly as he could away from the path, woods and park along the neighborhood sidewalks for home. Fearful that whoever was gunning for him might take another shot at any moment, he zigzagged down the street in the manner of a football running back tearing down the field. In excellent physical shape, the middle-aged Milo suffered no exhaustion even though his jogging suit was smeared with dirt, mud, sweat, rips and tears as a result of scrambling through and across the many obstacles. Running up the stairs to his front door, Milo focused his mind in an effort to sense if danger awaited him inside. He quickly came to the conclusion that his house was safe for him to enter.

Once inside he rushed for the phone to call Agent Cartright, the first name on his mental list. He dialed the number from memory and rapidly reported the attempt on his life with pertinent details. An even more urgent concern was for Veena's safety.

In a matter of minutes Seattle police cars arrived. With brakes squealing and squad car doors slamming, dozens of cops swarmed around the neighborhood blocking streets and searching potential hiding places. Answering the phone, Milo was relieved to hear Cartright assure him that Veena was unhurt, safe and on her way home under guard by two agents while her car was being driven home by two more FBI personnel.

"Where did you want your car delivered, to the garage or to the street in front of the house?" Cartwright asked.

Denying the need for any agents or police to be assigned to the inside of their home, Milo accepted Cartright's order for the rotation of four Seattle uniformed cops to be stationed at the appropriate locations outside the house twenty-four-seven until further notice. Actually,

Milo was given no choice in the matter.

"I was so worried about you," Milo whispered as he squeezed Veena in a powerful bear hug the second she entered their front door.

"I was afraid for both of us when I got the news," said Veena, her voice cracking as she hugged and patted her husband while kissing his cheeks.

Agent Cartright arrived, accompanied by two husky FBI colleagues. Seated at the dining room table, their conference began.

"Here is what I think is going on," said Cartright. "These terrorist organizations have become very clever about obtaining information. They know more about the CIA and FBI activities than we had thought. We think they have figured out how effective you have been in your work so far. For example, your input from the San Francisco interrogations resulted in our actions which destroyed their plan to smuggle in nuclear materials to California. They see you, Milo, as a uniquely formidable enemy. Compared to the rest of us working to restrain their terrorist attacks, you have become public enemy number one on their list of targets. We really didn't know this until now, but after that attempt to kill you this morning, it's clear."

Milo looked at the agent who was carefully recording their voices on his tiny recorder while another agent was diligently scribbling notes on a pad.

"So what happens now?" asked Milo.

Cartright cleared his throat and in a voice that dripped with sincerity said, "The first priority is to assure your safety."

"How do we do that?" asked Veena.

"There is more than one option, Mrs. Meeker. We can furnish a twenty-four-seven guard here at your house and assign a personal guard for each of you during your regular activities. This would necessarily be a temporary arrangement. We could arrange to place you on our witness protection program. If so, you would have to move someplace far from here. We could offer financial support, housing and appropriate jobs for you both in a different location."

"What do you mean by a different location?" asked Milo.

"Somewhere twenty-five-hundred miles or more from the Pacific Northwest," explained Cartright. "You would probably have a choice."

Veena spoke, "What about overseas?"

"That might be arranged," declared Cartright.

Milo stared into Cartwright's eyes, "Would I still be able to work for the FBI?"

"It's possible. We would have to work it out. I'm truly sorry about all that happened today and the changes you will have to make at this time in your life, but we cannot afford to underestimate the danger you are in."

Relieved that the meeting was finally over, the Meekers sat glumly at the table and looked at each other.

Veena spoke softly, "What do people do when their lives are turned upside down? We've got a lot to think about, Milo."

That night Cartright chaired a meeting with three of his highest ranking agents, "Here's what we need to happen for now," he declared. "Lynch, I want you to put a tap on the Meeker's phone and install security systems in their house. Gill, you relieve the Seattle cops from guard duty. Arrange for the Meeker's personal guards, one agent for each of them. One guard only at night. Our guys are to drive them wherever they need to go during the day. Arrange for the Seattle cops to have a patrol car cruise the immediate neighborhood on a regular basis day and night, starting with agent John Hill." Cartright growled, "Hill, I am assigning you to conduct a secret investigation to include every one of our agents here in Seattle and the San Francisco office as well. I suspect there has been a leak revealing Meeker as our secret asset, our own expert psychic." This brought some well-hidden smiles and smirks from the others. Cartright shook his head slowly as he spoke in a confidential tone, "It's unthinkable that we would have an informer or a mole in our midst, but I believe under the circumstances, it's my duty to look into it."

* * *

Veena and Milo slept in short intervals, but after their usual morning showers and breakfast, they both were eager to engage in their kitchen table confab which they both knew was very likely to result in a tipping point in their future together.

"Before we start," said Veena, "I need to explain something to you, Milo. It's about my past. I had a different career. You probably won't believe it, but in my younger days I was trained as a police officer and served for twelve years, long before I met you."

Milo was surprised but hid his feelings as he attempted to focus into his wife's thoughts.

"Police officer? Why have you never mentioned it?"

"When we were courting, I guess I thought if you knew I was an ex-cop it might frighten you away. I met my first husband when we were both patrol officers in the Seattle Police Department. Later he became a sergeant and then a lieutenant. He was killed in the line of duty at age thirty-nine. Not long after that I quit the force and went back to college to earn a teaching degree. Just a few years after that, I met you and you know the rest."

"Losing your husband at such a young age must have been very tough on you, Veena. I'm sorry for that, dear, but now I know why you never told me about your life before we met."

Veena sagged a bit in her chair, "It's all in the past," she said. "Now it's you and me, but here's why I bring it up. In the years when I served as a cop, my superiors thought I did a good job. I qualified for specialized training from time-to-time. I was well-trained in the use of weapons. I even served on the Tactical Squad. I also participated in drug bust raids where I was required to shoot at people."

"A weapons specialist, gun battles and shooting

people? My God, Veena, no wonder you never told me!"

"I'm telling you now because I need to show you something." From under the table, Veena slid a large box and lifted it onto the table top. Opening the box, Veena laid several guns on the table. "These were acquired by my late husband, who probably redeemed them from the evidence storeroom after they had been surplused. Here is a takedown AK47, a 12 gauge sawed off shotgun and two automatic pistols, a Glock and a Heckler, plus several magazines for each gun. I doubt if any of the ammunition here is still good after all these years of storage. We are going to replace the ammo tomorrow. There are also some holsters in the box. There is a shoulder holster here that I think will fit you, Milo."

"What will we do with all these guns?" asked her amazed husband.

Veena answered through clenched teeth, "We are going to arm ourselves and if those terrorist guys come after you again, we'll kill them. From now on, we won't be without the means to defend ourselves. This morning I want you to call Cartright and tell him to provide us with permits to carry concealed weapons. I want you to demand that he send us bullet-proof vests. He also may agree to appoint us as deputy FBI Agents or some damn thing just to keep us legal. Insist that he review my records as a former Seattle police officer."

"You must know, Veena, that I have no experience with guns."

A tiny light sparkled in Veena's dark eyes, "I'll show you all about it. Piece of cake, we'll start today."

Luckily, Milo connected with Cartright on the first try. Veena listened in on their second phone until the last request.

"I knew he'd argue, but I think you convinced him," she said. "Now let's sit here for a bit and figure out what to do from this point on."

Despite Cartright's wish for them to stay out of sight, they continued their regular schedules even though it meant dragging along their assigned body guards.

Wearing bulletproof vests were uncomfortable for both the Meekers, but both wore them for most of the first day and consistently thereafter. After work, Veena stopped at a local gun shop where she purchased some carrying cases for the guns along with ammunition, ear protectors and a supply of paper targets.

"That should take care of our needs for now," she declared.

*   *   *

That evening, their quiet conversation was about relocating to some far off place. Neither wanted to leave their friends from the bridge club, the chess club or the Ballard Elks lodge. They loved Seattle with the mild winters and cool summers, the nearness to the local lakes, Puget Sound and the majestic snowcapped mountains.

As the days and weeks passed, Milo was subject to thorough instruction on the rules and ethics of handling and maintaining their weapons. Veena's instruction also included mechanical details about each weapon and precise shooting techniques. Target practice was held in their basement, but not before Veena had schmoozed their immediate neighbors to ignore the strange sounds emitted from the Meeker's basement.

"We're conducting some very safe experiments for our Chemistry Club from time to time, so don't be alarmed," she told them.

Milo learned to take down and reassemble the AK47 automatic rifle just like he had seen the Marines do with the Garand M1 rifle in old World War II movies on TV. He surprised himself with his new expertise in weaponry. His powers of concentration had sharpened to a remarkable degree along with his physical development since his involvement with his doctors, advisors and trainers. He wondered if those experiences had helped make him a competent marksman, often outdoing Veena in accuracy as they practiced firing their weapons in the basement.

*   *   *

From the first, Milo had continued to be concerned about his psychic abilities. He wondered why he had not anticipated the attack when jogging at the park. He also wondered why he apparently could not predict when the assassins might strike again. Dr. Shah had cautioned him not to expect too much. The most accomplished psychics in the world could not always predict happenings or events in which they were personally involved. Maybe he needed to push his newly found powers past the traditional limits.

Perhaps he should push his limited knowledge about out of body travel. Maybe get himself in a deeper than ever altered state of consciousness and try to get to the Akashic record, deep into that other dimension, the source of all knowledge in the Universe. These were all things to ask Dr. Shah about.

*   *   *

Comfortably seated next to a small coffee table in Dr. Shah's office, Milo sipped a cup of green tea.

"May I hang your jacket up?" Shah asked.

"No, it's very lightweight. I'm comfortable wearing it right now," Milo responded.

Words came into Milo's brain. *You are wearing your jacket because you wish to conceal the fact that you wear your bulletproof vest and your Glock 9 millimeter automatic tucked in at the small of your back.*

Milo silently asked himself where the telepathic words that kept coming into his head were coming from.

"Now Milo," said Shah, "you continue to read those educational audio books, right? If you don't mind, I would like to give you a little informal quiz to measure your memory retention."

"Okay," murmured Milo.

"I will read a few lines from the books you've been reading. Let's see how closely you can complete the sentences, phrases or paragraphs."

41

The quiz ensued with questions from passages in various books. Milo found that tapping into his memory was quite easy. He could recall some passages from King Lear, quote from Adam Smith's book on Capitalism and recall the poetic lessons from the Koran with ease. As he asked himself what strange surgical procedures Dr. Claybo and others had done to his brain, he was startled to hear the voices attempt to answer him with a technical explanation. "Be quiet," he heard himself say as he received a quizzical look from Dr. Shah.

After a fifteen minute quiz, both Milo and Shah were impressed with Milo's retention ability.

"I'm amazed," breathed Dr. Shah. "Next, I have a regular book for you to study. It outlines the thinking of people of the Middle East. It will help you a great deal in your work with the authorities. Study it very carefully and give it a lot of thought."

Milo could feel his heart beat faster and his thinking seemed to leap into sharp focus. *So that's what you are about,* he thought, as he stared into Dr. Louis Shah's dark eyes.

*　*　*

Instead of heading for the gym, Milo headed rapidly down the hall toward Agent Cartright's office, hoping to catch him at his desk. Milo's bodyguard had to hustle to keep up. As luck would have it, Cartright was there. Milo carefully explained his newest revelation to Cartright.

"My God, Milo! You are accusing Louis Shah of being

a terrorist?"

"I'm not saying that," said Milo dryly. "You must understand that what I'm telling you are my honest impressions. Any psychic impressions are subject to latitude in interpretation."

Cartright's eyes narrowed, "Are you saying this is nothing more than guesswork?"

"Right now Mr. Cartright," said Milo, "you are thinking that accusing one of your own people as an enemy propagandist, a traitor, or a terrorist is completely irrational and unthinkable. How can I take such an accusation seriously coming from a little Nerd like you?"

Cartright shifted in his chair and scratched his cheek, "Now you think you are reading my mind?"

Milo uncharacteristically raised his voice, "Do you remember how my impression, during those recent interrogations, provided the evidence to get those terrorists out of circulation, tried and sentenced to Federal prison? All I am suggesting is that you put Dr. Shah under scrutiny and do a secret investigation. Shah is the man who leaked my identity to the terrorists and almost got me shot. Twice!"

For several moments the two men stared silently into each other's eyes. Milo stood and quietly took his leave.

*   *   *

"I have to tell you, Veena, that I am quite sure I can no longer trust everyone at the FBI. I have been betrayed and Cartright will not do anything about it."

"So it's that bad," said Veena. "How long do we have to continue to live like this? Let's focus on getting prepared to move very soon."

An hour before bedtime Milo settled in his study chair to begin speed reading the book that Shah had given him to study. The content of the book was pretty much as Milo had suspected with cleverly written comments, information and blatant propaganda about God's omnipotence and his intentions for people on planet earth as interpreted by the prophet Mohammed. All non-Muslims were regarded as Infidels with Americans described as the worst of the lot.

Milo placed his fingertips against his forehead and gently shook his head as questions came to his mind. *How is it possible that an educated man like Dr. Shah would think that I, after knowing me as well as he does, would think that I could be persuaded to believe the obvious propaganda employed by the terrorists? Wait, what am I hearing in my head? Louis Shah, actually Mohammed Shah, is from Pakistan, not India. This will take more thought,* he told himself. *From all I have been reading about people from the Middle East, it is certain that only a tiny percentage of them accept the viewpoint put forth in this awful little book.*

At home, in his favorite chair, the phone rang. "Hello," spoke Milo into the telephone. "Yes, what's up?" His face darkened. "Tomorrow? It's that important? Okay, I'll be ready."

*   *   *

44

The first class early morning flight to Washington D.C. afforded Milo an excellent breakfast and a chance to speed read an assigned audio book, "Super Brain," by Deepak Chopra. His bodyguard produced a miniature chess board, dying to find out if he might be able to defeat the psychic. Norman was astounded to receive a quick defeat on the first match and an even quicker loss on the second, causing him to stow the chess board in his flight bag and stare into his private movie screen. Seated comfortably, Milo closed his eyes and slipped into a zone of quiet meditation.

The pair was greeted at the airport by an FBI agent who drove them to a business class hotel a short distance from the Pentagon. After lunch in the hotel dining room, Milo was driven to a government building where he was quickly ushered into the office of a man with the title indicative of a high rank. Special Agent Morton greeted Milo courteously. Milo shifted his mind into an intensive degree of concentration as he listened to Morton.

"We called you here to Washington at the request of the head of the FBI himself." Apparently he has heard of your work. We have in custody a terrorist suspect of great importance to us. He is incarcerated here in this building. We have been questioning him with some success, but we know he is privy to a great deal more information that we need. We hope you can contribute some special information or insight. Would you be prepared to sit in observation as we question him again this morning?"

"All I need," said Milo, "is ten minutes in a quiet room alone before meeting with the suspect."

After his meditation, Milo was escorted to the interrogation room where he joined two other agents at a square table.

"Mr. Meeker, the man we will be talking to in a moment was arrested in Saudi Arabia. He has been a leader in a number of plots against the United States which resulted in many American deaths. Take whatever reading you can on him. His name is Abu Ben Ameer."

Hoping that his disguise would be effective, Milo nodded and adjusted his false mustache and sunglasses.

Led into the room by two formidable looking guards, Ameer was shown a seat at the table facing Milo and the agents. The suspect was short and husky with a greasy dark complexion. He wore a dark mustache, wild unkempt hair and a defiant expression. There appeared to be some small cuts on his forehead and dark bruises on his thick neck. Unlike the other interrogations Milo had witnessed, this one employed a darkened room and a strong spotlight directed into the suspect's face.

"Up to now, Abu, you have not been forthcoming when we asked you questions. As we have explained to you, your level of discomfort will increase dramatically from now on if you continue your uncooperative attitude. On the other hand, if you give us the information we ask for, your life in our custody will be greatly improved. Yesterday you hated the food we gave you, right? Last night we didn't allow you to sleep. You hate the primitive filthy toilet facilities in your cell, yes? If you give us phony answers to our questions today we are prepared to burn the nerves in your legs so you won't be able to walk and that's just the beginning. Do you understand all that I just told you?"

Milo could hardly believe what he had just heard. Was the agent just bluffing or had the FBI resorted to torture on its own soil? Abu gave no response except for the expression in his eyes which told Milo that he had understood perfectly.

"Now for the questions," growled Brady. "When you were meeting with your fellow Jihadists in Qatar last November, were you planning an attack on our Embassy in Beirut?" Abu was silent. Brady continued. "Were you in contact with spies in the American Embassy? You have no choice but to give us their names. If you continue to remain silent I promise you a great deal of discomfort, anxiety, excruciating pain and permanent damage to your sexual capabilities along with my other promises of a few minutes ago."

Abu swallowed with difficulty as his mouth began to move, "I can only tell you the truth. I was not part of any plan to attack anything. I remind you that America is bound by the Geneva Convention about treatment of prisoners of war."

"Who said you were a prisoner of war?" shouted Brady, "you slimy lying bastard."

Milo interrupted, "May I ask a question?"

"Ask," rasped Brady, giving Milo a disparaging look.

"When you were meeting with your comrades in Qatar, did you have acceptable housing?"

Abu smiled slightly and answered, "It was satisfactory."

Milo's voice took on a kindly tone, "I take it that two of your colleagues at that meeting have escaped our custody. Do they have satisfactory housing where they are living? In what country are they hiding out in?"

Abu answered with his straightest face, "I am sure their living facilities are most satisfactory. I am unable to tell you where because I do not know."

Milo cocked his head and looked at Abu with a skeptical glance, "Why don't you give us something we can go on? Speak up."

The suspect showed a slight grin as he spoke, "You would look much better to me, shorty, if your face was covered with measles."

"What about measles, what do you mean?" asked Milo. "Do you plan to infect Americans?"

Abu's smile grew wider, "Maybe smallpox would make you look even better," he said defiantly.

Agent Brady resumed the questioning about spies, names, locations, weapons and motivations with little if any worthwhile information. As Abu was led out of the room, he looked quizzically over his shoulder at Milo, as if to say, who are you and why those strange questions? As soon as his guards had hauled Abu out of the interrogation room, agent Brady looked accusingly at Milo.

"What the hell do you think you're doing butting in like that? You're just supposed to sit and keep your mouth shut!"

"I had good reasons for those questions," Milo declared.

Roberts, the other agent was curious. "What reasons?" he asked giving Milo a hard look.

Milo wiped his forehead and spoke softly, "When I asked Abu about his housing it was just to soften him up a bit. When he responded, a picture of the place where the meeting was held popped into his mind which allowed me to see it in my mind. When I asked him where the other terrorists were hiding out, the picture was of Montreal, in a south eastern suburb where many Muslims have emigrated in the past few years. If you act quickly you will have a good chance of capturing the two men you are looking for. My question about the measles provided more impressions."

"Impressions of what?" asked Brady. "I'm told that there is an ongoing plan to smuggle some infected people to the USA to create a deadly epidemic. Big time diseases like German measles, small pox and cholera." An awkward pause ensued. "May I be excused?" asked Milo politely. With no further questions or instructions, Milo and his bodyguard caught a cab to their hotel. "I'd like to shower," said Milo. "After that, let's go to the dining room for lunch."

"I'm all for it," said Norman. "In the meantime I'll check and see about our flight plans." Back in their hotel room for only five minutes, the phone rang. Norman answered. "Yes, of course sir, here he is," he said, handing the phone to Milo.

"Yes, it is I. To whom am I speaking?"

Ear glued to the phone, Milo listened intently. "Mr. Meeker, this is agent Howard Barnes. I have some disturbing news. We have taken your wife to the hospital. Do not be alarmed. She is not seriously injured."

"How was she injured?" asked Milo, alarm in his voice.

"A minor gunshot wound. She and Agent Hobart Brown were attacked by three assassins. Agent Brown was killed. The three gunmen are dead, shot by Mrs. Meeker who reacted to being attacked as a hero, a real warrior. She received only a flesh wound. A bullet passed through the upper corner of her left ear. She is receiving treatment at Harborview Hospital and will be there when you return in about three hours. You will be flying on our FBI private jet. We are dispatching extra guards for her here in the hospital and one more agent to fly home with you and your regular bodyguard. A car is on its way to pick you up at your hotel. Can you be ready in twenty minutes?"

"Of course," said a stunned Milo Meeker.

Less than four hours later Milo paused with his bodyguards at the entrance to Veena's hospital room and waited for the various guards to identify each other. Milo attempted to control his nervousness. *'Control your emotions and utilize your mind-body balance technique.' Where did that voice come from?* Milo asked himself. *Was it in my head?*

As he entered Veena's hospital room it was easy for him to see the loving greeting in her eyes as they filled with tears. As they hugged in a tight embrace, he whispered, "Veena, I love you so much. What was I thinking, leaving you here without me?"

Between sobs, Veena gurgled, "Oh Milo, I killed those guys!"

"Of course you did," he murmured, "but only because they were trying to take you away from me. I only wish it was I that shot them. I would have shot them ten times each, if anyone ever deserved to die it was those terrorists, those murderous rats." Both paused and looked deeply into each other's eyes.

"Do you know, Milo that I was shot six times?"

"Veena, what are you saying?"

Veena's jaw tightened, "The bullet proof vest saved me. Any one of those shots would have finished me."

*   *   *

At the breakfast table the next morning, Veena spoke, "Before getting to the big question, what can you tell me about your trip to Washington?"

"As you know, I'm not supposed to but I'll tell you anyway," Milo sighed. "I helped interview the man suspected of bombing the US Embassy in Beirut, and was able to give the agents a good lead on where his two conspirators are presently hiding out. I was also able to determine their plan to send infected Jihadists into the US to indiscriminately spread infections throughout the country."

Veena, pale and thinking of her Middle School pupils and their parents asked, "What diseases are you talking about?"

"Smallpox, German measles and cholera, the

deadliest. I'm quite sure the agents in the room did not believe in the validity of my impressions. Actually, I'm pretty sure the information I gave the FBI is correct."

"What gives you that idea?" asked Veena.

Milo's face took on a serious expression, "My spirit guide has confirmed it to me."

Veena's eyes widened, "Your spirit guide?"

"Yes."

"What's his name?"

"Veena," said Milo softly, "not everyone is aware of their spirit guide. One has to have a natural insight, which is very rare, or have developed a kind of heightened metaphysical awareness which provides the knowledge of one's personal spirit guide. It's a spiritual entity, like having an angel looking over your shoulder that sometimes acts as a protector and sometimes as an informant. Most people are not aware that they have such a companion, guide, informant and friend. Spirit guides usually communicate telepathically. They are valuable as a source of information about anything."

"Anything?" asked Veena.

"In the universe," Milo answered.

Veena's voice quavered, "Milo, what is happening to you?"

Milo smiled gently, "Don't worry; I am not going crazy, at least not according to most people's definition. I'm counting on you to give me the benefit of any doubts you may have about my sanity. My shrink says I am unusually intelligent. How about my IQ of 185? Not only that, but Dr. Claybo says that his brain surgery has opened up some amazing new channels suggesting even higher levels of intelligence and psychic ability. Please, can we let it rest there for now? What I want is for us to be as safe and happy as possible from now on. By the way, my guide's name is Lahz. Could we change the subject? Do you want to tell me about the gun battle?"

"I don't like even thinking about it," breathed Veena, "but I'll make it short for now. After school, Hobart drove me to my hair appointment at the Magnolia mall and just as we pulled into a parking spot, a car pulled in crossways behind us so we couldn't back out. Two men suddenly appeared from the front on either side of our car. Walking rapidly toward us they waited until they got really close before bringing out their guns, but before they did I sensed what they were about to do. I yelled 'guns' to Hobart and drew my Glock, quickly aimed and shot the guy on my side right through the throat. He fell backward immediately and I opened my door and jumped out, crouching low just as we were taught when I was a cop. I turned and fired across the hood of the car at the other guy who shot at me at the same time. The guy was firing a fully automatic machine pistol. I could feel the bullets striking my vest and bruising me everywhere they hit. The shooter had beaten Hobart to the draw and killed him before he could start firing at the son-of-a-bitch. I shot the bastard right through his left eye and he went down, but now the third guy had gotten out of his car and was coming for me. He was dodging around so I couldn't get a good shot at his body or his head, so I took a chance and sprayed where his legs seemed to be with three or four fast shots. I guess I hit a leg or two because he screamed, doubled up and sprawled on the ground where I scrambled over before he could still shoot me and shot him three times in the head. I was scared to death, but after all the time since I had been a police officer, some of the training at the academy came back to me." Veena began trembling a bit as she finished the account of her life and death battle with the enemy terrorists.

Deep in thought, Milo gently stroked his chin. "If," he said quietly, "we are ever required to travel somewhere again, we go together." His eyes showed an uncharacteristic twinkle. "I need my wife, the gunslinger, to keep me safe."

Veena's lips began to tremble again. "I feel so sad about Hobart," she said. Both were quiet as their thoughts turned in pity to their ex-bodyguard. An exceptionally nice and brave young man in the prime of his life and murdered for what? Milo felt a lump in his throat.

So many questions raced in both their heads. Veena took Milo's hand, "You have more than proven that your abilities are legitimate, Milo. Where do your metaphysical insights really come from?"

Milo drew very close and replied in a sotto voice. To Veena he sounded like someone else. "I must tell you a little more. Most people are capable to some degree of developing insight into the universal consciousness, but can't because of the closed-mindedness of society in general. It's because of many factors working against the true reality of the ever present and eternal universal intelligence. Some of the resistance factors include a cultural glorification of ignorance, firm and unyielding belief systems which include our education system, religious dogma, political propaganda and general ignorance of science, history, philosophy and critical thinking."

"Sounds like it's a good time to leave," said Veena. "For one thing, after I whacked those three assassins, the terrorists will probably keep after us from now on." She carefully scrutinized Milo's face. "Now for the big question, what do we do now?"

"Get ourselves to bed, try to relax and sleep 'til morning," Milo said softly.

That night both were aware of noises made by their numerous bodyguards stationed both inside and outside their house.

The next morning over bacon and eggs, their discussion reemerged. "Do you think," asked Veena, "that the witness protection offer is still good? Will the FBI let you go? Where can we go?"

Milo finished his eggs, fastened his gaze on Veena and answered, "Yes, yes, and any darn place we want."

* * *

Veena and Milo were strolling casually in the warm evening twilight, wearing shorts, T-shirts and wide brimmed sun hats. Veena smiled a huge smile and declared, "It's a relief not to wear the bullet proof vests anymore."

Milo was enjoying the fragrant smells of the eucalyptus and gum trees lining the pathway. "The vests are packed away forever, dear."

"Please tell me," asked Veena, "why you carry that little automatic pistol tucked into the belt of your shorts against your back where nobody can see it?"

Milo imagined he could imitate the tone of an FBI special agent and growled, "To protect you from a rogue Joey that tries to jump you."

Veena laughed. "There are no kangaroos around here."

"Well then," said Milo, "you might be in danger from a vicious Koala." He reached out and drew her close in a strong embrace, as his right hand found her left buttock. She couldn't restrain a schoolgirl giggle as Milo kissed her half-parted lips.

DO UNTO OTHERS

At first I thought I knew the man but as I looked closer I realized I had taken him for someone else. He was seated at a small table in the corner at the Sparta Restaurant, a quaint little seafood eatery on the shore of Lake Union, a few blocks north of Seattle's bustling downtown. As I entered, a familiar figure stood before me, smiling a greeter's smile. He was an old acquaintance named Chris Pallis, who managed the Sparta Restaurant. Our polite greetings ensued despite the very busy atmosphere.

"We're really packed today. There are no tables for one available, but if you don't mind I can seat you at the table over there in the corner with that other gentleman. He's a regular and doesn't mind sharing his table." I looked again at the man sitting at the corner table. He sported a white goatee and large round glasses.

"I think you'll enjoy meeting him," he added. "He's pretty smart and a bit of a nonconformist. The rumor is that he was a college professor somewhere. Follow me."

"I hope you don't mind," I muttered as I was seated across from the stranger.

"You are most welcome," the man said in a firm

sincere tone. Extending his right hand he said, "People call me Professor. What is your name?"

"Call me Larry," I said as our eyes locked in what seemed like a long moment. The Professor picked away at his shrimp salad as I perused the menu.

"I understand you are a regular here, Professor. What can you recommend for lunch?"

"Don't order anything with meat. Their coffee is never hot and you are not going to like any of their so-called sandwiches. Better to stay with seafood, salads and beer."

I ordered. He picked and sipped. After a few moments he asked, "So Larry, what makes you an interesting man?"

I looked closely at this person who might be in his late sixties or early seventies. He was bright-eyed, olive-skinned, and regular-featured with a large mop of wild white hair reminiscent of Albert Einstein. He seemed to be a bit undersized, perhaps at five-nine and one-forty-five, give or take. He wore what I judged to be a perpetually bemused expression behind a pair of thick round glasses which exaggerated the size and roundness of his gaze. When he spoke he seemed to exude a quiet but vibrant energy which went along with a pair of beady dark brown eyes and the look of a predatory prehistoric bird. A pterodactyl? Perhaps. In response to his unexpected question, I faked a smile and said, "Not very interesting. I'm just a writer."

The Professor scratched his cheek with a forefinger ala Vito Corleone. "Do you make a living at it? If so, what do you write about?"

I tried to put a friendly look on my face and declared, "My experience includes working as a small-town newspaper reporter. Later, I worked as a feature writer at the Seattle Times. I've been fortunate to have two novels published. I enjoy writing about special people. I might like to write about someone like you."

Loud laughter escaped from the Professor's mouth. "Like me?" he roared. "There are none like me," he guffawed. "I suppose I should be flattered, but I am well past my ego phase, or I hope I am."

"I'm sure," I said, "that you have extensive knowledge and compelling opinions which would make interesting reading."

The Professor issued a sound like a quiet grunt. "The ideas and opinions that I have at this time may or may not be of interest to anyone. In any case I think that my thoughts would be difficult to grasp or at best be considered absurd to your average reader."

This really caught my interest. "I can't say I agree with you, sir. I'm sure your thoughts would be of great interest to readers, if I am any judge."

"That's kind of you to say, Larry, but it's okay to disagree."

I felt his penetrating beady eyes. Was there a challenge in that stare? "What would you say if I were to request a real interview?" I asked.

The Professor looked amused. "For what purpose?" he asked.

"For a human interest feature," I said. "Maybe there

would even be the possibility for a book." I smiled a genuine smile as he glared at me.

"You know very little about me," he declared. "If you did, you probably wouldn't entertain such thoughts."

I said, "Well, here's another thought. Subsequent to an initial interview, how about letting *me* decide if the idea is worthwhile to pursue?"

The Professor blinked a few times as he thought it over. Then he said, "We just met, Larry. I'm not sure I can trust you. How old are you?"

I looked away for a moment. "Thirty-four," I said, "six-one and one-ninety." A silence took over as we sipped our coffee.

The Professor wore a stern expression as he quietly spoke, "Maybe you should know what I am concerned about."

I said, "Please tell me."

The Professor leaned forward. "I mean to transform things," he stated.

*   *   *

The interview took place in a dark corner at Pedro's bar, a shabby little place in the Fremont neighborhood overlooking the ship canal. After the compulsory handshakes and semi-friendly greeting, the two of us sat opposite each other and ordered fried eggs, blackberry pancakes and virgin coffee. I spoke first. "I have a few questions for you, Professor, just to get things rolling. Is that okay with you?"

"That's fine, Larry, I don't much care for the usual small talk anyway."

"I think you will find our conversations to carry some substance. Here's a question for openers: What did you mean when you said you intend to transform things?"

The Professor looked at the ceiling and said, "Big changes take time. Transforming anything is usually a long term process. I will get to it as our discussion, or is it an interview, moves along."

"That sounds like you have some short term objectives as part of a long-range plan of some sort," I suggested.

The Professor's amused expression accompanied his words. "Sure, would you like to hear some of the minor issues that I intend to deal with?"

I nodded.

The Professor continued, "As the late comedian George Carlin used to say in his social commentary, 'Here's a list of people and things I can do without.'"

"For example, why have we allowed ourselves to accept the fact that the volume on our television sets automatically increases when the commercials appear on the TV screen? When television first began in America, the FCC imposed a limit on the number of commercials that were legally allowed relative to the length of the program on the screen. It didn't take long for the big corporate advertisers to get rid of such rules. As time went on, the number of commercials increased and got even louder. There seems to be no limit to the morally questionable images on movie screens. As

61

everyone knows, the proliferation of downright dirty words in movies and television is outrageous. Outright pornography is now accessible on everyone's home computers. Is decency disappearing for good? Respect for the English language is disappearing as well. How many times in the past week have you heard people use the word 'incredible'? It's incorrectly and constantly overused in everyday conversations and by people on radio and television. Why is it that professional communicators mispronounce the names of foreign countries like Iran and Iraq? The letter 'I' is correctly pronounced as we pronounce 'E.' Even some of our elected politicians, including some presidential candidates, indulge in abysmally ignorant use of the English language. Even some of our numbskull military leaders mispronounce 'Al Qaeda.' The polls indicate that somewhere near fifty percent of Americans deny the facts of evolution and global warming. It makes you wonder if there is any limit to intentional ignorance."

As I picked away at my breakfast, I was unsure if I could accurately read the Professor's facial expression. Was he being serious or just putting me on?

"Professor, are your comments to be taken seriously?" I asked.

"My comments about such tiny issues are not of real importance in the scheme of things, but they are not inconsequential as symbols of serious decline in American culture. Each month when you examine the bills from your utility and energy companies, are they invariably accurate? They are usually inaccurate and never in your favor. You know I'm right. The same goes for insurance companies, television cable stations and supposedly trustworthy banks. Some of us remember when it wasn't necessary to carefully examine our accounts, assets and bills to protect ourselves against false advertising and blatant cheating, along with all kinds of fraudulent schemes and scams. There used to be an unspoken trust between American business and their customers. Now there seems to be an overriding general attempt to cheat people out of their hard earned money."

In an attempt to simplify his commentary, I said, "So the smaller crazy issues are symbolic of a larger craziness?"

"Yes, indeed!" murmured the Professor. "We must keep in mind that all things are connected. I'll give you a few more examples. Any American of average intelligence must wonder why we think our country must continually fight, invade, slaughter and destroy armies, soldiers, innocent civilians and devastate cities, towns, villages and everything we can set our sights on. It must be that we believe that we are continually threatened by other countries intent on invading our shores. We seem to be continually told that we are the virtuous ones and our enemies are pure evil. Ever since our revolutionary war, we wage a new war every generation or so." The Professor raised his left hand to shoulder level and began showing his fingers as he kept track of a series of historical events. Counting continued with "The War of 1812, the Mexican War, the Civil War, the Spanish-

American War, World War One, World War Two, the Korean Conflict (a euphemism for a major war), the Cold War, the Vietnam War, the Desert Storm War, the Afghanistan War and the Iraq War. That doesn't count the many battles with Native American tribes and the many invasions of Mexico, Central American countries like Honduras, Nicaragua and Panama. In 1813, we even invaded Canada. In fewer than two centuries the USA has fought ten major wars. Do we believe that all those wars were really necessary? It's for sure that the billionaires who profit from sales of military weapons would enthusiastically agree that wars are absolutely necessary without any doubts whatsoever."

An anti-war tirade, I thought. *Are politics next?*

"Not only that," said the Professor, "but the ugly issue of racism is rampant again here in America. If that isn't enough, the concentration of wealth in this country is so extreme that in a short time all the wealth and the overwhelming power that goes with it will result in a totally different system of government. Nothing less than Oligarchy, which translates into all government policies and decisions being determined by a relative handful of billionaire corporations and families who will wield ultimate power to affect every aspect of life in the USA. Can you define Fascism?"

"Professor," I said, "Where are you going with all this?"

The Professor showed a buck-toothed smile, "You ain't heard nothin' yet," he declared.

I turned it over in my mind and said softly, "You

must admit that all this commentary will sound quite radical if disseminated as your opinion in the media. Is it your intention to make your opinions about these issues known to the public?"

The Professor's eyes lit up as he leaned forward with an attitude which seemed to say, pay attention and listen, "Aren't you going to ask me if I intend to remedy all this stupid behavior I have described?"

"Okay, I'm asking. Do you intend to do something to make things right?"

The Professor hardened his look, stuck his chin out and growled, "You're God damned right!"

*   *   *

Our next meeting was held at Lincoln Park in West Seattle, distinguished by wide shady pathways under the branches of enormous native trees. The circumferences of the many Douglas firs' trunks often exceeded eight feet. Hemlock and spruce trees were every bit as large, stately and magnificent examples of the Pacific Northwest forests of the past. The wooded grounds of Lincoln Park also included some very large deciduous trees such as giant madrona and maple species. Native shrubs formed elegant boundaries to the manicured pathways throughout the park.

The Professor paused near a park bench. "Shall we sit here?" he asked. He was unaware of my tiny little voice recorder hidden in my shirt pocket. I wasn't sure why I thought I should record his remarks but I felt compelled to do so for one of those mysterious motivations that nobody can explain.

"Well, Larry," said the Professor, "as I was telling you the last time, there are far too many things in this world that are out of control and one thing leads to another. Sooner or later things begin to break down, unravel, split apart and result in disaster. This occurs in the tiniest systems in nature as well as all of man's creations such as any institution and organization. Scientists have a word for it. They call it 'entropy.' It's really quite easy to see, if anyone would stop and think about it for a minute, that the pace of technological advancement is running out of control right now. Most futurists predict the possible end of the human species as a result of artificial intelligence outsmarting us and taking over."

I studied the Professor's facial expression to determine the tone of my next question. "I assume there is a lot more commentary about the many ironies in the various aspects of the culture in general, Professor, but is it premature for me to ask where this is going?"

"Yes it is," he said, "but I can share just a bit of an overview if you are getting impatient. You see, Larry, I haven't yet decided if I can completely trust you as yet."

"Well," I said, "you are the one to determine the degree of trust you may or may not have in me. I understand, but if it means anything, I give you my word that none of what you have told me and anything you might tell me from this point on will ever be disclosed or repeated to anyone else without your permission. I would appreciate hearing more."

The Professor scratched his forehead in thought. "Okay, Larry," he said, "I can give you the benefit of the doubt for now. How would you define the 'Golden Rule'?"

"My definition?" I asked.

"Yes," he murmured, "can you accurately define it?"

I drew in a breath, "Do unto others as you would have them do unto you."

"Is it from the Bible?" the Professor asked.

"Yes," I answered, "and from other religious philosophies as well which go back even further in time. It seems to have been forgotten in today's world."

The Professor seemed to take on a sort of sly look, like he had a secret. "How is it you have never asked my name?" he asked.

"I didn't want to probe too much until I got to know you better," I mumbled.

The Professor squared his shoulders. "My name is Edgar Rule. I have an interesting middle name which I rarely use. My mother and father were good and virtuous people. They were very idealistic and hopeful that they could somehow play a part in making the world a better place. They were not being playful when they gave me a middle name, Golden. My legal and official name is Edgar Golden Rule."

I needed a few moments to digest what I considered a kind of revelation. It gave me the courage to ask more personal questions. "Where have you worked as a Professor, Mr. Rule?"

"After earning my PhD at Princeton in New Jersey, I taught for almost forty years at three universities until my retirement about a year ago. The first was at Reed College in Portland, Oregon, an elite private school for only those with the highest academic qualifications. The second job was at Amherst in Massachusetts, another exclusive school for the rich and privileged. My third educational assignment was at Howard University in Washington D.C. You have heard of Howard, of course. The student body is virtually all African American by intention. Its founders wished to offer an affordable higher education opportunity for black students who were denied admittance to most other colleges and universities in many places in the country at the time. After only two years at Howard, they kicked me out. I was fired." The Professor revealed a sad smile.

"Good Lord," I exclaimed, with such an apparently outstanding record in higher education, how did that happen?"

"I would probably still be teaching someplace, but after they dumped me at Howard, I couldn't get another job. That's why I live out here in Nowheresville hanging out in quirky little eateries and making plans."

Now I had to ask, "Don't you want to tell me what happened at Howard? And what is it you are planning?"

The Professor was now glowering at me. In an unusually gruff tone, he said, "You are asking two questions."

I said, "You don't have to answer."

"I will answer the first one," he said. "The reason the dean at Howard canned me was because he said that I hurt the feelings of my students in a couple of my classes by acquainting them with a social reality. This was in a sociology class."

"What made them think that their feelings had been hurt?" I asked.

The Professor looked thoughtful.

"I was lecturing about responsibilities in a sociological context and generalizing about the behavior of people living in ghettos and other black neighborhoods in America. I told them that despite the inequities in their lives, it would be slow going to achieve total equality without measurable change in the behavior of those members of the black community that were perceived by the white population as being hooligans, thugs, participants in drive-by shootings, outright criminals, inner-city gang-bangers and with disproportionate numbers involved in murder and other serious crimes. The statistics cannot be waived even when there is a general awareness of limited opportunity in so many ways in the black communities. I was careful to include comments which acknowledged my awareness of social, legal and traditional white privilege and the myriad of laws, and outrageous discriminatory traditions. Despite all of that, they nailed me and ruined my reputation along with what was left of my career. I simply voiced an opinion."

Then I said, "College people pride themselves on their objectivity. Do you see that experience as an example of hypocrisy?"

"Of course," he said, "hypocrisy is everywhere. It's positively pervasive in these times in politics, religion, education, science, government, the military, the legal system, business, in charitable organizations and in the hearts of otherwise well-meaning institutions and individuals."

I couldn't help chuckling quietly at the irony of his comment. The Professor and I watched as a casually dressed middle-aged man strolled by and flipped a cigarette butt into the grass a few feet away from our bench. The Professor stared at the remains of what had likely been an instrument of destruction to the poor sap's health, perhaps leading to an early death.

"It's going to be difficult to deal with the problem of these people deliberately destroying themselves," he said softly.

*   *   *

Our next meeting took place at lunchtime in an upscale restaurant called the Palisades, located a mile northwest of downtown Seattle on the shore of Elliott Bay at the foot of Magnolia Bluff. The interior was contemporary, spacious and classy in every respect. The Professor and I were seated adjacent to enormous windows with a knockout view of a Carnival Line cruise ship tied up about two hundred yards away across the water from our vantage point. "Great view," I said as we were seated by a young lady who, for the moment, I was sure was the virtual reincarnation of Elizabeth Taylor.

After ordering what promised to be some scrumptious salmon and oyster choices, the Professor peered into my eyes and asked, "Do you think these little rants I have uttered are worthwhile for your purpose, Larry?"

"I can't really tell yet," I responded, "but I'm hopeful." I joshed a bit with the waitress as we ordered from the enticing delicacies offered on the menu. "I've thought a lot about your comments, Professor," I said. "I look forward with great anticipation to what you will be telling me today."

The Professor quietly sipped his coffee, "I have more for you, Larry."

"Most people in America have no knowledge about the 'Robber Baron' period of big business in the late nineteenth and early twentieth centuries. Those were the times of greedy monopolies and out-of-control business interests which begat virtual slave labor and widespread poverty. Anti-monopoly laws were passed and over time resulted in forcible break-up and reorganization of many of the biggest companies. This proved ultimately beneficial for overall economic and humanitarian purposes. The anti-monopoly laws are still on the books. At this time we have dozens of monopolies among our big corporations which meet the definitions of illegal monopolies. No cases have been pursued by the government since the 1980's, so don't be surprised if the federal government will soon be virtually controlled by those super big business organizations. They continue to destroy all competition, manipulate the trade policies and economic decisions for their own selfish purposes. Thus, the US domestic and foreign policies will be controlled and coordinated by a top level collusion between the insurance companies,

Big Pharma, all banks, manufacturing companies, Wall Street speculators and a handful of politicians bought and paid for by a relatively small group of billionaires." The Professor paused and gave me a glowering look.

"You are getting pretty political," I said.

"I'm just stating the truth," he said. "Not only that, but Americans of this generation have attitudes quite different from those of, say, two generations ago. Too many young people today are ill-mannered, inconsiderate, uncaring, drug addicted, pistol-packing loud-mouthed ignoramuses. Not all of them, but a vast majority fit the description. Most people would not agree, but those are the younger ones who don't remember the older days when there was a value placed on civility and respect for others to a much greater degree than in present times."

"That's a pretty broad generalization," I suggested.

"Most older people," declared the Professor, "would agree but they are afraid of being challenged, attacked and becoming involved in an uncomfortable controversy." Taking a bite of his broiled salmon, he gently chewed and blotted his lips with his napkin.

I voiced a question: "Do you think it possible that there could ever be a revolution in the United States of America? Whose interests would it serve?"

The Professor replied, "Theoretically it could serve the interests and needs of the bottom eighty or ninety percent of all America, but it would have to occur within certain parameters to be successful."

"How do you see such an event ever taking place in this country?" I goaded.

"It would have to take place as a huge grass-roots movement, of course. It would take an enormous amount of money, political and military involvement and unprecedented will on the part of many factions of our society to peacefully accomplish such an earth-shaking endeavor. I emphasize the peacefully part. The organizers would need complete and total control of the military. The army and marines would have to temporarily incarcerate every government official including everyone in the congress, white house and pentagon if necessary. After a successful coup d'état, martial law would ensure the control of all state and local governments as the transition continued. Don't think it can't happen. It's happened to other modern governments in a very smooth fashion. The new philosophy would then have to be imposed along with the dissemination of pertinent information to the public as the changes take place. All communications, computer and energy systems would be tightly controlled and our military would be put on alert for danger of threatening actions toward the USA by foreign nations."

I sipped my coffee and asked, "Would a takeover of the government be in violation of many laws including the Constitution itself?"

"Of course," said Professor Edgar Golden Rule, but it wouldn't be the first time. We remember the Confederate secession in 1861, the Jim Crow decision in 1893 and the imprisonment of Japanese-American citizens right after Pearl Harbor in 1942. Many powerful forces both within and outside the government have violated the

Constitution in the past and gotten away with it." The Professor smiled proudly as if he believed an important declaration had been delivered.

In a very low serious voice, I asked, "Are you aware of plans by subversive forces in this country that might actually be planning such a life-changing takeover, coup or revolution such as you describe?"

My question evoked a stern look through those big round spectacles and his wild hair seemed even wilder. His mouth twitched a bit as he squared up in his chair. For such a small man, he had the ability to somehow make himself appear as a very big and important figure. "There are always radical forces planning or hoping for such things. Nothing like it has ever happened because there has always been such effective security in the vulnerable places."

"Look, Professor," I said, "please don't take me wrong. With all due respect, from the way you talk I would almost suspect that you could be sympathetic to a revolution such as you describe to me."

"To answer your question I would need nothing less than your sworn oath to never betray me for anything that you know or even suspect about me, my beliefs, plans or intentions about absolutely anything."

I looked him squarely in the eye, thrust my jaw forward and hissed, "I'll do exactly as you ask. If you require an oath-swearing ritual, a signed document or both, let's get on with it."

The Professor held my stare. "Are you one of those Christians?" he asked.

"Close enough," I said.

"Then I'll bring my Jefferson Bible." The Professor gestured with his hand as if something had been resolved and spoke, "Let's meet tomorrow at ten."

*　*　*

I didn't sleep much that night. The Professor's remarks kept repeating inside my brain, preventing me from falling into my normal sleep routine until early morning which resulted in a tardy arrival at the Professor's designated meeting place. The address was easy to find. It turned out to be a rather small, neat-looking apartment building on Green Lake Way, about a block from one of Seattle's three charming lakes located within the city limits.

After announcing myself at the doorway of the Haida apartment building, I entered and found my way to the Professor's small, tidy apartment. "You found it," he said, "and almost on time."

"You have a very nice apartment, Professor," I said. "It looks like you have two bedrooms."

"So I do. My second bedroom is used for my computer and all the stuff that goes with it. Let's get down to business. Sit here at the table." I could see the little recorder along with a printed contract, a legal-looking document and a skinny Bible. He said, "Maybe you have read the Jefferson Bible?"

I stared at it and inadvertently uttered a little cough. "I've heard of it. Is that the one that Thomas Jefferson edited to include only the pronouncements and actions of Jesus in which everything else was left out?"

"This is the one," smirked the Professor. "Real Christians don't seem to like it much. Put your right hand on it, Larry, and repeat after me." As we began the oath, he turned on his little digital recorder. The verbal oath, the official looking document and the contract were similar in content. The strange little rituals were designed as a total loyalty commitment to the Professor's thoughts, opinions and plans. I was even required to cross my heart a couple of times. As we finished, the Professor gathered the recorder along with the documents and carried them into the other bedroom to store or to file. He was smiling as he served coffee and a tasty butterhorn.

"Now," he said proudly, "we can be trusted friends!" I nibbled on the fresh pastry, sipped my coffee and gave in to a comfortable state of relaxation. This was a rare feeling when in the presence of Edgar G. Rule. My own tiny recorder which was hidden in an inside pocket, continued to record everything.

"Now that we have established a trusting relationship," I said, "I need to hear more about your plans to change things for the better."

"I take it that you sincerely wish to be part of my plan to change the United States of America." He smiled and glowed. "Are you in?"

"You bet, I'm your man," I declared.

He rested his elbows on the arms of his chair and placed the fingertips of both hands together, just under his chin and began to speak. "I have an appointment in less than an hour. I will give you a brief version of the plan for now. As we proceed in the next few weeks, I'll fill in more details."

I nodded. "Please proceed. I'm all ears."

"Here's a rough outline of the benefits everyone in America will derive. We will not only maintain most of our entitlement programs, but we will enlarge and extend them to provide increased health, happiness and protection for all. These generous programs however will be subject to new rules for the purpose of eliminating financial waste, dealing efficiently with bureaucratic nonsense and imposing common sense principles. These principles will insure the highest level of efficiency by means of great emphasis on accountability on the part of all administrators, managers and workers up and down the line. New very stringent laws will be imposed to protect our fragile environment which has been inexcusably abused for far too long. State 'right to work' laws will be declared unconstitutional and trade unions will be encouraged to flourish, although with intense scrutiny. The IRS tax laws will undergo a complete review. Corporate welfare tax loopholes will be eliminated. All pure food and drug laws will be upgraded and enhanced. Our tax revenue policies will include sensible increases for most multibillionaire corporations, resulting in increased income for the Federal Treasury. Trade tariffs will probably need to be increased, but renewed scrutiny will be in order. Since the problem of the increased proliferation of guns has become unmanageable, we will reverse the present trend by dealing with the problem in some ways considered radical by some, but sensible and necessary by right thinking people. Just wait until you see what's going to happen to those crooks on Wall Street who have had an unprecedented run of profit through fraudulent shenanigans. Laws will be passed requiring mandatory voting for virtually all American citizens."

I raised a finger to signal for a pause. "Some of these 'reforms' will seem to violate the Constitution," I suggested.

"Of course," said the Professor, "but that won't stop us from making the necessary corrections. We have plans to deal with the contradictions. You understand that a coup means a takeover of government without armed conflict or bloodshed. As I explained to you yesterday, by virtue of our control of the military and martial law, we will be able to govern by means of a temporary dictatorship, not by a single individual but with a three-man triumvirate, backed, of course, and advised by a nine-person council. At this point, we have virtually decided on which individuals will serve. I can tell you that the most brilliant people in this country will guide us through the transitions back to a familiar version of the USA."

I gave the pause signal again and asked, "How long would this temporary dictatorship remain in place?"

The Professor's eyes gleamed. He hesitated and the words slid out of his mouth. "Not more than a year or two. We will need that much time because there will be so much to accomplish and we Americans are not used to big changes, not to mention rapid progress and efficient work. One of the first things we have to change is the matter of too much money in politics. We have to put a strict limit on the contributions by the donor class. Our politics now are ensnarled in a system of legalized bribery. We will get rid of the lobbyists in Washington D.C. This will allow congress to fulfill the wishes of their constituents instead of accepting bribery money from the special interests. Too many businesses are guilty of cheating the public. Banks and credit card companies seem immune from charges of usury, de facto bribery and other illegal devices to provide unfair financial advantage. Under our rule, the authorities will expose them and prosecute them as never before."

"Professor," I interrupted, "surely you know that these measures will be severely challenged and criticized by those who fear we will cease to be a capitalist republic and become some kind of freaky combination of a socialist dictatorship or another Soviet Union."

"Yeah, I know," said the Professor, "but I have a special earth-shattering method of achieving this new age of making things right for the betterment of all people everywhere, thus becoming a model society for all time to come. This will be far above and beyond anything ever attempted in the history of the world!"

That was a surprise. "Now you have to tell me," I said, "what this new movement consists of."

"It has a name," he whispered. "It goes by the initials GR, we call it the GR movement."

I mouthed the words. "The GR movement? Does GR stand for Golden Rule?"

"Yes," he said in a hoarse voice. "The motto is 'Do unto Others.' The GR movement will soon become the national passion and become the fulfillment of the greatest dream of mankind. It will set an unprecedented ethical and moral standard of behavior and lead to a better world from every possible viewpoint. It will renew mankind's eternal hope for a better life on the planet for all time to come."

The Professor's passionate remarks begged the question, so I had to ask, "How do we instill the Golden Rule philosophy into the hearts and minds of hundreds of millions, or is it billions of unsuspecting people?" We both had to chuckle over the word "unsuspecting."

The Professor raised his voice a bit and his words seemed to have a sharper edge. "That part will be easier than you might think, but let me give you a short sequential summary of some background and how the action will go. My planning committee consists of about a dozen of the most brilliant loyal courageous people you could imagine. We have high-level politicians, military generals and admirals, world-renowned economists, Nobel-winning scientists, computer technology wizards and a very large number of revolutionary activists. We have been working intently on our plans to take over for the past three years. Our secret is apparently secure, even though we have had to 'take out' a few who we suspected might betray us. Control of the Treasury will help with the funding. Our governing group will do their work from the bomb-proof office in the Capitol basement. The big changes will then begin and proceed smoothly and efficiently. It will take time, but when the public realizes the enormous benefits conferred on them by our new government, they will accept, adapt and be happier than ever before."

I interrupted, "Professor, how can you be certain that such a takeover of the US government would not result in counter revolutionary violence?"

"We don't think so," he snapped, "are you aware of the recent breakthroughs in brain research? Some Cal Tech researchers have been working on constructing a large size artificial human brain, complete with the billions of complex electro-magnetic pathways and connections precisely like the human brain. The various locations in the human brain that function as memory, perception, motivation, emotional feelings, reasoning and every human function have been installed in the Cal Tech artificial metal and plastic three feet long counterpart of our natural flesh and blood human brain. Some of this research has become available to the drug companies. Some of their ongoing research overlaps or dovetails with the world- shaking discoveries by the brain research scientists. This has resulted in many experimental drugs being produced. It is hoped by the Big Pharma people that we may have drugs in the near future that will have powers to virtually cure cancer, dementia, diabetes, epilepsy, malaria and many of our debilitating diseases. Not only that but it will be possible to alter our thinking, our perceptions, our judgements, our attitudes, our philosophy, our religious convictions, self-awareness and our deeper consciousness. They now know for sure that our brain is the facilitator for most everything we do in life. Just imagine that in the very near future we all would be afforded access to a little pill that would provide motivation to adopt the Golden Rule as our overall guide for every activity and every relationship in our lives. Now let me tell you a secret. There is such a drug and I have access to it in unlimited quantities. It may not be easy to believe me, Larry, but I have acquired some big time connections and thousands of loyal followers eager to do my bidding."

This latest was a mind-boggling revelation to me, so I spoke up. "Just how are you planning to impart the Golden Rule into everyone's consciousness, with some kind of brainwashing procedure?"

The Professor smiled, "There are many methods available to us to install a 'Do unto Others' consciousness that is efficient, well-intentioned and effective. It requires intensive planning along with noble intentions. It, of course, would be one of civilized man's greatest achievements if we can successfully carry it off. I believe that no less than the survival of the species is at stake. Can you perceive all this in accordance with the way I have described it to you?"

"It's a lot to digest," I mumbled. "You have given me an insightful perspective. Are you going to tell me exactly what part *you* will be playing in this revolution?"

Professor Edgar Golden Rule drew himself up in his armchair and faced me looking directly into my eyes. His arms were slightly extended with his open palms facing up and said, "I will be heading up the triumvirate and supervising the nine-man council. I will have total charge. It will all take place exactly six months from this very day."

*   *   *

Those were the Professor's words about two years ago. I have been incarcerated for almost the same amount of time. There is supposed to be unspeakable shame for any murderer sentenced to a lengthy prison term in a penitentiary, even if it is a 'white collar' prison like where I am locked up now as I write this story. One would think that capital murder would usually bring the death penalty, but in my case there were extenuating circumstances. In my youth I had served in the Marine Corps and sworn to protect the Constitution. I considered it a lifetime commitment, therefore when I divulged the Professor's plans to the FBI, I felt in my heart, I was doing my duty as an American citizen. The FBI investigation wasn't getting anywhere, so I took the matter into my own hands and strangled the little bastard.

There are many unjustified reasons for taking the life of a fellow human being. Having 'taken out' the Professor, I think of myself as an instrument for the avoidance of imminent disaster imposed on the United States of America. It caused a major stir in the media. Some people think of me as a martyr.

I can only hope you agree.

HONEST COP

Marty Griffen sat on the edge of his bed. "It's great to sleep in," he thought, "after all those years on the job. Thirty-one years of getting up at six-thirty. I lost out on a lot of weekends too, when Connie and the kids left to enjoy the cabin or the beach but I was too restless and distracted to be part of it. Being a cop twists your thinking. It makes a damn weirdo out of you."

Looking at himself in the tall bedroom mirror, he judged himself to be in pretty good shape for his age of fifty-five, at five-eleven and one-eighty-five. He was still pretty muscular and had no fat to speak of, just a little here and there. *Not bad, Marty, but you could do with more exercise.* Glancing at his wife who was sound asleep in the bed, he decided that she was still quite a beauty. *I think I'll start the day with a nice hot shower.*

Marty struggled a bit keeping his focus on the business at hand, which was not overcooking his scrambled eggs. As he washed his breakfast down with black coffee, his thoughts continued. Now three years since his retirement from the Seattle Police Department, he was successfully settled, notwithstanding his pathetic retirement pension. At least that's what he told himself every day.

Come on, Marty, he said to himself, don't be a jerk, appreciate all that God has given you. A nice house in a decent neighborhood, a loving loyal wife who goes along with just about everything you want to do. Then there are our three grown kids, all living their own lives and a few good friends at the bridge club. What more could you ask for? Wait, he told himself, I'm not done thinking about it yet.

The phone interrupted his reverie. The name of Marty's best friend, Perry Jarvis, appeared on the screen. "What the hell do you want?" barked Marty into the phone, trying his best to hold back a laugh.

"Am I speaking to Marty, the douche bag?" a hoarse male voice asked.

Marty spoke loudly into the phone, "This must be the guy everyone calls sewer mouth. Is it really you?"

"You up for lunch today, big shot?" Perry asked.

Marty paused, "Yeah, why not? I think Connie has some kind of appointment. Have you picked out one of the choke-and-puke eateries you like so much?"

"You probably won't puke but I can't guarantee the choke part. We'll shovel grub at a place called Faro's on lower Queen Anne. On second thought, knowing you, I wouldn't be surprised if you puked your guts out right at the table. We'll find out soon enough," said Perry in a tone that sounded like an old street cop comment.

"That sounds perfectly delightful, Mr. Knuckle Butt. See you there at noon."

*   *   *

Without admitting it, both Marty and Perry enjoyed their lunch. The friendly insults continued off and on throughout lunch, interrupted by some pleasurable reminiscing about the sometimes bizarre and crazy occurrences which are a normal part of every police officer's daily experience. Leaving the restaurant, both were in good spirits as they casually strolled down the sidewalk toward their car, parked half a block away.

"Do you know that Ike Hargett lives about three blocks from here?" asked Perry.

"Old Sergeant Ike? He's been retired for how long, about eight years?" asked Marty, answering his own question.

"Let's drop in on him," suggested Perry, "just for the hell of it."

"I hope old Sarge isn't going down the tube," murmured Marty as the two ex-cops stepped onto the front porch of the shabby-looking house.

"Are you sure this is the right address? What a dump." Perry rang the doorbell. After a short wait, Ike Hargett greeted them with a big smile accompanied by ritual handshakes, hugs and punches on arms and slaps on backs.

"It's great to see you guys," growled Ike. "It's been way too long."

"How's it going, you old buzzard? Nobody ever hears from you," scolded Perry.

At that moment an attractive fifty-something woman

walked into the room. "Hey," shouted Ike, "this is Candy! These are two of my old comrades, Marty and Perry. We were on the job together back in the day!"

Candy appeared to be in good physical shape, but looked tired. Sporting a fashionably short haircut, painted eyebrows, shiny red lipstick, with large brown eyes and ample breastwork, she boldly ogled the two strangers. "Don't you remember me, Marty?" she smiled.

"Oh my God," exclaimed Marty, "of course I remember, it was so long ago. Wait a second, it's Candy, right? Its been over twenty years. What a surprise! Candy, do you live here?"

"Yeah," she said, in a throaty voice, "right here with Ike for the past three years. Ain't that a coincidence?"

Ike said, "Candy's a waitress at Clark's downtown restaurant at Fourth and Union. They know her as Mary."

"I'm on my way to work right now, so I've gotta dash for the bus. Maybe we'll see you fellas again soon."

"Nice to meet you," said Perry. After Candy's departure, the three ex-police officers sat at the dining room table and looked at one another.

"Great to see you again, Ike," said Marty.

"Relax guys," said Ike Hargett, "let's have a drink and catch up."

*   *   *

After returning home, Marty sat in his easy chair just as the phone rang. "Hey, Long Dong," Perry's voice came over the line. "Is anybody listening on the line?"

"No," said Marty, "Connie hasn't returned."

"Am I mistaken, or did you have some kind of thing with Candy back when you were a young cop at the Central Downtown precinct?"

"If you don't bring it up, it will stay forgotten," said Marty in a grim voice.

"I could use it for blackmail," giggled Perry.

At that moment Marty was pleased to see that Connie's car was pulling into their driveway. After giving his wife the usual squeeze and soft peck on the lips, Marty plunked himself onto his most comfortable lounge chair and assumed a position of exaggerated relaxation, closing his eyes and shutting off all distractions. The telephone on the adjoining coffee table rang. Marty picked up, "Hello," he growled.

An unfamiliar man's voice said, "Hello, I'm trying to contact Mister Marty Griffen."

"Speaking," Marty said.

The voice said, "I hope that you will bear with me for a very short few minutes as I have an opportunity and an interesting offer for you."

"What offer?" snapped Marty.

"I represent a firm that specializes in providing security services. We have a need for a part-time security guard on some jobs that might be of interest to you. I can tell you that the pay for this work is very generous. For example, this Thursday a nine-hour shift would pay up to three-hundred dollars. I should tell you that recruiting men for this kind of work is easy for me, but we select only the best qualified in terms of experience, competence, decision-making abilities and loyalty. We know something of your stellar reputation as a former police officer and that's why I'm calling you, Mr. Griffen. You might think of it as an opportunity to work two or three days a week for a period of weeks or months." The caller paused. "Does this sound like it might be of interest to you?"

Marty's jaw hardened, "Who is this? What is your name and who do you represent?"

The voice said, "You may call me Damon. I represent a legitimate security firm well-known and respected in the industry. If you show serious interest, Marty, may I call you Marty? Then I will answer all of your questions and concerns."

"Well," said Marty, "I'll have to give it some thought. You need to furnish me with proof of who you are, or at least virtual proof. So far you haven't convinced me that you are who you say."

"How about this?" said Damon, "I need an answer for Thursday. Suppose you think it over and give me a definite answer when I call you again at ten o'clock tonight?"

The phone call over, both men hung up. Connie appeared from the kitchen and paused for a moment in the doorway. "Who was that, Marty? I didn't get much from what I heard you say on the phone."

Marty looked at her and said, "Sit down, Honey and I'll tell you about it."

Connie said, "Are you saying you could make three

hundred dollars a shift and work two shifts a week? At six hundred a week, that's twenty-four hundred a month!"

"Not so fast," he said, "I haven't even agreed to anything yet. I don't know enough about this guy who calls himself Damon and the rest of his story."

"Oh, Marty, you'll never get over being a cynical cop. Suppose this is a legitimate offer? If you did it for six months at twenty-four hundred, we could save enough for a trip to Europe, the trip we've always dreamed of and never could afford. Assuming that the offer met your standards, whatever they are, would you be willing to take the time for a part-time job? You know that many ex-cops take security jobs for the extra income."

Marty couldn't suppress a grin, "When you get wound up you really are cute."

Connie came closer, threw herself into his lap and placed her arms around his seventeen-inch neck "Promise me you will give it some serious thought," she murmured.

Marty had to admit to himself that he very much enjoyed the closeness of Connie's body and face, her large lovely eyes locked into his, her lips only inches away from his own. The result was that Marty relaxed and his facial expression softened. "Well," he said softly, "the way our lives seem to be going right now, I have to admit that I'm enjoying my free time. But I suppose I could take a part-time job now and again so that we could add to our savings. Our financial cushion is nowhere near what it should be, no secret about that."

Connie responded by planting a soft kiss on Marty's

mouth, the tip of her tongue succeeded in touching Marty's and surprised him. After the kiss, Marty looked intently into Connie's eyes and breathed, "For you sweetheart, I would do anything." They both laughed. "Well," he said, "almost anything."

*   *   *

As expected, the phone rang precisely at ten p.m. Marty put the phone on speaker. "Hello, Damon," spoke Marty.

"Good evening, Marty," said the voice. "Have you had enough time to think about my offer?"

"I've given it a lot of thought and I am leaning toward a positive answer. Before doing so, I need more information."

"Sure," said Damon, "go ahead and ask."

"What is the name of your organization?"

"Guardian Services Agency," said Damon. "Look it up and you will be convinced of our outstanding reputation."

"How strenuous is the work?"

"Not strenuous at all. About one shift in ten there could be some form of action, if you could call it that. The action I refer to is almost always a minimum risk situation because our officers are true professionals and understand how to defuse any serious danger."

Connie listened intently.

Marty asked, "How should I dress and what should I take with me?" Damon's answers seemed acceptable to both Marty and Connie.

Marty arrived forty-five minutes early at the assigned destination in the Woodinville suburb. As described, the building was a two-story brick office building with a concrete porch and access stairway. Marty entered and opened the door to the first office on the right as instructed. Three men sat inside – two big guys and a smaller one who rose and stepped toward Marty.

"Glad to see you, Marty," Damon declared in a pleasant baritone voice. "I'm Damon Garchik," he said, extending his hand for a firm handshake.

Marty's experience allowed him to very quickly take in virtually every detail about the appearance of Damon Garchik and the other two men as well. Damon was no taller than five-nine on a thin frame and skinny neck topped by a head a bit larger in proportion than normal. Topped by thinning black hair and a receding hairline, his narrow face contained a prominent nose, thin lips and very dark deep-set intelligent gray eyes.

"Let me introduce you," said Damon, "to these two gentlemen you will be working with today. The two men stepped forward to shake hands as they were introduced. "This is Rocky Dukich, a good man to work with, a very brave and loyal guy. Meet Biff Lonsky, as good a partner as you could ask for." Biff was the taller of the two wearing a graying crew cut, a sallow complexion and a flat nose which had obviously been broken more than once. Biff carried a strong-looking athletic physique. Rocky stood about five-ten with a husky build and a full head of black hair. A coarse featured round face appeared as if Rocky had survived a few physical battles himself. Marty perceived Rocky's black darting eyes as a giveaway to an 'undependable' character. More specific evaluations of his new partners would no doubt come into Marty's judgment as things moved along. Further instructions were necessary before their security shift began. Marty sat in a chair at the front of Damon's desk as he familiarized himself with the man's check list.

"You have dressed appropriately, Marty. I see you have provided yourself with a tie, a jacket and your lunch box. On the table over there are our black caps. They are similar to army officer's baseball-style caps with our GSA logo emblazoned on the front. Your flashlights and night sticks are there as well. I'm sure you remember carrying them back in the day when you used to walk a beat." Damon grinned. "Back then we called them 'billy clubs' or 'batons.' You are 'packing,' are you not?"

Marty kept looking Damon directly in the eyes, "Yes," he said, "I have my Glock nine automatic in a holster flat against my lower back, nicely concealed as per your instructions."

Damon spoke quietly, "Your job today will be to work with each other to patrol the area around the building. If the teenage hoodlums who have threatened to graffiti the outside of the building show up, you guys are to intimidate them with your presence. Do not fight them or hurt them unless forced to do so. I want Biff to call the sheriff and me if the situation becomes threatening. If that occurs, all three of you are to position yourselves at the entrance of the building in a military stance showing your night sticks. If your shift ends peacefully you are free to go home at two a.m. Do you have questions?"

The three security guards sat around a small table. Biff Lonsky spoke first. "If a fight starts or the deputies don't show up we have the right to defend the building. If it comes to that and we have to use our clubs, we are supposed to just knock 'em down and bruise 'em up, but don't bash their heads in and avoid killing any of 'em. Remember, if it comes to a fight, we are in a self-defense mode, got it?" The two other men nodded.

Marty said, "You fellas sound like you are experienced. I retired from the Seattle Police Department three years ago. I was on the job for thirty years. If you don't mind my asking, what are your backgrounds? I like to know something about the guys I am working with, especially if there's the possibility of action."

"I worked for twenty-five years as an officer for the King County Sheriff's department," replied Biff Lonsky.

Rocky Dukich said, "I was an Army MP for three enlistments – twelve years in different places around the world as well as the USA."

Based on his training and experience, Marty guessed that Biff and Rocky had worked together on similar assignments.

*   *   *

As the shift began, the three security guards separated and walked slowly around the exterior of the building. The neighborhood was quiet. Marty and the other two guards took turns retreating into the building to eat their lunches. After reassembling, the three relaxed by sitting on the front porch and discussing the latest news about the Seahawks and the Mariners. As evening approached the three men became noticeably more alert. As they patrolled the area around the building their movements became cautiously sensitive. Their previous experience in law enforcement led them to sense and anticipate that something was likely to happen.

Just as it turned dark, a pickup truck and two aging cars came into view moving slowly down the street. As Damon had warned, the vehicles appeared to contain as many as thirteen or fourteen teenage boys. The three guards assumed a defensive position, brandishing their billy clubs and projecting a fierce glare toward the new arrivals.

The kids in the truck and the cars stared back, assessing the situation, perhaps thinking, "Only three guards. What could they do against more than a dozen of us if we attacked them and gave the building a spray job?" The nineteen-year-old long-haired driver of the pickup stepped to the sidewalk and yelled, "Everybody on the sidewalk!"

As the boys piled out of the vehicles to line up on the sidewalk facing the building, Biff Lonsky spoke into his cell phone to call for backup from the sheriff's headquarters. Unfortunately, he thought, the Sheriff's deputies would be coming from their office as far as three miles away and would not be able to help if these kids really attacked in an aggressive way.

Rocky suddenly recalled that protective shields were available on a table inside the office. He quickly turned and darted into the front door of the building, immediately returning with the two-foot by three-foot shields. All cops were familiar with the shields employed by police tactical squads when used in confrontations with demonstrators or mobs of some kind.

Biff spoke so his two partners could hear, "What do ya think guys?"

Rocky's eyes glittered as he responded, "We don't run from punks like these little shits!"

Biff added, "The law's on our side. If they come, smash their body parts but not their heads!"

Marty had been in many confrontations in the years he was on the job and was always able to suppress any real feelings of fear, perhaps because of confidence in his ability to fight if necessary and not be intimidated by the threat of violence. Despite his disciplined thinking, he had to wonder what he had gotten himself into.

The big kid in charge hollered, "Let's get the job done, guys, GO FOR IT!" All thirteen teenage hoodlums ran forward in a massive charge wielding their spray paint cans and their clubs, a few of which were full-sized iron crow bars. Three of the boys seemed to be assigned to throw firecrackers into the melee, possibly as a distraction to the guards opposing them or maybe just to add to the excitement. The plan of attack was obviously to overwhelm the three guards with superior numbers. Aware of the kids' strategy, Marty and Rocky left Biff's side and moved to a new defensive stance on each side wall, thus forcing their attackers into three smaller groups. The men weren't sure how seriously aggressive the teenage attackers were. Could it be that they were just having fun?

Marty knew immediately when the attack began that the boys were out for blood, so it was no holds barred. Four of them came at Marty swinging their clubs and attempted to squirt him with their cans of red and black paint. The two tall seventeen-year-olds and two smaller kids seemed confident that their superior numbers would take Marty off his feet. Marty used his shield to deftly ward off a stream of red paint aimed directly at his face, at the same time sweeping his billy club swiftly, low to the ground. It smashed into the first kid's ankles sending him screaming to the ground, probably with a broken ankle. Side-stepping to his left, Marty greeted a second boy with a crushing blow to his thigh rendering his left leg useless for the moment. As the kid tumbled to the ground Marty clubbed him on his lower back. The lightning fast action didn't keep Marty from remembering his instructions from the police training academy instructor. "Take their legs out from under them and hurt them enough when they're on the ground so they can't get back up." Marty made short work of the two remaining attackers with some agile footwork and savage use of his shield and club, leaving the two young idiots sprawled on the ground out of action. The boys' yells and screams of pain did not deter Marty for a second as he charged forward to help Biff in his battle

with four boys. The number was now only two since Biff
had beaten two of them senseless. Marty quickly moved
in to put one of the two boys down. By the time Marty
and Biff charged over to help Dukich, the fight was over
with the teens still on their feet running for the safety
of their pickup truck, cars, and the delinquents on the
ground, beaten and bleeding.

Police sirens cut through the night as the Sheriff's
van arrived. The driver and four deputies disembarked,
armed with shotguns. The deputy in charge quickly
evaluated the situation as he barked orders to the
other officers. The teenaged attackers who were not
seriously hurt were handcuffed and hustled into the
van. The injured kids were gently laid out in the small
yard surrounding the building. Three ambulances had
been called.

Two deputies were assigned to gather the paint cans
and other evidence. At this time the High Sheriff arrived
in a county squad car. Damon Garchik also pulled up
in his Cadillac to immediately identify himself to the
police and seek out his three security guards. Damon's
first order was to Biff, "Collect our clubs and shields and
put them in the trunk of my car. Here's the key. Do it
quietly and don't attract attention. Dukich and Marty,
come with me to the office with the sheriff."

When the ambulances arrived, four deputies stood
by as the attendants loaded the wounded aboard. Inside
the office, the sheriff utilized a digital recorder to obtain
commentary about the battle. He also queried two of the
deputies present along with Damon. Marty, Biff and

Dukich were required to fill out personal information forms. The sheriff then surprised everyone by having one of his deputies take still photos of each of them. Marty, Biff and Dukich were then required to be videotaped in a manner similar to a short deposition. Each man was required to speak describing his involvement in the earlier incident.

As the men sat closely grouped at the table, the sheriff looked into each of the security officer's eyes, "By doing this paperwork and taking photos, I have tried to save you the inconvenience of trips to my headquarters. I think I understand your role in all of this and I believe you are blameless, but if the lawyers get their hooks into these kids' parents they may wish to pursue lawsuits and make trouble for all of us. We can be in touch later if necessary. You may go home now, gentlemen, and best of luck."

*   *   *

On the drive home, Marty tried to evaluate his feelings about the whole experience. He had to decide what to tell Connie. He surely was not used to a long day away from home, the stress of a serious fight and the emotional letdown afterward. It brought back memories of the many violent incidents of his years on the job. At the same time he felt an afterglow of excitement. He had survived what could have resulted in serious injury or worse. Because of his quick wit, resourcefulness and courage in the face of danger, he had survived. So much for pride, he thought. He had been generously paid and that's what counted, right? Despite all these feelings, Marty genuinely felt sorry for the boys who had suffered injury at his hands. There was genuine regret and sympathy in his heart for the kids who had attacked him. But, self-preservation is necessary in times when your life is in danger.

Connie was waiting in the living room dressed in pajamas and bathrobe. "How did it go?" she asked with concern.

"Just fine," Marty grinned as he handed her four one-hundred dollar bills.

She fingered the money as she asked, "And you weren't in any danger?"

"Absolutely not," he lied, "but I'm really tired. I need a hug, a shower and lotsa sleep."

*   *   *

Three days later Marty received another call from Damon. "I've got an easy one for you, Marty," he said.

"Where and when?" asked Marty.

"Tomorrow night. That's the first night, then three more after that. You will be the only guard. It's the Evangelista Ladies' residence building. They've had some threats, probably from crackpots. Your shift is from seven to three a.m. Wear the same clothes as your last job in Woodinville. Be sure your badge is showing and you have your private detective ID. Carry a big flashlight and flash it around a lot as you show yourself.

I want you to scare the bad guys away and make them think the place is continually guarded. Arrive early and present yourself to the director, a Mrs. Snellman. She is expecting you. Keep in touch with me on your cell."

The Evangelista was in a three-story building at the corner of University and Boren Avenue on Capitol Hill, just a few blocks from downtown Seattle. Nice building, thought Marty as he drove slowly around the neighborhood surveying the Evangelista and its surroundings.

In Mrs. Snellman's office, Marty survived a short interview and learned that the ladies' residence kept a secure environment for unmarried women with certain residential limitations such as the eleven p.m. curfew for all residents, to ensure their privacy and safety.

Marty found it easy to patrol the exterior of the building, keeping his big flashlight in play and keeping the beam from shining on the residents' windows. At the same time, his background in law enforcement did not allow him to lessen his vigilance even for a moment. About midnight, Marty had turned his flashlight off while he ate the contents of his sack lunch. He sat on a flat rock in the garden area of the property finishing the last bite from an apple. His eyes continued to keep a careful watch when he thought he saw some movement in the backyard of the building next door. Marty figured it was possible that whoever was moving around next door might be the suspect who had made threats against the Evangelista. If he turned his flashlight on, he might scare the suspect away, but if he just kept quiet the guy might reveal himself, and capturing him would remove the problem. He decided to see what happened.

Suddenly a dark figure appeared. It was a man running in a crouch heading toward the building. Marty dashed toward him, his powerful flashlight in his left hand and his police baton in his right. As Marty caught up with him, the man stopped running, blinded by the flashlight beam shown directly into his eyes. The guy grimaced, at the same time brandishing a hammer in his right hand. As Marty saw the hammer, he set his feet into a position to respond if attacked. Unable to see Marty clearly, the guy swung the hammer in a wide sweeping arc in a desperate attempt to put his opponent out of action. Anticipating just such a move, the ex-cop timed his smashing blow to the man's right wrist knocking the hammer to the ground. A thought went quickly through Marty's mind when he felt the impact of his club on the intruder's wrist. "Damn, I may have broken this guy's wrist," whispered Marty. Ignoring the screams of pain, Marty deftly threw the perp to the ground face down and applied plastic handcuffs, one of the essentials he was required to carry while on duty. With both wrists and arms secured behind his back, the suspect was virtually immobilized.

"Time for the law," said Marty to the poor sap lying face-down on the grass and moaning in pain. Just one button on Marty's cell phone connected his call. "Murderous intruder captured at the Evangelista apartments backyard at Boren and Madison, in need of immediate response. Martin Griffen, night patrol security guard." A patrol car must be close by, thought Marty, when he heard a police siren within three minutes.

The police cruiser turned into a parking space in front of the Evangelista, emitting two uniformed officers who hustled into the back yard, one carrying a flashlight, the other carrying a shotgun. "What's happening here and who are you?" Were the first two questions asked.

Marty quickly showed his ID and explained the situation in words the two officers easily understood. They both wrote in small notebooks. The bigger of the two officers, patrolman Ralph Jackson, said, "We will take this guy and book him. They'll keep him in jail until we can find out more about this incident tonight. Will you be here every night?"

"I'm not sure about that," replied Marty, "Here is a business card for my employer and me."

"You may have to testify in court," Officer Jackson said, "but that's for later. From what we can see it looks like you did a very good job here tonight."

*　　*　　*

Back home Marty slept until a late morning hour at which time he gave Connie a brief account of the night's activity. He omitted the parts where Connie might sense there had been danger.

*　　*　　*

The next call from Damon came a few days later. "It's an evening job," he said. "It's on Saturday night, four days from now at the Columbia Tower building on the seventy-second floor."

"What's the occasion?" Marty asked.

"A group of wealthy businessmen." said Damon, "A big expensive banquet where they have a view of the city lights and enjoy thinking that they are the ones who decide what happens in the city. They represent big money and power so they are always a bit nervous when they show themselves in public. Maybe it's because they remember all the toes they've stepped on. Anyway, we are hired to keep them safe. You will be one of four guards. Wear a black tux, black tie and be sure your badge and gun are well hidden and not noticeable. You are to blend in. See you in the lobby at four-thirty on Saturday evening."

Something told Marty that it would be wise to change his appearance. Somebody at the Columbia Tower banquet might recognize him and identify him as an ex-city cop. I don't want that to happen and I'm sure Damon doesn't either.

Along with the rental of a very nice-fitting black tuxedo, bow tie, cummerbund, suspenders, cufflinks and patent leather black shoes, Marty also found that from the same rental store he was able to obtain a black wig, false eyebrows, mustache and horned-rimmed semi-dark glasses. That should do it for his disguise. Maybe he could get Damon to pop for the bill. If the other guards were going to use names as they communicated between themselves next Saturday night, then maybe I should use a phony name too, thought Marty.

*   *   *

Damon and the four guards had no trouble finding each other in the swanky lobby of the downtown Columbia Towers building. Damon gave cursory introductions to his four security guards. As he touched Marty's upper arm with the back of his right hand, he declared, "For tonight this man's name is Visco."

The three other hard-faced men softened their expressions a bit as they murmured something that sounded like, "Good to meet you," or "Okay, Visco." Trained to remember names, Marty acknowledged Keel, Bull and Bart, his partners for the evening. A few more instructions were in order. "Do not engage in conversation with the guests. Be very polite. Keep your mouths shut. Keep your eyes on anyone who seems out of place. While the odds are against it and it may seem farfetched, there's always the possibility of an assassination attempt. The men at this banquet are very wealthy and powerful. They have all made enemies along the way. Watch very carefully for anything that strikes you as unusual. If so, quickly take control of the situation. I count on your experience and professionalism, so good luck and do a good job tonight."

Marty's first assignment was to stand by the elevator on the seventy-second floor along with Keel and greet the arriving guests and say, "Good evening gentlemen," and nothing more, while carefully looking at each of them as they stepped out of the elevator. Marty was especially glad for his disguise, since some of the guests

106

were familiar to him from his days on the job. The ones recognizable were mostly familiar underworld guys, a few of whom Marty had arrested back in the day. Marty had mixed feelings about his involvement with these underworld characters. Although morally uneasy, he was not very surprised. It was just "part of the job."

The tuxedo-wearing guests were not street thugs but authority figures, some Marty could identify as notable mob hierarchy, many of whom had prison records. Memories of their names echoed inside Marty's brain. Names like Anicello, Ferraro, Mancini, outnumbered the occasional Cohen or Friedman. A name like Olson or McDougall never seemed to pop up which was no surprise to the four ex-cops on guard duty. The other two cops were assigned to general surveillance in which they kept a low profile combined with careful scrutiny of everything on the seventy-second floor banquet hall. After twenty minutes, the four guards changed places and continued an intent observation of everything in sight.

The diners were obviously enjoying their elegant five-course dinner laced with choices of expensive wines. As they ate, the men engaged in lively conversation, much of which was about their work which mainly was concerned with racketeering, extortion, conflict with the law and other sins. The four guards kept effectively out of sight pretending that they heard nothing from the elegantly dressed men at the dining table. The four waitresses were all twenty-something, attractive and efficient, smiling as they served and hustled back and forth from the kitchen. Carefully observing the waitresses, Marty was amused at the clever way the ladies avoided the many attempts by the diners to aggressively flirt with them, even when some of them tried to pat or squeeze their buttocks. The waitresses disappeared as the VIPs were finishing their dessert.

The main man at the affair was a swarthy, balding, heavy-set, sixtyish man seated at the head of the table. Everyone there, including the guards knew him as Vincent Carabba, the local mafia boss. Carabba put his spoon down, glared around the table at the guys and cleared his throat. Suddenly all were quiet. Remaining seated, Carabba was totally in charge as he began speaking. "Gentlemen," he said, "thank you all for coming. As we all know we have some problems to resolve. First, about the territory dispute. West Seattle has been yours, Frank Russo, for about five years. In the meantime..."

A heavy-set, middle-aged black-haired waitress suddenly appeared carrying a tray with three wine bottles, moving rapidly toward Vincent Carabba at the dining table. Marty was suddenly alert. Middle-aged waitress? Heavy-set? Moving too fast? Marty charged forward even as the questions entered his mind. Vincent Carabba continued, "...the south end has been growing in population, so we're gonna have to make..."

The waitress reached the table before Marty and quickly set down her tray and pulled a gun from her blouse. The blasts from the waitress's nine-millimeter pistol resounded loudly inside the banquet room, deafening those at the table. At very close range, the first two shots entered Carabba's head, one directly into the back, the second into the right temple. The third and fourth shots found the forehead of Alonzo Bertini, seated just to the right and one shot landed in the chest of Mario Faccone, the man just to the left. At that moment Marty smashed into the waitress with a vicious flying tackle sending her crashing to the floor and sending the pistol flying through the air landing on the carpet eight feet away.

Despite the fact that the waitress was obviously hurt and no longer a threat, the three other guards arrived and hurriedly handcuffed her. They also tied her ankles together with a length of plastic twine. The entire banquet hall was in an uproar. Many of the guests had drawn their weapons (mostly small revolvers and automatic pistols) and moved away from their chairs and assumed a defensive crouch, pointing their weapons every which way. The looks on their faces and their body language were a mix of fear and an aggressive urge to shoot at somebody.

Down on the street level, a traffic jam rapidly developed. Police vans clogged the streets as they unloaded scores of police patrolmen, sergeants, lieutenants, captains, detectives and photographers. Included in the mix were coroners, doctors, medical aides and newspaper reporters fighting to get through the door. Within ten minutes this army of first responders invaded the seventy-second floor of Seattle's tallest building.

Some of the first to be questioned were Damon Garchik and his four security guards. Everyone on the top floor of the Columbia Towers including the cooks and waitresses were questioned. Some of the guests were arrested for previously issued warrants, some for illegal possession of weapons, many of which were confiscated. After many photographs, the corpses were cared for and properly dispatched. The murderer, the middle-aged lady posing as a waitress, was identified as Winona Sharpton, widow of Neil Sharpton, the late CEO of Pacific International Cruise Lines, headquartered in Seattle.

Marty dragged himself home at one a.m. As he quietly slipped into bed next to Connie, he said to himself, "Here's hoping she's not too upset when she hears the news in the morning or I'll never hear the end of it."

*   *   *

Connie was fascinated with the channel 5 accounts of the previous night's gruesome killings, especially Marty's heroic action in subduing Mrs. Sharpton. "My God, Marty, if you hadn't knocked that woman down she might have killed a dozen more of those guys last night."

"I was doing the job," said Marty, "Even so, I may have hit her awfully hard. They're not telling you that she broke her left leg when she fell. Then when they got her on the gurney, do you know what she said?"

"No, what?"

Marty's face took on a grim expression, "She said, 'No matter what happens, I'm glad I shot that dirty Dago. He had my husband killed. Now he can rot in hell along with those other two killer WOPs in his gang!'"

"I'm saving all the money you've been making in a special hiding place," Connie said. "Promise me you'll be careful, Marty."

* * *

Three nights later, at ten p.m., the Griffen phone rang. "Hello Marty, this is Damon. Is anyone at your house listening on this line?"

"Absolutely not."

"Okay then listen. The people who hired us to protect those guys last Saturday night are upset with us for not protecting the guests. I pointed out to them that more lives would have been lost if you hadn't responded as quickly as you did, and knocked that woman down breaking her leg. They are somewhat understanding because they also realize that that kind of whack job often happens when we think we've got it covered. No matter how smart we think we are, in these matters unpredictability is always a big factor."

"Yeah, I know," said Marty, "but I still feel like I failed. It's a bad feeling."

"Well, if it makes you feel better, Marty, the people in our organization think you are a hero." Marty was silent. Damon continued. "My boss wants to meet you. I think he has some kind of reward. Don't get too excited, it's not that big a deal. He also wants to give you an opportunity to make some real money. Don't tell him what I just said, okay?"

"What's his name," asked Marty.

"You'll find out on Thursday. Come to the Claremont Hotel on Sixth and Lenora, Room 301. Park in the alley. There will be a security guard at the back entrance who will be expecting you. Use the back stairs. Don't talk to anyone until you get to the room. Got it?"

"Sure," said Marty, "I'll be there."

* * *

Marty arrived at Room 301 at three-fifty-five and gave a sharp rap on the door. Through the barely opened door a very big man with a shaved head glowered at Marty.

"Who are you?" he growled.

"Marty Griffen."

"What's your member name?"

"Oh," stammered Marty, "uh, Visco."

The door opened. "Come in, Visco," said the skin head, "Stand here," the big guy commanded. Another man immediately stepped forward and Marty allowed the two guys to frisk him. "He's clean," the biggest man called out.

The hotel room appeared to have been converted to an office with a large important-looking desk at the far end with chairs organized in a semicircle facing the desk. The chairs were occupied by four almost-respectable looking Caucasian dudes. At the big desk sat a heavy-set middle-aged man wearing rimless glasses and sporting a full crop of wild, out of control black hair. Squinty dark eyes, a wide face, prominent nose and sallow skin completed Marty's visual impression of the man who was obviously the boss, but on what level?

Damon appeared with a handshake and warm welcome. "Come over and meet these gentlemen, Marty." The man at the desk stood up as did the others. "First," said Damon proudly, "I want you to meet our esteemed leader, Tito Nowitsky."

"So very pleased to have you join us," said Nowitsky with a wide smile in a basso voice. Polite introductions to the other five men, including Biff, Keel, Bull and Bart with whom Marty had worked previously.

"Please sit here," said Damon, indicating a comfortable chair directly in front of Nowitsky's desk.

Everyone in the room took their seats as Tito Nowitsky spoke, "I have been fully informed of the outstanding work you have done for us over the past few weeks." Marty looked into Nowitsky's eyes but kept silent. "To show our appreciation, we are presenting you with a bonus." Marty accepted a letter sized manila envelope. "Don't open it now. It's a token of my respect for outstanding performance and courage that you have shown on our behalf."

Later at home, Connie would squeal with excitement when she saw the twenty five hundred dollars that Marty slid out of the envelope.

Nowitsky continued. "When you served on the Seattle Police Department, were you an effective cop?"

"Yes sir, I believe that my record bears out the fact that I had a distinguished record with the SPD."

Nowitsky looked him up and down. "Now in your

retirement years, do you ever feel that you are bored or marking time, or that you would be happier with a definable purpose in your life? By the way, call me Tito, everyone else does."

Marty was not surprised by Tito's questions. What was surprising was that this interview was not private, but taking place with an audience that appeared to be a group of twenty or more men, all listening carefully to every word.

Marty maintained a respectful demeanor as he responded, "I have been retired for three years. I have been constantly analyzing my feelings about my life in retirement. I admit that my family's financial resources and income fall short of what we would like them to be. I have thought a lot about taking a full-time job but I haven't yet come across the kind of job where my experience in police work would fit or be of use."

"How much formal education have you had?" asked Tito.

"I had completed my sophomore year at the University of Washington when I joined the SPD. While working on the job, I took advantage of opportunities to complete college classes, so I have earned the equivalent of about three-and-one-half years toward a degree in criminal justice."

Tito showed a tight-lipped smile and said, "You are obviously a man of high intellect, Visco. Now I want to invite everyone here to enjoy some snacks in the restaurant downstairs. Visco and I will be here for an hour or so when you return to continue our meeting."

The men all obediently stood and shuffled their way toward the door, except for Damon who stopped by Marty to whisper in his ear, "Tito owns the hotel." With a big smile and a sharp pat on the back, Damon headed out with the others.

Tito spoke through his teeth, "Excuse my curiosity, but what did Damon just whisper to you?"

Marty displayed a friendly smile and replied, "He said that he thought you were almost beginning to like me." They both chuckled and sipped their coffee.

"Let's cut to the chase, Marty. I am inclined to create a spot for you in my organization. Working for me you could count on an income of at least three times what you receive now from your SPD pension with the possibility of a lot more as time goes on. How does that strike you?"

"You must know how tempting that is, Tito, but is it only part of any agreement? I would have to know what your organization is all about and specifically what my responsibilities would be."

Tito squinted through his rimless glasses, "During the three times you have worked for our Guardian Services organization, have you noticed the names of your coworkers and the names of the men you met here today?"

"Yes," said Marty, "the surnames sounded like Polish or Yugoslavian or maybe Russian names to me."

"Would the word 'Slavic' be appropriate?" asked Tito.

"Yeah, that's right. I remember my father telling me about my Croatian ancestors from three generations back. They changed their last names to fit in as Americans."

Tito couldn't contain a knowing smile, "Did you know that you are actually a Janusevich? He was your grandfather. Your wife's grandmother was a Krakovsky. They met as immigrants in Chicago and soon after married and changed their name to Griffen. They probably thought it sounded like a real American name. You must know that millions of immigrants from just about everywhere have done the same thing over the years."

"Congratulations, Tito, you have done some research about my background." Tito smiled and continued, "Our organization originally began as a charity to support the needs of our Slavic relatives in the USA and in Europe where after World War Two, millions of people in Slovenia, Croatia, Serbia and Kosovo were struggling to survive. Over time we have sent tens of millions in aid overseas. We have also extended a lot of aid to American residents in Slavic communities here in the USA. As time went on, we extended our activities to include applying various methods of pressure, yes, including intimidation, to help right some obvious wrongs within our local Slavic communities."

Tito pulled his earlobe, "Alright, Marty, I will tell you some confidential information, just between the two of us, okay? I'll tell you more about our organization. I'll tell you about my role and I'll tell you about what I expect of you. The police are suspicious of our organization because they think we are engaged in some kind of illegal activity or some kind of racketeering, but they are wrong. They seem to interpret what we do as illegal. I admit that

116

some of the things we do edge pretty close to what the Italian Mafia mob does right here in Seattle. Those guys are the real criminals. The cops somehow mistakenly blame us for what the local mob does. That includes extortion, gambling, prostitution and drugs. We are more like a charity. We have our own methods of financing the good work that we do. Most of the people we help are struggling economically and from other social and political pressures."

"Political pressures?"

"Sure, many countries in the world know nothing of democracy. We help them with financial donations and everyday goods when and where they are needed. In the past few years this has amounted to millions of dollars in aid to people we are ethnically connected to, mothers, fathers, sisters, brothers, family members and others who benefit from our help. There are local pressures also from city authorities and bureaucrats who enforce zoning laws, administer public schools and dictate policies used by the police. Occasionally there are confrontations not only with the police but also with the local Italian mob. Sometimes we lock horns with them, sometimes our access to our financial resources compete with them. To be frank, there is a rivalry. We believe our motives are honorable and theirs are not. They focus on making money and they use unscrupulous, illegal methods to get it including kidnapping, smuggling, drugs and murder."

"Both the cops and the mob are always misinterpreting what we do. We usually resolve those problems easily enough, but sometimes it's difficult to put them in their place. The recipients of our charity receive cash and material goods. We regularly do the same for our local people of the Slavic culture who live in our Seattle neighborhoods. The people I refer to are connected by religion, language, food traditions, traditional rules of personal relationships, family customs and notions about fairness and justice which are sometimes similar to our own and sometimes very different. The Slavic based languages are spoken in the Czech Republic, in Poland, Russia, the former Yugoslavian countries and Bulgaria. Slavic speakers far outnumber other language speakers in all of Europe. We have helped them all and are continuing to do so. We keep in close touch with their leaders. We send hundreds of thousands of dollars on holidays like Christmas and Easter. We donate to their churches. Those people respect us and love us for the help they receive from us. My organization limits our membership – for the most part – to people born to the Slavic traditions. Solidarity is important to any organization. We refer to it at times as the 'SIC,' which means Slavic International Community. SIC has a bit of symbolic significance. It's the same as saying to a fierce guardian dog, 'SIC 'em!', when confronted by an enemy. We can be pretty tough when we have to. Some of our members are pretty tough guys. We need to be tough because we have some serious pressures on us from time to time."

"Pressures?"

"Yes, economic, political and social. For example, some of our people who live in neighborhoods like Rat

City, Beacon Hill, Rainier Valley and other places. Sometimes they have troubles with city authorities about zoning, unfair rental and leasing contract issues. Often they are preyed upon by banks and real estate people, insurance companies and phony billing policies on the part of energy companies who cheat on telephone, internet and television billings and contracts. That's when we step in and use our persuasive abilities. Yes, this includes intimidation sometimes in order to resolve these problems in favor of our people who have no one else to turn to." Tito's intense gaze into Marty's eyes confirmed what Tito thought was some skepticism.

"You know," said Marty calmly, "that I am fully aware of what you mean by intimidation, or do I not understand you?"

"Oh, come on, Marty, intimidation takes different forms. I'm sure you would approve of leaning a bit on an unscrupulous landlord who was abusing a poor family named Janusevich. That's about as far as it ever goes. It's unimportant in context of doing the right thing for our people who are struggling to get by. Now I will tell you more in my attempt to answer your questions."

Marty sat up straight in his chair, "Yes, about your role and possibly my own, if I join you."

"We are not a democracy. I am the leader; I initiate everything we do. All policies, decisions and actions must be approved by me and supported by every member of the SIC I need to tell you about last week's Columbia Tower banquet. Those mob guys aren't as smart as they think they are. They never would have hired us as their guards if they had known. They mistakenly hired from our SIC because we sometimes function under different company names. Front names, if you will. The three guys who were whacked were the main leaders of the Seattle mob. As you saw, some of the others were arrested under previous warrants or charges of one kind or another. This means the gang isn't functioning right now. Most of their business is disrupted. Some of their clients have fallen away from the mob's control. This is our opportunity to move in on some of their operations."

Marty leaned forward, "Which operations?"

"For quite a long time the WOPs have subjected certain West Seattle businesses to illegal extortion and have gotten away with it. Over time, this has amounted to some very big money for these Guinea thugs. As we talk, our organizers are taking over, offering protection from the mob at half the cost. These businesses will be asked to voluntarily donate instead to our SIC charity organization. We keep it all legal. That's an example of one of the ways we finance our organization. Don't be shocked, Marty, you're not sheltered by the police department anymore. It's time to face the real world, which you know is unfair, crooked, cruel, illogical, twisted and weird beyond anything we could have imagined fifty years ago. This job I have created has worked out well for me. I deal with a pragmatic reality on what it takes to survive in comfort and purpose in the world we live in.

"Now about you, Marty, from what I have researched and observed about you, I think you may be the man I have been looking for. I think you might be a loyal and efficient factor in what we are trying to do. You appear to have the special qualities of experience, courage and decision making talent that could take you beyond just working as a security guard. Tell me, from where you are now in your life, what would be your fondest wishes for the future?"

"I would like more income. I would like a better house in a nicer neighborhood. I would like to have a greater variety of friends and more social connections. My wife would love to afford a membership in a golf or tennis country club. We would both enjoy having new cars. She has always dreamed of taking a month long trip to Europe. I've never told anyone things like this before, Tito. What's gotten into me?" Both men grinned at each other.

"Well, I asked you and you confided in me. What would you say if I offered you a full-time job at a salary of, say 200k per year? Combining that with your present income, would total more than 250k per year. Not only that, but you could count on more. If things worked out the way I think they would, after a very few years you'd be looking at up to seven figures."

"Leg breakers aren't paid that much, Tito," said Marty with an obvious twinkle in his eye.

Tito twinkled back, "Forget that. I want you to be a decision maker like me. If I am any judge, you must always be your own man, no matter what. I could work with that, but there would be times when you would come close to crossing that line you have always respected. If you truly want the life you wish for, you have to make compromises in the real world." Tito rubbed his forehead and said, "So now you have an opportunity to live the good life, so to speak, a challenging job as a leader doing work that you are very good at and enjoying the rewards which translate into big money. Some ego satisfaction may also be part of the package as you see your plans work out and the people who work for you admire and respect you. Now Marty, I have tried to acquaint you with some of the advantages of the job. What I need is trust between you and me. When I give my word I keep it, no matter what. I want you to join us. I expect you to say you need to talk it over with your wife and then I'm going to say, 'man up and tell me you're in.' There is no need to sign anything, just give me your word."

Marty looked thoughtful. "All right, Tito, I'm inclined, but I have a reservation. I can't totally commit until we agree on a trial period of, let's say, three months. After that, a full commitment if everything goes well."

Tito stood, smiled and offered his hand, "Deal," he said, "welcome aboard."

*　*　*

Driving home, Marty decided to stop at Perry's and relate to him what had just occurred in Tito's office. Marty called on his cell phone. They agreed to meet at Brody's bar, close by.

Already seated at a table inside, Perry's face brightened as Marty approached, "Hello, numb-nuts," greeted Perry, "what's up?"

Marty couldn't help grinning, "Hey Ugly, I have to talk to you."

Perry looked into Marty's face, "Sounds serious," he said quietly. They both sat and signaled for beer.

"I have been at a meeting with Tito."

Perry's face darkened, "What did Darth Vader offer you?"

"You must be psychic," growled Marty, "he offered lots of money, a full-time job and bonuses like a house, cars, memberships in exclusive clubs and advancement."

Perry blinked a few blinks, "Are you gonna tell me you bought it?" He looked at Marty incredulously.

Marty spoke quietly, "I agreed to a three-month tryout period."

"For three months?" Perry spoke sharply as he grasped the sleeve of Marty's jacket. "After one month, Tito the Anti-Christ will have you so captured that you'll never be able to get out."

"Get out of what?" asked Marty, "My agreement with Tito?"

"Of course," shrilled Perry, "and out of the SIC, out of being part of their racketeering, shakedowns, blackmail, virulent attacks, extortion, torture and tax violations. Sooner or later you will be arrested and in for a long prison sentence. You won't be able to get out of that, either!"

"I have a promise," said Marty in a shaky voice, "that I will not be involved in that kind of crap. Anyway, I will be able to analyze the situation during the three month trial period. How is it that you think you know so much more about Tito and the SIC than I do?"

Perry's expression seemed to darken further as he talked across the table to Marty, "During our careers in the department, the best time for me was the five years you and I were partners. I think we were great cops and did everything right, the best way we could. A big part of that was because of your idealism. You were always a model for all of us who worked with you, an honest cop, through and through. I have always looked up to you and still do. I was even envious of you when you had that thing going with Candy twenty-five years ago." Both snickered a bit. "There were so many years on the job when I was working with other officers and indulged in unethical activities which you probably never heard about. In the course of all that, I got to know quite a number of bad guys, con men, mob guys, thugs and criminal types. Believe it or not, some of those guys became semi-friendly acquaintances. Even now I keep in touch with a few of them. These guys know all about underworld organizations like the one you just joined up with. You might need my help on this one, Marty."

*   *   *

Marty had plenty to think about as he drove home. As he suspected, Connie was very curious. "So what happened at your meeting?"

Marty showed her a half-smile, "Starting tomorrow, can we live on sixteen thousand a month more than we get now? I just took a three-month temporary job to see

124

if it fits."

Connie's mouth dropped open and her eyes popped open wider than normal, "Is this for real? Are you serious?"

"By now you should be able to tell," he laughed.

Connie took two steps closer, "Will it be dangerous?"

Marty put firm hands on her shoulders, "A lot less dangerous than being a cop. I will be managing some security guards."

Connie gave Marty a questioning look and asked, "They are paying you a lot of money to do a job you can do with both hands tied behind your back."

Marty's smart-assed look betrayed his next comment, "If they want somebody with outstanding abilities, like you-know-who, they're gonna have to pay! With that kind of money, we'll be able to take our trip to Europe next summer maybe."

"Can you get time off work?"

"That's part of the deal," said Marty.

*　　*　　*

From the very first day Marty was to be known as Visco. So be it. He met with Tito at eight a.m. on the first day. They shared a warm handshake. "You're not afraid to fly, are you, Visco?" Visco shook his head. "If not, I have an interesting project for you this morning. I want you to take Dukich with you. I have made arrangements for you to fly to Lummi Island up in the San Juans. Have you ever been up there?"

"Yes," said Marty, "it's a beautiful area."

"Go to the south shore of Lake Union where they keep the float planes. Ask for a guy named Stan Klacov. He is the pilot. You will be landing in a little bay on Lummi Island. A real estate guy named Barry Mortenson will meet you on the dock. He will show you some property I am thinking of buying. Collect all the details about the cabin, access, property values, tax information and bring it to me this afternoon so I can make a decision."

Located less than a mile north of downtown Seattle, the south shore of Lake Union was teeming with boats, boathouses, restaurants, apartments and waterfront businesses. How the area managed to accommodate the float plane traffic in the middle of such activity without accidents or injuries would seem to be a problem, but all things seemed to fit into place as the float planes constantly kept taking off and landing in close proximity to the entire goings-on.

Marty met Rocky Dukich at the dock accompanied by one of Tito's men named Savich, who seemed to Marty to be out of character compared to the other men that Marty was aware of in the SIC organization. Small in stature, a slumped posture, unkempt hair and mustache, he wore a sloppy-looking ball cap and confused expression. Savich could be described as a *nebbish*. As one of Tito's men, how could a little guy like that be good at anything? Maybe he is just a gopher or something, thought Marty.

Stan the pilot invited them aboard the plane. It was a bit more spacious than Marty would have expected, with seats for four passengers. Stan's plane was one of a half dozen single engine pontoon monoplanes tied up at the Lake Union moorage. The plane was known as a Cessna 206. As the guys strapped themselves into their seats, Stan started the engine. As he shoved the throttle forward the engine roared and they were on their way. Stan banked the airplane to the west for a few minutes until flying over Puget Sound and then turned north, flying high above the water. Their estimated time of arrival at Lummi Island was only about fifty minutes after takeoff.

Cruising at five thousand feet above the blue waters of Puget Sound, Dukich unstrapped and handed Savich a plastic sack.

"Tito's orders, Savich, we all are instructed to leave our valuables and identification on the plane when we go ashore. Put your stuff in this bag for now. Make sure your wallet, watch, credit cards, car keys and any ID goes in this bag." Savich looked puzzled but complied. Marty looked on, but was puzzled as well.

After five minutes Dukich leaned across the aisle to whisper into Marty's ear, "Listen Visco, we will be having a little action in a few minutes. You are to sit still and watch. Do you get me?" Marty nodded.

Dukich stood and headed for the rear access door. "Come with me, Savich, I want you to see how the island looks from above." He opened the door about ten inches and said, "Look out there."

Savich cautiously approached. In a very quick move Dukich grabbed Savich by the left wrist in a powerful grip with his left hand. Dukich's right hand hooked into

Savich's belt holding it against Savich's lower back, shoving him out the door. Dukich watched Savich's body rotate slowly as he fell five thousand feet to certain death in the deep cold waters of Puget Sound. Dukich closed the door and went to his seat. Leaning a bit toward Marty, he said, "Now you are as guilty as I am, Visco. You are an accessory. Now you are one of us."

The float plane landed smoothly at the bay on Lummi Island. After tying up to the dock, the three men stepped out of the plane to be met by Barry Mortenson, the real estate agent. Marty knew he was going to have to adapt his emotional state to overcome the shock of witnessing a murder.

Marty and Dukich were driven to the property about which Marty was expected to examine, evaluate and express an opinion for Tito's consideration. With Mortenson's input, Marty was able to compile the vital facts about the waterfront setting, the large ranch-style cabin, the maintenance obligations and the tax particulars. Marty was favorably impressed with the entire package except for the price of the property.

*   *   *

On the flight back, Marty struggled with his conscience and was unable to focus on the San Juan Islands from the air, one of the world's most entrancing sites. It was difficult, but once back and meeting with Tito to discuss the property, he felt that he did an acceptable job of keeping his concentration and impressing the boss with the Lummi Island data.

*   *   *

The following two weeks were spent mostly around Tito's hotel office acquainting himself with the basic procedures of the organization. After that, it was obvious that he was going to function as a go-between serving Tito and his employees and sometimes in a supervisory role similar to Damon's job.

At first, Marty was not required to be present at the nighttime security guard assignments, but as time went on his orders required his presence at night. Marty was pleased to discover that he had a natural talent for supervisory and leadership roles and he felt good about it. From time to time he was given lists of the employees along with e-mail and phone numbers, but never the complete list of all personnel specifics. Only Tito had the complete information about personnel and most everything else.

In Marty's second month, he was often sent out as a representative from SIC to settle or resolve matters involving city and county zoning authorities, landlords and bank managers on matters of suspected overcharging, usury and fraud against their Slavic immigrant customers. In the course of assuming these assignments, Marty was to meet and interact with many, if not most of the men working for SIC Marty was proud of the apparent rapport he achieved with the SIC guys despite the difference in their intellectual capacities.

Marty felt that he did a good job in winning them over.

Perry continued to be persistent in his frequent calls, urging Marty to back out of the deal with Tito and quit the SIC.

As Marty's third month anniversary approached, he felt he had a good working relationship with those in the organization, even becoming somewhat friendly with a few of the brighter ones.

* * *

At their most recent lunch together, Marty and Perry indulged in an unusually serious discussion in which Perry seemed quite upset, "Look, Marty," said Perry, passionately, "if you don't quit that underworld mob, you are going to force me do something about it!"

What the hell does he mean by that? thought Marty. "Come on, Perry, back off, I know what I'm doing."

In the days that followed, Perry's remark came back into Marty's mind frequently, even though he tried to forget it.

* * *

The call came at three a.m. Sunday morning. Marty forced himself from a deep sleep. "Hello," he murmured into his bedside phone.

"This is Damon, Marty," the voice said, "Tito has been killed. His car was bombed. It took his wife and Dukich also. Meet me at Tito's Claremont Hotel office.

There are some matters we have to attend to."

*   *   *

Both men had learned to keep cool in a crisis, but Tito's murder meant that many associate's lives were to be deeply affected. As Marty well knew, when confronted by a sudden tragedy, many, if not most, lost their ability to think rationally and became emotionally disoriented for a time, as they recovered from shock. Both Marty and Damon felt that they were better able to pull things together than anyone else in the SIC.

Damon's keys provided entrance to Tito's office where Marty and Damon ignored Tito's desk as they sat at a small conference table in the middle of the room.

"The first thing," declared Damon, "is to retrieve Tito's keys to his files, his combination to the safe, his secret files and the cash. I'm not supposed to know about Tito's hiding places, but I peeked a few times when Tito wasn't looking."

"Can you find the cash first?" asked Marty.

Damon gave Marty a hard-faced look as he thought the question over, "Yeah, I think so, as long as all of this is just between you and me," he said, "Come with me and I'll show you a few of Tito's hiding places."

Marty was amazed by Damon's ability to pick locks. After emptying the safe hidden in the next room and cleaning out the contents of Tito's desk, they placed all they had found on the conference table to examine it.

There were financial ledgers, binders containing

tax records, payroll and expense accounts, charitable activities, financial sources which surely must include payoffs from blackmail, extortion, smuggling and insurance fraud, if indeed the SIC was a criminal organization as described by Perry Jarvis. One interesting discovery was an old gavel, unusually heavy, which Marty presumed Tito had received as a gift after serving as a chairman or president of some local organization.

It was four a.m. when Marty and Damon moved onto examining the eight shoe boxes of cash from the safe. They both carefully counted it as Marty marked the amounts on a legal pad. When finished, they gave each other incredulous looks.

"Tito sometimes bragged that he kept a million on hand in his safe," Damon said quietly.

"Well, whataya know," said Marty, "here we have two-point-five million, right here in neat stacks of hundreds and twenties. I suppose the best thing to do is to put the money back in the safe, don't you think?"

Damon had taken on a glowering look, "Wait just a minute," he blurted, "this money is unaccounted for. Nobody even knows of its existence. You and I could keep it and nobody would ever know unless one of us was stupid enough to tell somebody. Even then, there would be no proof, so what is all this bullshit about putting it back? A million bucks would guarantee a comfortable life for each of us."

Marty stared back, "It's about doing the right thing, Damon!"

"What planet have you been living on, you idiot?"

asked Damon. "This is the break of a lifetime!" They continued to glare at each other, both trying to decide what to say next. Damon spoke first. "If you don't want the money, just say so and I'll take it and you can go to hell!"

Marty held his eye contact with Damon and said calmly, "Please don't talk that way, Damon, relax, we can work everything out. Let's not steal the organization's money."

"Damn you," shouted Damon, as he pulled his twenty five caliber automatic from inside his coat and leveled it at Marty, "For two and a half million, I might even whack you! Get down on the floor, face down!"

Marty's senses sharpened as he stood and slowly shuffled toward an uncluttered space on the floor. This brought him much closer to Damon who continued to point his gun at Marty's chest. As Marty bent his legs slightly as if he was beginning to slump to the floor, he kept his right hand on the table as if to support himself as he descended. In a lightning quick movement, Marty's left arm stretched to his left with his index finger pointing at the door.

Damon was not about to be distracted but he couldn't avoid turning his head quickly in the direction of the door for a nanosecond. It was just enough time for Marty to whisk the gavel from the table and smash it onto Damon's hand, knocking the gun out and sending it skidding across the floor. In the same second, a strong leg drive sent Marty charging into the smaller man, knocking him backward where he landed with a loud thump, as his head smacked into the floor with a sickening crack.

I don't like that sound, thought Marty. Damon's body felt limp. "Man," said Marty out loud, "you're out for sure."

For Marty, picking Damon up and carrying him downstairs was easy enough. He opened the door to his trunk, moved his car jack and flashlight to the back floor of his car and dumped Damon into the trunk. Gagging and tying Damon's wrists and ankles finished the job for the moment.

Back upstairs to the office, Marty set about placing the cash and the files back into their original hiding places. When the office looked presentable, Marty moved one of the comfortable chairs next to Tito's desk so that he could sit facing the empty room. He checked the time on his watch. It was six a.m. Marty was sure that at least some of the SIC employees would show up. Some would be in shock over the terrible news of Tito's assassination. All would be anxious about their futures without Tito's leadership.

A few minutes later Marty heard footsteps on the stairs. Three men entered the room. Marty had worked a bit with them but didn't know them well. Two men came in followed by four more. Polite greetings ensued. Marty did his best to greet each man. The room was soon filled to overflowing.

"Visco, call the meeting to order," somebody shouted.

Marty stood with his palms raised and shouted, "Gentlemen, let's have it quiet, please."

Someone else yelled, "Get behind the desk, Visco!"

As the men became quiet, Visco spoke in a loud authoritative voice, and described the facts of Tito's murder as he understood them. Angry voices came from the crowd demanding revenge. Many loudly accused the Italian mob of Tito's murder.

"Hold everything," shouted Marty, "Do we have any evidence? If not, we need facts to go on! Let's not go off halfcocked!"

"We need a leader!" shouted another. Biff Lonsky stood and walked forward. Standing in front of Tito's desk where Marty sat uneasily, Biff faced the crowd of uneasy, anxious and angry men.

"I have been on the phone talking to our people about this," said Biff, "I have talked to most of you in the past few hours. Right now we need a leader, at least temporarily. Almost everyone I talked to agreed. The man we have in mind is one of our newest employees but we who have worked with him know him to be very smart, dependable and gutsy. We have all come to trust his judgement. We want you, Visco, to take over, at least for a while until we can sort everything out and we can't wait. How do you guys feel about it?" The men seemed to agree. Some cheered. "Well, then, let's have a voice vote right now. All in favor say "aye." The room exploded with favorable yells. Biff turned to Marty, "For now Visco, you're in charge. What's our next step?"

Marty drew himself up before the crowd and spoke. "Thank you for your confidence. I will do the very best I can. I will be working on next steps over the next day or two. Plan for a meeting here at eight a.m. on Tuesday. Do not take action on any issue or project without conferring with me first. I share your profound sadness. Each of us will be dealing with a natural state of mourning or grief for a while, so I encourage you to keep your cool. That's what Tito would want. Gentlemen, you will find some degree of consolation by keeping in touch with your friends and comrades in the SIC. In the meantime, we must love and respect each other as never before. This meeting is adjourned."

*   *   *

Back at home, Marty's edited explanation seemed to make sense to Connie who was especially proud of the part about Marty's appointment as CEO of the SIC organization. It assured a greater income. Connie thought the fact that Marty was the leader of a large group of employees and managing a charitable organization was sure to result in a higher social status.

Marty was seated in his favorite lounge chair. Connie walked toward him with an amused expression and a fetching smile, turned her body and sat on Marty's lap. Throwing her arms around his neck with her mouth next to his ear, she whispered softly, "Marty, you are becoming a man of importance and I love you for it."

Marty and Connie Griffen made love that night and Marty couldn't remember a more exciting or pleasurable experience. *Why does the word 'thrilling' come to mind?* he asked himself as he lay next to Connie. She slept, but Marty, feeling restless, got up and headed for their second bedroom which served as their office and for Marty, a sanctuary of sorts.

It was three a.m. and Marty sat at his desk trying to organize his thoughts. He allowed himself to understand that, in his heart, he knew Perry was responsible for Tito's death.

I know he did it to shock me into bailing out of the SIC Deliberately killing three people is unforgiveable and unthinkable. Even so, it looks like I still have choices. I could back out of the SIC and continue life as a retired cop with no money to speak of. Life with Connie is good. I'm sure glad I was able to turn Damon over to Biff and Keel right after our meeting today. I'm still not sure if the poor bugger is still alive. If not, then I've made my bones for the second time. How in hell can I justify that to myself?

If I keep the job with SIC, I'll be going against my own conscience. I could be really good at taking over for Tito, but I would be working as a gangster, a racketeer. I'm afraid I would too easily become the kind of arrogant crook that I used to love to put in jail. Every time I went on a security guard assignment and had some action, I felt excitement and a strange exhilaration. I can't deny that I loved it! What's wrong with me? If I stayed with this job we would be into the big bucks. Connie would be proud of me. What has happened to my pride in doing the right thing and being an honest man, an honest cop? I have to think this through. How can I decide? I have to decide what to do. I have to think...

I cannot vacillate any more. Fate has determined that I have become Visco. So I am now a confident, resourceful

137

and strong leader. Damn it, it's my calling! From this moment on, I am a real leader to look up to, a man to be admired and feared. From now on, I am Visco!

THE ANNIVERSARY PARTY

Meeting and reminiscing with old friends is always a great pleasure for me. At a luncheon a few years ago, I had such a meeting with two of my closest boyhood pals. The three of us were often together as kids growing up in the Maple Hill neighborhood, a suburb of Seattle. This story may or may not have meaning for the reader, but it gives me pause to ponder whenever I think back on it. Ponder what exactly; maybe it's just thoughts about human relationships and family loyalties.

Kyle Garrett and Danny Stern were seated at Poncho's Restaurante Mexicano. As I arrived, they jumped to their feet and began punching and hugging me. To anyone watching, it must have appeared unseemly for three guys in their seventies to act like unruly teenagers. Hugging, slapping and laughing together were simply part of our tradition as friends going back to our boyhood. Even though we had not been in close touch through the latter years, the affection was still in our hearts. As we settled into our chairs, the expected banter began, "Did those big bloody scabs on your ass ever heal, Kyle?" asked Danny.

"They did, but I noticed your mange is still eating away at your hairline," retorted Kyle.

Sure enough, Danny was balding, but still retained traces of kinky graying hair. Danny's face, prominent nose, black brows and dark perceptive eyes revealed an unusual degree of sensitivity and intelligence. Only five-foot eight, Danny appeared as husky and strong as he was as a football star fifty-seven years ago. Kyle Garrett was tall and fair with lots of white hair. His blue-gray eyes accentuated an outgoing personality, creative, sensitive and intellectual awareness. I admired both of my old friends for their ribald senses of humor and youthful attitudes which had carried over into their senior years.

"What about you, Pete," asked Kyle, "have you given up masturbating three times a day?"

"Oh, I've cut down a lot in my old age," I answered, grinning at the thought. More friendly insults continued along with the chuckles and laughter of old friends remembering their restless, mischievous and hilarious days spent together so long ago. As they ordered lunch, the guys couldn't help teasing the waitress (and each other) about the menu selections and the restaurant atmosphere. Along with the banter, we all enjoyed the spicy food and the usual drinks.

"It doesn't seem like two weeks ago since the party," said Danny.

"It was quite a wonderful fiftieth anniversary party," I said to Kyle.

"You did a great job putting it together," offered

Danny. "I understand you planned the whole thing. Your wife and kids did a few things, but mainly it was your party, right?"

Kyle just grinned, "I thought it worked out just fine."

"Since the party," I said, "Danny and I have discussed it. We wanted to talk to you about it."

"Why, did something go wrong?" Kyle asked.

Danny spoke up, "The reception party was great, forty people, relatives, friends, drinks, snacks, visiting and background music. It was all terrific."

"The setting was beautiful as well," I said, "a very classy place with a view of the lake, very stylish décor and tasteful appointments. Kyle, your introductions were no less than professional as you circulated around the tables with the microphone. That was nicely done. A short compliment about each person there made them feel especially important, not just one of a crowd. How did you remember all those names and all the information?"

"Damned if I know," smiled Kyle.

"The food was great and the short movie about your life, Katie's life and the kids as they grew up," said Danny. "It was entertaining. A great job."

"Then, about the speeches," I commented. "Your speech about your courtship, your life with Katie, was quite touching. The part about your love and respect for your wife was very sweet, very moving. One of your three, forty-something- year-old kids spoke, mostly about his mom."

"He didn't say much about you," said Danny. "How come?"

"He talked about his dad," I said. "Two whole sentences. What about your other two offspring, Kyle, are they deaf and dumb?"

"Wait a minute you guys aren't being fair, besides that's too personal," growled Kyle.

"We are your oldest and dearest friends," said Danny, in a serious tone. "It's not too personal because we love you."

"We are discussing this for a reason," I said. "So listen. At this point in your anniversary party, after fifty years of a great marriage and three successful offspring, why was all the talk about Katie, which was great, but almost nothing about you?" My question gave Kyle pause.

"What did you expect them to say?" asked Kyle.

"For starters," Danny said, "how you worked for years at the equivalent of two jobs so your wife could be at home with the kids. Didn't any of your kids remember how their dad read to them at bedtime, almost every night when they were small? Didn't their dad teach them how to ride a bicycle, throw a ball and teach them how to swim? Didn't they remember how they rode on his back when they rode down the hill on a sled, how he backed them up dozens of times in school, in the scouts and in campfire girls? The many times their dad took them on outings to the ocean, horseback riding, camping, hiking, Disneyland, on boats, rivers, lakes, every kind of adventure you could think of? Don't any of them remember how you have always been there for them, backing them up, supporting them in every goddamned thing they ever did in their lives?"

I jumped in, "Not to mention when the one kid was in serious trouble, you helped him out to the tune of thirty thousand bucks? Kept him out of prison. I remember when you said, 'Well we took a hit on that one, but if he needed more, I would have given him everything I had.'"

Then Danny asked, "Why did your wife Katie, just sit there and say absolutely nothing?"

"I don't know," said Kyle.

"That was the time," I interjected, "right after your speech about your wonderful family, when they could have offered just a few words about their dad. It looked like they kept silent because they did not feel they could offer any compliments, any words of appreciation for all you have done for the family. That's what it looked like. It looked like they not only do not love you, but don't even like you. Otherwise your wife and two other kids should have said *something!* Now, after all that, we want you to know something: *We* know what a really good man you are and always have been. We know who and what you are and *we* appreciate and love you. So there you are. We got it off our chests about the anniversary party."

Danny's eyes were moist as he spoke, as were mine. "Okay, Kyle, now we have told you our thoughts. We want to know how you honestly feel about all of this."

Kyle was thoughtful as he spoke very slowly. "Yeah, I admit it bothered me, but maybe you are helping me get over it."

"Bullshit," said Danny. "You don't have to admit it, but it damn near broke your heart at the party."

Now Kyle's eyes showed tears. "Don't worry about

me, guys, I'll be fine. You do me a great honor to be my friends."

Danny and I didn't meet with Kyle after that. A man lives a lifetime mostly devoting himself to the most important thing in his life, his wife and family and right near the end he discovers that they don't give a damn about him. One can only wonder how really painful that was. Enough, maybe, to make a man die of a broken heart.

Three months later Danny and I attended Kyle's funeral. The cause of death was never announced by his family.

ART, LUST AND SELF DEFENSE

It was a foggy day in December. The Union Gospel Mission was in full operation in the old Seattle Skid Road district. The free food was a huge attraction for the poor population living in the Yesler Square neighborhood.

After finishing her shift as a volunteer server, twenty-year-old Kim Rogers was in a hurry to catch her bus up to Capitol Hill in time for her art class at the Cornish School of Allied Arts. Walking north on First Avenue, she was aware of the many drunk and stoned people in the neighborhood and kept a fast pace. Just then, a bedraggled guy wearing a hoodie staggered out of an alleyway reaching out his hand to grab her. Ever alert, Kim produced a can of pepper spray from her shoulder bag and aimed it directly at the man's left eye, squeezing the trigger. She followed up with a powerful kick to the man's crotch then continued along First Avenue at a run, the man's moans echoing in her ears. *I've never heard a man scream quite like that,* she said to herself. *It looks like that self defense class was worth it after all*, Kim reflected as she boarded the bus.

After arriving at the Cornish school slightly out of breath and feeling shaken from her encounter with the man in the alley, Kim was now standing at her easel with her painting gear in place, issuing friendly greetings to the other classmates who were all waiting for class to begin. She was determined to shake off the feeling of anxiety that lingered beneath her friendly smile.

Painting instructor, Ivan Markov paused in the doorway, peering into the room before entering. Markov played the role of sophisticated Russian immigrant fine-art painter, and seemed to thrive on the respect and admiration of his students in the new unsophisticated world of American art. At five-ten and one-sixty-five, he sported a rather unkempt mustache which extended down to the corners of his mouth and an untidy goatee beard which appeared plastered to his chin. His gaze stopped on Kim Rogers, taking in her blonde pony-tailed hair, her oversized intelligent eyes, short nose, and cherry red lips. Though mostly covered by an artist's apron, Kim obviously was endowed with what was pretty close to a classic figure. Kim felt a great deal of admiration for her painting teacher, and had taken this class specifically to learn his technique. She looked up from her easel to see him staring and bestowed a friendly smile. Frowning, Markov looked away, forcing himself to focus on his duties. "I'm here!" he yelled to the roomful of art students, each of whom had made a special effort to arrange their busy schedules to attend this two-hour painting class each Wednesday afternoon during the dark winter months.

Ivan Markov strode to the center of the room and addressed the class. "Our still-life project began last week, as you recall," he said in his heavily accented English. "We work for two more class sessions and then you take home finished oil painting which you will be very proud of. The still-life set-ups are stored on little tables back in the northwest corner of room. Now we need our helpers to fetch and place them in this room exactly as they were last week so everyone may start to work right away. I will circulate around and coach each of you while you get started. Then later, I demonstrate."

The students scurried about, retrieving their unfinished paintings and setting up their easels and other accessories.

Each of the two still-life table arrangements contained an apple, pear, wine bottle, a glass and a cooking pot. Both set ups were illuminated by a portable electric lamp on a side table. The students were to paint the arrangement carefully, considering the rules of composition, the relative shapes of the objects, the shadows, highlights, reflected light and textures of the various objects.

Markov, while making his rounds, removed Kim Rogers' canvas panel, wet with oil paint from her easel and set it against the wall. Placing his own blank stretched canvas on her easel, he began his demonstration. As he mixed his colors on the palette, he lectured as he painted, describing his technique. As the students watched and listened, he applied paint over his preliminary drawing in swift confident strokes. Calling attention to how he worked to affect light, shade and reflected light on the wine bottle, the highlights on the neck and rounded top of the glass and echoing the shiny texture of the glass bottle.

As the class came to an end, Kim became aware of someone standing behind her. It was Drake Gilson, a classmate. Kim had briefly spoken to him at a prior class and was not unaware of the twenty-three-year-old's good looks and pleasant manner.

"Excuse me," he said, "but you seem to have a lot of art supplies to put away. Do you need any help?"

"Thanks, but I'll get it all together in just a few minutes. I won't need any help," Kim responded.

"It's very dark and windy outside right now," said Drake, "can I walk you to your bus stop?"

With a smile, Kim asked, "How do you know that I am taking a bus?"

"Because when I was entering the building, I saw you running up Roy Street, obviously having just stepped off the Broadway bus. You are a pretty good runner, Kim. I'm Drake Gilson."

"Nice to meet you, Drake. I was a sprinter on the track team in high school."

"Nice. What else did you do in high school?"

"I was on the gymnastics team. Why am I telling you this?"

Drake looked directly into her eyes, smiled and said, "I think it's probably because you had the kind of parents who taught you good manners, like when someone asks you a question, you give them an honest answer."

Kim gave Drake a questioning look, but kept silent.

"Come on," he urged, "let's walk to the bus stop."

*   *   *

Bundled up against the wind, Kim and Drake trundled toward the nearest bus stop a block away. As they got closer, Drake spoke in an urgent voice. "Look, it's past my usual suppertime and I am as hungry as a starving grizzly. There's a cafe over there. Let's get something to eat before we both collapse from starvation. The bus will still be running in an hour or so and we can catch it then, with a full stomach."

Kim looked up at him with a tired grin and said, "I admit that you have tempted me. Let's do it but only if it will be Dutch!"

Inside the little eatery, Kim and Drake enjoyed their hamburgers and coffee. The conversation was about themselves out of a natural curiosity about each other. Their main interests were about the art class, their instructor and their ambitions to be known as outstanding "fine-artists." Both had been successful in their previous college art classes and dreamed of becoming competent at the activity they loved the most, expressing themselves through the process of drawing and painting. Maybe they could discover a way to make a living at it. Perhaps that dream was pure fantasy, then again, maybe not. It certainly is fun to talk about it with someone with the same interest. In Kim's case the word "interest" might be changed to something like a "consuming passion."

Finally, Kim looked at her watch and said, "This has been great Drake, but I really have to get home."

He gave her a long look and in a low voice said, "May I call you sometime?"

Kim paused and said, "I'll tell you what, I'm so busy this week, why don't we plan on having a snack here again after class next time?"

In an attempt to hide disappointment, Drake murmured, "I'll look forward to it, Kim Rogers." Grinning he said, "Maybe I'll even dream about it."

Kim blushed, "Okay then. I'd better catch that bus."

Drake waited for her bus to arrive and waved as it left the stop. "Nice guy," Kim thought as she watched his figure fade into the distance. She would also look forward to next week.

*   *   *

After Drake's farewell to Kim Rogers at the bus stop, he was not about to spend his time riding connecting busses home and simply used his cell phone to call a cab to take him to his elite neighborhood. The entrance to the Broadmoor community was protected by an elaborate gate, a guardhouse and an armed guard on duty twenty-four hours each day. It was required that every entering car stop and show identification. The guard peered through the open driver's window and shone his flashlight on the faces of the two occupants.

"It's only me, Fletcher," said Drake as he held up his Broadmoor resident ID.

"Good to see you, Mr. Gilson," said Fletcher, the guard. "Is everything alright?"

"Sure," replied Drake, "this is Ahmed, my driver. He's just going to drop me off at my house."

"Okay, Mr. Gilson, pass on through!"

At age twenty three, Drake thoroughly enjoyed living with his parents in a post-modern, four-thousand square-foot mini-mansion, complete with four bathrooms, a sweeping 150-degree view of Lake Washington, the foothills of the Cascade mountain range, and a dramatic view of fourteen-thousand-foot Mt. Rainier to the south. He didn't mind having the cook and the maid to order around either, if he were being completely honest with himself.

No one seemed to be around when Drake arrived home so he headed directly to his study desk in the corner of his large bedroom. Studying for tomorrow's lecture was the order of business tonight. Drake sat at his desk thumbing through his second year architecture text book. "Let's see," he said out loud, "I hafta try and memorize as much as I can about posts and beams, stresses and strains, wood and concrete strengths per square foot."

Drake was typically a motivated student but tonight was different. Unable to get Kim Rogers off his mind, he thought of how the highlights shone in her hair.

I've never seen such hair on a girl before, he thought. *And she is gorgeous all over. Don't you love the way she talks and the way she walks? She seems unusually smart and sweet all at the same time. Is this girl perfect or what? Wait a minute. Nobody's perfect. Have you fallen for this girl or have you gone nuts? I have read about love at first sight. Has it just happened to me? Oh, come on Drake, get real. Thinking of Kim is a distraction. The strange thing about it is that it's never happened to me before. Short term infatuation maybe, but nothing like this.*

Looking around the room he had grown up in, Drake wondered what Kim would think about the fact that he still lived at home with his parents. He always tried to avoid confessing this to others and realized that Kim's opinion suddenly mattered quite a bit.

Drake's father, Fred Gilson, was a prominent corporate attorney whose clients included some of the wealthiest and most important corporate business firms in the region. Drake had often wondered how much money his father actually controlled – a couple of hundred million at least he guessed. Drake was the only child of Fred and Louella Gilson, who were well liked members of the most prestigious country clubs and charity organizations in the Seattle area. Drake had not been left out of the family fortune. Upon turning twenty-one, he had come into his trust fund and now had five million dollars in the bank and various investment accounts.

Fred Gilson had spent a good deal of time with his son Drake from the time the child was born all the way through his young life, providing him with everything a bright kid could need. Fred tried his very best to generously provide the actual needs as distinguished from the unnecessary desires of any spoiled rich kid. Fred went along with the notion that parents should allow their children to choose their own careers based on their natural interest in what was to be their life's work. From his earliest years in school, Drake's main interest was in his art classes, although sports were firmly in second place. Football, wrestling and tennis were foremost since Drake Gilson earned a place on the starting lineups and distinguished himself in all three sports. In his high school years, his father pressed him a bit to choose a career so they could set their sights on the best college. Sometime during his sophomore year Drake informed his father that he would be happy in his adult life if he could be an artist. Some serious discussions ensued after the boy's declaration in which Fred discovered how persuasive young Drake could be. Fred however was a much more experienced debater and eventually convinced his son that he could be even happier by being a fine-arts painter as a sideline and commit himself to being an architect and by doing so make an important contribution to society and the world in general without the risk all artists take which, more times than not, ends in frustration. "Every architect must be a capable artist," Fred said.

*　　*　　*

Kim's home was halfway up the steep slope of Queen Anne Hill, one of the seven hills on which the original town of Seattle was built in the mid-nineteenth century. The house was a typical early twentieth century Seattle bungalow. Its three and one-half bedrooms, two bathrooms and dramatic territorial view had been a comfortable family home for twenty five years. Kim's father, Wayne Rogers had barely qualified for a mortgage obligation, but he had somehow scratched together enough for a minimum down payment at the time of purchase as well as a steady job in the Seattle transit maintenance garage. Shortly after moving into the house, Wayne and his wife, Clara, welcomed their firstborn, a baby girl named Megan. Four years later, baby Kim joined the family. When Kim was eight her world was turned upside-down when her mother succumbed to colon cancer but it was her sister, twelve-year-old Megan, who was the most deeply affected. Not long after the loss of her mother, Megan began exhibiting bizarre behavior. Kim felt compelled to become a caregiver to her older sister. Though Wayne made a huge effort to see to his daughter's welfare, he became so bewildered by Megan's psychological problems that he was compelled to seek professional help. Her psychoanalyst recommended confinement to the Western Washington State Hospital near Lakewood, forty-five minutes away, which was the state hospital for patients with mental, psychological, social and behavioral problems. Megan's confinement began at age sixteen and continued until the authorities at the hospital declared her competent to deal with life on the outside at age twenty-five. Although Wayne and Kim had visited Megan as often as they were allowed to over the past eight years, they were nervous about the adjustments to their lives which would be required when Megan returned to the family home. Kim was busy not only with her painting class, which was her true passion, but with her other pursuits which helped her father to maintain the house and pay for Megan's medical bills. She worked multiple jobs as a teacher of Hatha Yoga and a general fitness and Zumba dance teacher as a local gym and several Senior Centers along with her volunteer work at the Mission. Still, Kim was excited about the prospect of having her sister back.

Soon after Megan's return home, both Wayne and Kim became aware of Megan's limitations. Despite the care and treatment that Megan had received at Western State Hospital, it was unlikely she would be able to successfully hold a job, live by herself or be competent in managing her own affairs. Wayne and Kim had been advised of this by the medical authorities at the hospital who also informed them that she was unlikely to improve by continued confinement there.

Kim found that her beautiful, twenty-five-year-old sister, Megan, was a gentle sort and easy to get along with. Her long black hair flowed down her back well past her shoulders. Her dark brown eyes always seemed to be shadowed, while her delicate, beautifully proportioned facial features indicated a mysterious shyness which everyone who saw her found deliciously compelling.

Kim was most excited about the fact that Megan also had an artistic bent. She happily included Megan in her own pursuits, including plans to invite her to attend her oil colors course.

*   *   *

"Are we ready to go to class, Megan? Do you have all of your materials in the big bag?"

"I'm so excited," called Megan, as she gave a final glance at the contents of her bag of art materials. "It's so nice of you to take me to your painting class, but I'm still not sure I'll fit in!"

"Of course you will, Megan, you just have to trust me. Everything will be fine. You're gonna like it a lot!" They both shuffled off for the bus stop carrying their big sacks of precious art tools.

*   *   *

As the class was preparing to start, Drake saw Kim talking to their instructor and gesturing towards another young woman. Drake could recognize that this other woman was also beautiful in a different way from his Kim and noticed that her charms were not lost on Markov who was soon setting up an easel for the new girl even though students were never allowed to join after the first two class sessions. Markov even gave her some one-on-one attention, demonstrating how to begin a charcoal drawing prior to painting.

Drake kept himself in the background until he thought it was the right time to speak to the lovely Kim and she was no longer distracted. Approaching her after class, he had the opportunity to meet the dark-haired woman, whom Kim introduced as her older sister. Since he and Kim had arranged to share dinner that night, Drake successfully maneuvered Kim and Megan to the restaurant. This time, Drake offered the women a ride home rather than an escort to the bus. Kim was very appreciative as it had been a long day and agreed to let Drake take her to lunch the next Monday when her schedule allowed a one-hour lunch break.

*   *   *

In the weeks that followed, Drake put his creative abilities to work figuring out how he could spend enough time with Kim to win her over. By now he was convinced he wanted to marry her and the sooner the better. Drake was not consumed with a mindless infatuation. He assured himself that he knew exactly who Kim Rogers was. He knew, he thought, who and what he was. He knew that if he could charm Kim into marrying him, both of them would be better for it. He thought of the line by Jack Nicholson, "You make me want to be a better man" and knew that he would strive to be an even better man if he won Kim. He found himself daydreaming about the kids they would have. He found that he could think of nothing but her for more than thirty seconds. When he was with her he found himself deliriously happy and when not, he was restless and unhappy.

*   *   *

Over winter months, Kim continued to be quite happy in her work and spending as much time as possible with Megan, escorting her to lectures, stage performances and movies. She and Megan enjoyed making art together in their home studio.

But more than anything, she had become attached to the handsome Drake and found herself won over by his personality, common sense and subtle demonstrations of his sincere love for her. It hadn't taken long for them to become intimate and when Kim finally let her guard down, she fell head over heels in love. When they announced their engagement, both families approved wholeheartedly.

*   *   *

The impending marriage between Drake and Kim was a matter of frequent discussion between Drake and his parents. They understood his impatience but believed the couple should get to know each other better before taking the plunge. They also felt an obligation to tradition, their social position and obligations to friends and relatives. Drake's parents finally persuaded him to set the date for six months down the road, in December, just about one year since they first met. That would give Louella plenty of time to make plans for a magnificent ceremony and celebration.

*   *   *

Ever since Megan came home from the hospital, Kim worried that she might be spending too much time alone. This was of special concern now that Kim was working full time and spending so much time with Drake. Megan had convinced Kim that she was competent to travel by bus to and from Capitol Hill. Megan jumped at the chance to attend full-time art classes at the Gage academy, an art school only four blocks from Cornish. The prospect of taking drawing, painting and design classes was enormously exciting for Megan. Kim was pleased to arrange for Megan's tuition, art supplies, instructions on preparing and carrying her daily lunches. A list of emergency phone numbers was installed inside Megan's lunch box.

Megan bubbled over when relating her version of the classroom events, the teacher's quirks and the other students' work which she invariably admired so much. Megan was also able to continue the still-life painting class with Ivan Markov, who coincidentally, taught a figure-drawing class at the Gage academy.

Kim was gratified to hear that her teacher had been giving her sister special instructions in class, sharing his insight and coaching her in the use of her painter's tools.

*   *   *

Driving home from her job at the senior center, Kim reflected on a recent experience during dinner at the Gilson's in which one of Fred Gilson's good friends, a

159

principal partner in a prestigious architectural firm spoke to her about Drake's work in his architecture class which he'd had the opportunity to review. These projects had earned Drake top grades. The architect told Kim that he believed Drake had the potential to become one of our great American architects. Kim couldn't help the tears of pride filling her eyes, as she thought about Drake and her responsibility to support him in achieving his promise. But right now she wanted to take a rare moment for herself to have a chocolate chip cookie and take a short nap before Drake came over.

As she drove into her driveway, she was surprised to see an unfamiliar car parked in front of the house. "Who could that be at this time of day?" she asked herself. Upon entering the house, she called out, "Are you home, Megan? Who's here?" Kim began to worry as she tramped through the living room, dining room, the hallway and the kitchen calling for Megan, who suddenly appeared in the outside her bedroom door wearing her bathrobe, looking confused and a bit tousled. "Why the bathrobe, sweetie? Are you sick?"

Megan looked away and murmured, "I'm not sick, Kimmie."

"Well then, tell me what's wrong. Whose car is parked in front of the house?"

"It's my car," said a deep, heavily accented voice. Ivan Markov stepped through the bedroom door fully dressed and stood behind Megan who hung her head as if ashamed.

Megan showed her typical shy smile, "We are lovers,"

she breathed. "He is going to marry me ."

"We'll see about that!" yelled Kim. "Megan, you take a shower and get cleaned up. Mr. Markov, you go into the living room and wait until I tell you that you can go! If you even think about leaving I will have you arrested and put in jail today!"

Megan went into the bathroom. Ha!" exclaimed Markov, "arrested for what?"

"For raping a mentally challenged woman, you bastard!"

Wayne and Drake arrived at the house at about the same time. Kim met them at the door. "How's everything, honey?" asked her dad.

"Whose car is parked in front?" asked Drake. "Come here and give me a hug, you little rascal. Why the long face?"

Kim explained as best she could what had occurred since she'd arrived about an hour before. The three of them walked into the living room and discovered Ivan sitting on the sofa calmly smoking. Wayne lunged to attack Markov. Drake, in a quick reaction, grabbed Wayne in a powerful grip and held him by the arms as he whispered to him, "Wayne, hold it. Wayne, you will just make everything worse." Wayne calmed down a bit as Drake held him and continued to talk in the lowest of tones. "I understand your anger, but we need to talk. Later on if you still want to kill him, maybe I'll help you."

Drake directed everyone to sit around the dining room table and relax. Drake spoke, "Kim, what's best for Megan at this point?"

Kim looked angry and determined, "I want to take Megan to a doctor right away. There's a walk-in clinic about four blocks from here. They are open until about eight or so."

"Okay," said Drake, "but if her exam shows a disease of some kind...?"

"She has no disease, you fools!" shouted Markov.

Drake continued, "or if she is pregnant, what do we do?"

"You people are crazy!" shrieked Markov.

Drake gave him a steely gaze, "Keep quiet or I will slap you silly."

"Do not make mistake of underestimating me," growled Markov. "I served in Russian Cossack cavalry. We learned how to disable enemy in half a minute and kill within a minute. If we fight, I may not give you a choice!

Kim stared at Markov and said, "You are twice the age of Drake. You are out of shape and you're known to be an alcoholic. Drake is a college wrestling champion. I have taken self defense classes. I think I can take you myself. You just sit there and be quiet."

Drake looked at each person sitting at the table, "If Megan happens to be pregnant, Wayne and Kim, how do you want to handle it?"

Wayne stroked his chin and spoke slowly, "I was raised a Catholic and went to Catholic schools. I guess I am considered a fallen Catholic, but I am still a believer. I have never believed in abortion and never will."

"Me neither," said Kim, as her eyes filled with tears.

She rose to her feet and stood behind Megan's chair. Megan sat with her elbows on the table, her hands covering her eyes. Her body language seemed to reflect sadness, shame and a kind of hopelessness. Her gentle sobs were heard by everyone at the table.

Wayne sat slumped over. The sadness in his face made him look twenty years older than his sixty-three years. Tears were apparent as they ran down the wrinkles in his face.

"Come on, hon, we're going now," Kim said to Megan. "It probably won't take more than an hour. I'm depending on you all to be here when we get back."

Wayne went to the kitchen to make coffee for Drake, Markov and himself. As he served Markov, the Russian spoke to him in a quiet voice, "Would you happen to have bit of vodka?"

"You are lucky to get coffee," snarled Wayne.

The three men at the dining room table grew fidgety as one and one-half hours passed before the return of Kim and Megan. "Here's the report," said Kim in a sober voice. "Megan is in good physical health. She is about three months pregnant." A pathetic groan was heard from Wayne as he sank deeper in his chair.

Drake looked across the table and his eyes met Kim's, "What will you do, Kim?"

Kim blew her nose and dabbed at her eyes, "I think I will need to stay right here in the house and look after Megan. She will need lots of support, especially after the baby comes. I will take care of them both."

"But Kimmie," asked Wayne, "won't this affect your

163

marriage plans?"

"There's nothing I want more than to settle down with Drake and start our own family, but right now I'm in a state of shock. I know that I have to take care of my sister no matter what. This is a time when we all have to do the right thing for her. That's why we have to postpone the wedding, hopefully for only a short time. Drake, I need you now more than ever."

All concerned with these new circumstances, with the exception of Ivan Markov, agreed they adapt as best they could.

* * *

Kim gave up her teaching jobs which might have resulted in a complete lack of income for her except for Drake's generous supplementary checks every two weeks. He helped her connect with one of Seattle's finest gynecologists. Drake's subsistence checks also allowed for the necessary art supplies. Megan relied on Kim for virtually everything, including seeing to her medical needs and the loving companionship that her sister unselfishly provided. Drake pursued his studies with an even greater energy and commitment while continuing to visit the Rogers' girls ever third or fourth day.

On weekend days, when Wayne could serve as caregiver to Megan, Drake tried to take Kim out for some kind of entertainment or cultural activity which he knew was necessary to provide a pleasant diversion. Wayne kept plugging along at his job but continued to worry about what the needs would be for a grandchild and Megan in light of his impending retirement.

As the weeks and months went by, Kim referred to books about baby care and tried to make sure that Megan understood as much as possible when she shared the information. When the time of the baby's birth was close, there was excitement in the hearts of the Gilson and Rogers families as well as serious concern for the futures of some family members.

While at the breakfast table, Megan put both hands on her abdomen and cried, "Something's happening, Kimmie!" A quick look by Kim confirmed the fact that her water had broken.

* * *

Two days later, Megan and the baby were secure back home. Megan was tired and weak from the ordeal of giving birth. The baby boy was perfectly healthy with a normal routine of sleeping, eating and crying. The decision to name the child was left to Kim. Accepting the responsibility, she named the boy what she thought was a masculine, contemporary-sounding name. The little guy would be known as Brian Rogers.

* * *

Marianne Parker, Kim's loyal girlfriend, was on the line in the latest of their frequent telephone conversations. "Yesterday I bumped into two of your old classmates from Ivan Markov's painting class at Cornish. They said that Markov has been acting really strange lately."

"How so?" asked Kim.

"They say he looks and talks like he is deranged, sorta nervous and really scary."

"I hope he doesn't call or show up here," said Kim.

The very next morning she answered the phone and heard Ivan Markov's voice, "Is this Kim? Mr. Markov here. You say I am baby's father?"

"Yes," said Kim, "You are, and according to our agreement, you were required to begin sending child support payments to Megan starting two days ago."

A pause ensued, "How much is payment?" rasped Markov.

Kim replied in a no-nonsense voice, "Five hundred a month, as you well know."

"I want to see baby boy."

"You must send the child's support money starting now," said Kim.

Markov shouted, "You cannot stop me! I have right to see him!"

Kim spoke calmly, "Okay, we will allow you five minutes to see him. When can you come over?"

"I need to see baby today!"

"All right," said Kim, "Come at four o'clock. You may visit for five minutes or so and you better be sober or we won't let you in the front door." Her call to Drake was answered on the first ring.

"Hello, sweetheart, I am at the campus library doing some research. What's up?" Kim recounted her call with Markov.

"Okay, I'll be there at three thirty and keep a close eye on him. Are you sure you don't need a nurse to help out with Megan and the little pee maker? I told you I'd be glad to hire a good one."

"Drake, this is my chance to practice for when we have our first baby. I have all we need for now. I can't wait to hold my hero in my arms again. It's been two whole days since I've seen you."

Drake was amused at her many cute references to himself. "Did you say hero?"

*   *   *

Drake parked his Mustang in front of the Rogers' house at three-thirty and sprinted to the door, anticipating the hugs and kisses he had been looking forward to. They were plentiful and greatly enhanced by some groping and loving caresses. During a passionate kiss, Drake told himself, *Hold your tongue, man, you don't have time for more right now. The Mad Russian may arrive and spoil everything.*

"Megan is napping and I just fed and changed the baby," Kim whispered between kisses.

Drake said, "That's good, but let's get ready for Ivan."

Kim said, "Remember I told you what his students have said about him lately. He has been acting like he's nuts."

Suddenly they were both aware of Markov's car pulling up outside on the street.

"Let me handle him," Drake he said in a whisper.

As Drake opened the front door, Markov stepped into the room wearing his usual worn out gray suit jacket, baggy black trousers and a striped dress shirt, which had seen better days, open at the neck.

Drake couldn't keep his eyes away from Markov's rat like little black eyes which were rimmed with an unsettling reddish glare. "Are you okay Ivan?" asked Drake, staring into Ivan's face.

Ivan attempted to stand like a proud Cossack. He looked both Kim and Drake up and down and growled, "I need to see baby."

"Come this way," said Drake, "We will go to the spare bedroom which is used as the baby's nursery." Reaching the doorway to the nursery, Drake said, "You can see the cot over here where Megan sleeps every night to be close to the baby. When the baby wakes up, he needs to be fed. Right here is the crib with the sleeping baby. That's what the little tyke does most of the time."

"I want to see my baby alone. I'm his father. I want to be alone for few minutes. This is first time I see my little boy."

Standing next to the crib, Drake spoke slowly and distinctly to the older man, "I will leave you here with the baby for just a few minutes. You are not to pick him up or wake him. You may very gently touch him, but that's all." Drake still felt a strange nervousness about the unusually weird look on the older man's face, but felt he had to give the old fool the benefit of the doubt for only a very few minutes. "I will be right outside and I will open the door in a few minutes. Then you must leave. Do you understand me?"

"Yah, I know," hissed Markov.

Drake stood with his ear to the nursery door and thought he heard a movement which he thought likely indicated Markov was looking at the tiny baby's face from more than one viewpoint. Kim stood watching from about ten feet away in an adjoining hallway.

Everything was quiet. Suddenly the nursery door slammed against Drake's shoulder and Ivan bumped Drake's arm as he brushed quickly by, heading for the living room. Out of the side of his mouth, he mumbled in a gravelly voice, "We talk now," as he scurried past.

"In a minute," said Drake, who stepped into the nursery. The baby didn't seem to be moving. Drake rushed to the crib to inspect. "Oh, my God!" He screamed as he got no response from the little form in the crib. No heartbeat and no respiration. The little boy was limp and turning cold to the touch, obviously dead.

"Why? Why have you done this you monster? Oh my God," he kept repeating as if he could find no other words to express his shock. Drake gently covered little Brian's face before turning to catch Markov who was standing defiantly in the living room. His expression was a mixture of smugness, defiance and hatred as he faced Drake who had half-staggered into the living room, obviously emotionally upset. Drake was virtually at the tipping point of being out-of-control with grief, sadness and shock with an overriding mix of indescribable hatred for the man standing before him, the brutal murderer of his own child.

Markov held an envelope in his left hand from which he withdrew some papers. "Look here," he gloated, "this problem now gone away!"

Drake's eyes narrowed as he confronted the Russian, and his body assumed a slight wrestler's crouch as if anticipating combative action, but he could not resist glancing at the papers that Markov thrust at him. They were obviously clippings of articles about the infant crib death phenomenon. Markov displayed a half-grin showing his yellow teeth marked with dark stains. His eyes seemed to glitter as Drake's stare penetrated Markov's look of a raging insanity, "Now ve have no more money problem with kid, everything legal and everybody happy."

Drake peered at him with an incredulous look. "You are a demon straight from hell; you are the devil himself and you are a despicable monster, a sniveling cowardly rat-bastard! I should kill you myself with my hands just like you murdered that innocent tiny little soul in the nursery. If you think you can fool the authorities or anyone else about the cause of death blamed on crib death syndrome, it just confirms the fact that you are a hopelessly insane murderer."

Markov's eyes flashed as he reached into his pocket to pull a switchblade knife, holding it in the palm of his right hand with the blade pointed up between his forefinger and thumb. A challenging gesture that all had seen in the movies. Kim stood in the opposite corner of the room watching and terrified. She saw the knife flash as it caught the light.

Poised to charge toward Drake, Markov sneered, "Now I keel you!" Lunging forward, he swept the blade in a swift slashing circular motion. Drake anticipated the move and skillfully shuffled to the side, even though he knew another murderous maneuver would rapidly follow hoping to catch him unaware. The next thrusting slash was avoided by means of more quick footwork by the ex-wrestler, and this time Drake's competitive instincts came into play as he grabbed Markov's hand with the knife and gave it a powerful twist that sent the knife bouncing across the floor. Markov continued to attack as if out-of-control like a mad dog, foaming at the mouth, spitting, kicking, biting and swinging with both fists, charging forward with all his strength like a demon empowered by an overload of adrenalin.

Drake's physical combat experience provided him with the strategy for fighting an angry opponent. An opponent, who charged straight ahead like Markov, was always vulnerable to his antagonist who might give way just enough to take advantage of the speed and momentum of the charge. As the attacking Russian's advance drew him very close to his retreating opponent, Drake deftly sidestepped and tripped Markov, at the same time placing his right hand on Markov's back and giving him a powerful shove forward, enhancing Markov's charge. As Drake rolled away to the side, his opponent's charge was expected to end in a sprawl on a wrestling mat as in the gym, but this fight was in the Rogers' living room. Markov's momentum carried him rapidly forward in a headfirst dive as his head crashed into the brick fireplace wall with a sickening thud like a cantaloupe dropped to a concrete sidewalk. Markov's body stiffened, shuddered and fell limp.

Kim had followed the action from the hallway. She watched in horror and was sickened when she realized that Markov was dead and Drake would no doubt be accused of murder. At this moment she and Drake's eye's met in a terrifying silence.

Drake's lips moved, "We have to call somebody. Who shall we call?"

Kim's jaw and lips began to quiver uncontrollably. Drake took her arm and walked her to the nearest sofa. His voice deepened and he spoke slowly, "Before we call anybody let's try to think clearly about this. First I need to call my dad and he will call his lawyer. The authorities will accuse me of murder, second degree or maybe manslaughter. You will be kept out of it. We will just tell them the truth and they may agree on self defense and drop the charges, but any court trial is a crap shoot. That's what all the lawyers say."

"Hold it, Drake, don't call anyone yet. We need to discuss it some more. What happens to your career if you go on trial for murder? Even worse, what happens to our marriage plans? If you go on trial, all those headlines and gossip will wreck your reputation. You can't afford it and neither can I."

They both were silent and stared into each other's

eyes, "You're right, but Honey, I have to do the right thing. I'm bound to tell the truth and whatever happens, happens."

"No, wait," pleaded Kim, "here's the way we can do it. You leave here right now. Then I call 911. You stay at home and keep quiet. The cops will get here pretty soon. My dad will be here right after work. I will call your dad and he'll get your lawyer for me and bail me out tonight. You can hire that caregiver or nurse you have been talking about and get her over here to help with Megan."

"You know," said Drake, "that I can't let you do this!"

Kim grabbed his arm, "Think, Drake, mine is a sensible plan. They are less likely to convict me than they are you. I am thinking about our future, you and me together. We tell the cops you were never here today. I will make them believe that I pushed Markov into the fireplace wall as he attacked me. Go arrange your alibi. Now get out of here!"

Kim procured a large tarp from a closet and covered Markov's body and blocked the nursery to prevent Megan from seeing what she should not be allowed to see.

In order to get Megan out of the house as soon as possible, Kim called Marianne Parker, and luckily found that she was available to come over immediately and take Megan to the shopping mall. Marianne would arrive in ten minutes. She went to Megan's room, got her on her feet and into her shoes. Megan seemed eager to go shopping with Marianne. Kim sat in her room to use the telephone. The cops should be here shortly she surmised.

173

While Kim was involved for a few moments, Megan put her jacket on preparing to leave. She walked out of her room and absentmindedly strolled into the living room where she saw the switchblade knife that had fallen from Markov's hand in his struggle with Drake. She paid no attention to the tarp covering Markov's body, but merely assumed that it was part of another of Kim's cleanup projects. Her attention was instead focused on the knife which she deposited with the blade still exposed into the dishwasher in the kitchen.

"Marianne is here!" called Kim.

Marianne hustled Megan into her car and drove away.

*   *   *

Cars descended on the Rogers' neighborhood and parked up and down the street where two murders had occurred on the same day. There were cars from the police department and other official-looking cars which carried policemen, detectives, photographers, coroners, newspaper reporters, radio and television people and various support staff. The inevitable yellow plastic police ribbon indicating a serious investigation surrounded the house.

Kim Rogers' predictions were all coming true. She had been interrogated, arrested and sent to police headquarters downtown. She was met by Drake, his father Fred, and their lawyer, Clive Harrington, who arranged for bail. She returned home that night and was happy to see that her father was looking after Megan, who was confused about the hubbub. They all were pleased that Drake had dispatched a nurse who would be staying on to care for Megan.

Police investigators revealed that baby Brian was smothered to death by Ivan Markov who also broke the neck of the helpless baby in the brutal process. Kim Rogers was charged with second degree murder. She and her attorney would insist that the prosecutor drop the charges and declare her to be innocent since they insisted the killing of Markov was obviously in self-defense.

The trial began one month later. The prosecutor and assistant district attorney were unusually aggressive and pursued the case as if a conviction was the most important thing since the Lindberg kidnapping. The knife that Markov used in his attack on Drake might have assured an acquittal for Kim based on the self-defense issue. The knife which had been removed from the scene by a completely unaware Meagan before the investigators arrived at the Rogers' home was of no consequence. A fact of great importance was that Kim was experienced in self-defense tactics and that she was in unusually good physical shape as evidenced by her standing as a physical training instructor.

Everything seemed to go wrong for Kim and her attorney in the three-day trial. Ipso facto, Kim was convicted of second degree murder. The jury unanimously advised the judge that a first degree manslaughter conviction was appropriate under the circumstances. The judge agreed and sentenced Kim to serve six years at the Washington State Women's Correctional center at Gig Harbor, often referred to as "the Women's prison at Purdy," about thirty five miles from the Rogers' home in Seattle.

*　*　*

That evening at the Roger's home, the attorney, Clive Harrington, met with the devastated Gilson and Rogers' families. "We are filing appeal papers and we will fight this conviction with all we have. To be completely honest, the chances of a reversal are slim. Our best estimates pretty much assure us that Kim can expect to be released on parole in about four years. I regret with all my heart that justice in this case was not served."

The collective mood of the two families was what anyone might expect after what the Rogers' and Gilsons' had endured in the previous weeks. A mood of darkness, pessimism, anxiety and trauma combined with the big question of how Kim and Drake's futures would be affected. Drake was crazy with worry about how the time in prison might affect Kim. Even assurance by their attorney that Purdy was not a 'hard time' institution was not much comfort to Drake and Wayne. Three or four years in any lockup environment were cause for profound worry. Serving a term in prison might result in a serious psychological change in anyone.

*　*　*

In the week before Kim was expected to start her sentence, she and Drake were together constantly. One evening when together, Kim cuddled in his arms, Drake attempted to describe his feelings of profound sadness and regret that she was about to be punished for his actions. Tears overflowed his eyes and ran down his cheeks as he kept repeating, "I'm the guilty one. Now you go to prison in my place! It's all wrong! How could it have come to this? I never should have listened to you when we were waiting for the cops to show up and you sent me home. It shows how wonderful you are and how rotten and cowardly I am."

Kim abruptly sat up and drew very close, their faces inches apart, "Quit talking like that," she scolded. "We did it with our eyes wide open, Drake. It made sense at the time and it still makes sense. I love you with all my heart and when this prison thing is over we will start our lives together. We will still be young. We will raise a beautiful family and enjoy each other for a lifetime."

"Honey, I'm so very sorry," he sobbed.

"Drake, you have a brilliant future ahead, that's why this is the best way. We can be in close touch the whole time they have me locked up. I can be very adaptable. I have a lot of patience when it's called for. I'm pretty tough, too, when I have to be, so please don't go off the deep end worrying about me."

* * *

The second year after Kim's incarceration saw

Drake Gilson graduate and begin his promising career at Empire Architects.

Megan seemed reasonably content under the care of her nurse while Wayne Rogers doggedly kept going to his job and looking forward to retirement in two years.

Like the other prisoners at Purdy, Kim absorbed her ups and downs in an atmosphere which required constant adjustment and adaptation, while counting the days to her release. The weekly art class in one of the prison's classrooms felt like a lifesaver to her. When in an art environment, even behind prison walls, she felt like she was in another dimension, free from ordinary frustrations, obligations and limitations. She felt free to experiment using watercolors, felt markers and a variety of colored pencils. Art paper with different textures and surfaces were also employed in her work. After her first two or three classes it was obvious to the prison staff that Kim was genuinely talented and brought a certain inspiration to her classmates, all prisoners like herself. Since Kim obviously possessed more background and training than the others in her class, she was encouraged by the prison staff to share her knowledge and skill-techniques with her classmates. Because of her background as an accredited instructor in physical fitness classes, she was also assigned to teach exercise classes to the other inmates. Along the way, Kim also became interested in the service-dog training program. These activities were enjoyable to Kim even though she was required to take her turn at some of the so called 'dirty-duty' assignments in the kitchen and the laundry. Kim became a leadership figure and handled it with a mixture of charm and poise beyond her years.

Drake drove to the prison virtually every day he was allowed visitation privileges. During their visits they were allowed to hold hands across the table and have a twenty minute conversation in which their loving remarks were exchanged.

*　　*　　*

After three years of Kim's confinement, she was aware that Drake became extremely busy and was unable to be as consistent in his visits as he had been before. During the last part of Kim's third year of confinement, their talks became less intimate with fewer mentions of love, fidelity and commitment to each other. Drake had continued that mode of conversation but Kim had made it obvious that she was uncomfortable with such intimate and loving talk. Drake tried mightily to understand why the tone of their conversations had taken such a turn but he felt that talking frankly about it might cause Kim to become even more distant. Finally, on what turned out to be his last visit to the prison, Kim informed Drake that she did not want him to visit again.

"My God, Kim, what has come over you? You're breaking my heart!"

Looking directly into Drake's eyes, she said, "I may as well come right out with it, I am in love with someone else. She is serving a sentence in here just like I am. Her name is Jackie Morris."

Drake's mouth dropped open as he stared in confused silence.

Kim continued, "We think we will be getting paroled at about the same time. We intend to spend the rest of our lives together. We are exactly right for each other, Drake, and that's the way it is and it won't change. You were right when you described yourself as a coward for letting me serve time for your crime. It's all over for you and me, so please don't come back here on visitor's day. Go back and live your own life as a spoiled millionaire brat."

That night as Drake lay in bed unable to sleep; he anticipated the difficulty of winning back his precious Kim. I'm not going to let her get away from me no matter what. It's pretty clear to me that this lesbian, Jackie Morris, has bad mouthed me to the point where Kim thinks she has to dump me. Along with the other pressures in that hell hole of a prison, the loneliness and despondency of prison life has resulted in Kim turning to that Jackie woman. Apparently Kim has decided that she feels secure with that queer bitch to the point where she thinks that spending the rest of her life with another woman is the answer, for her, my poor confused Kimmie.

None of this will tear her away from me. I will formulate a plan to win her back and I will act on my plan until she returns and we will be together as we have dreamed so much about. Drake swallowed the lump in his throat and rasped, his words out loud, "Nothing will stop us from being together again someday."

DADDY

Casey Brannon couldn't help it. He had a passion for murder. He was also enthralled with kidnapping, thievery, assassination, blackmail and robbery.

A moderately successful crime-fiction writer, Casey had often declared that his stories and books were the products of his own creative imagination as well the serious people-watching he engaged in wherever he went. Then there were the shady characters he had interviewed as research to ensure his books were realistic. He did not start writing his stories with so-called "dark themes," but they just always seemed to tend in that direction. Casey believed that if he ever attempted to write comedy or love stories, it would be a total failure because his brain just didn't think that way.

In contrast to the lawless lives portrayed in his books, Casey lived a cultured, healthy and orderly life with his wife of sixty years, Norma. Together they had raised a family, then when the kids grew up, they'd been free to pursue their own interests such as travel and dancing.

As anyone who has ever tried writing a memoir

or an autobiography will attest, the more one delves mentally into his own past, the more he remembers. Now eighty-four, Casey took pleasure in his memories and was profoundly thankful that, unlike many of his contemporaries, his mental awareness was still functioning virtually as it had ten years earlier. Many of his fondest memories were of his role as "Daddy" to his three wonderful children.

Casey met his oldest son, Rico, more than fifty five years earlier, walking across a parking lot in downtown Seattle. The little dark-skinned, nine-year-old kid had attempted to snatch a briefcase out of Casey's hand. He was met with the quick reactions of the then twenty-four-year-old Casey who had seen the kid charge, and caught the boy with one hand, kicking his feet from under him and slamming him on the asphalt surface of the parking lot. Neither of them could suspect that this was the beginning of a lifelong parental relationship.

Casey couldn't help feeling empathy for the little guy struggling bravely within his grasp. It was not the first time that nine-year-old Rico had been frog-walked from place to place by a strong adult. But this time Rico's captor led him to a restaurant and bought him a hamburger, two hot dogs, a mountain of French fries, two mugs of root beer and two scoops of spumoni ice cream. During this impromptu lunch, Rico opened up a bit and answered some of Casey's questions, revealing that his father had died two years ago and that his mother had packed her suitcase and left about two months ago and he hadn't seen her since. He survived by begging and stealing. He slept in alleys, in the woods and deserted buildings where he wished for a warm blanket. He had been confined in the juvenile detention center a couple of times, but escaped. He hid from cops and anyone else who looked like they might want to catch him. As time passed, Casey and Norma could see the boy's natural intelligence reveal itself. They found that Rico's sense of humor and sensitivity marked him as a very special, courageous and remarkable young man. Norma and Casey agreed that they wanted Rico to become part of their family. They never thought of Rico as anything other than their own natural son. They felt great pride in his accomplishments including earning a pre-law degree at Western Washington University and accepting a government job.

Six years after they had welcomed Rico into the family, they were blessed with the arrival of Janet, a remarkable young girl who not only earned top grades in school but also distinguished herself as a star of her high school track team. At Nathan Hale high school, Janet topped off her accomplishments by serving as a class officer in her senior year and receiving the honor of being named the Salutatorian at graduation. She accepted one of her many offers of a full scholarship at Central Washington University. Now at age fifty-one, Janet Brannon Keeler was a young widow, having recently lost her husband, a successful attorney, to cancer. Janet had one son, twenty-four year old Leland who worked as an engineer at the Boeing Company.

Six years later, to everyone's surprise, their son

Nickolas was born. Casey was filled with enthusiastic affection and attachment for Nicky from the time of his birth. At age eighty-four, Casey still doted on Nick, who was now employed as the City of Seattle's Head Deputy Prosecutor and receiving frequent public praise from his boss, Head Prosecutor Michael Swain.

To Casey, it felt that the fantasy world of his stories had manifested in Nick's profession. And Casey had often relied on his dad's keen insights into the criminal mind as a key to breaking tough cases. On one occasion it looked like the crime-fiction writer might even get the chance to experience his passion first-hand.

*　　*　　*

Casey was working on his computer at home when the phone rang at seven a.m.

"Good morning, Dad," said Nick calling from his desk at the prosecutor's office.

"What's up, Nick?" chirped Casey.

"I'm not supposed to talk about any of this but I have to get your reaction. It's the Snark murder case. We have been counting on two witnesses who can assure a conviction. As of two days ago we have lost contact with both of them – two women who are Snark's neighbors. They are officially missing. The police have had a search going on as of yesterday. The question is, would my favorite criminologist have a feeling, some insight or theory about this latest turn in the case?"

Casey was silent for the moment as an invisible

switch turned on somewhere deep in his psyche. "As you know, Nick, I have been keeping up with this case by reading the accounts in the papers. I think the Snark family are bad asses of the worst kind. I hope I'm wrong but I think it's highly likely that they have disposed of your witnesses."

Nick felt his face and body tighten, "I hope you are wrong too, Dad, but thanks for your opinion."

*　　*　　*

Every few weeks, Nick and his wife, Monica, hosted a family dinner and an evening of conversation at their home for Casey and Norma. After a memorable dinner of baked salmon with all the trimmings, the family members including Nick and Monica's ten year old daughter, Joy, took the comfortable seats in the living room, each holding a cup of coffee or an after-dinner drink. Relaxed and ready, each one was prepared with research on a pertinent topic for discussion. This was in accordance with Casey's suggestion that each person "bring something to the table," meaning that each member prepare him or herself with some interesting facts or thoughtful opinions to enhance the family conversation.

When Nick's turn came, he related some particulars about a case he had been working on, being cautious about the confidential details. Casey immediately recognized it as the Snark case. A man named Herman Snark had been accused of being an accessory to a double murder. Snark was a father of four, two boys in their twenties, Adam and Jacob and two pre-teens – a boy, Eli and a girl, Ruth. It was alleged that the developmentally delayed pre-teens were born from incest and murdered by the two older boys with the knowledge and consent of Snark and his wife Lydia. Someone in this family had threatened their accusers and the family appeared to be deadly serious about intimidating witnesses who had been lined up to testify against them.

Casey shifted his weight to relieve the pain in his right leg and stared intently across the coffee table at Nick. Being legally blind only allowed an extremely blurry look. "Has your office received any threats?"

Nick took a sip of amaretto, "Not as yet but we have been advised to be alert."

The old man blinked a few rapid blinks, "I have heard of such threats to judges, lawyers and prosecutors. A few in the past have had bloody results. I have researched a number of them. I even wrote a couple of stories based on those cases."

The conversation shifted to another topic, but Casey's mind continued to mull over what his son had said. He was worried.

*   *   *

Early the next morning Nick called Casey, "Good morning, Daddy."

Casey answered brightly, "Listen, Mr. Prosecutor, do you have access to a bullet proof vest?"

186

Nick was silent for a moment, "Come on, Dad, aren't we being overly fearful?"

"Don't forget that you are speaking to an expert on criminal behavior."

"Daddy, your creative mind may be working overtime because you are naturally protective of your family, including me. I am not fearful and you shouldn't be. I am not convinced that I should wear a bullet proof vest around the prosecutor's office with the entire police department right next door. My colleagues here at the office will think I have chicken blood."

Casey responded with an amused little snort, "I wasn't suggesting wearing it around the office. I think you should wear the vest when in your car and when you walk anywhere around town and in your own neighborhood. It's just being smart. Nick, even you can't imagine how much I have learned about the criminal mind. I've studied it all my life."

"You probably know more than anybody, Daddy. I respect your experience and insight. I will think seriously about the vest and keep in close touch, but right now duty calls so I have to hang up and get back to our work on the case. We'll be in court with it next week."

*　*　*

Rico Brannon was half-dozing in his favorite chair accompanied by a rapidly cooling cup of coffee and the morning newspaper which was slowly drifting from his lap to the floor when his cell phone rang. "Hello," he grunted into the mouthpiece. "Oh, it's you Daddy," he said quietly.

"What's up in your world these days? We haven't been in touch since three days ago, Rico. Is everything okay on your end?"

"Yeah, I'm fine except for the lonely part. Can you believe it has been three years since Elena passed away? Right about now I'm wishing we had produced some kids but I guess it wasn't in the cards, so I have to get used to being a lonely widower ."

Casey spoke in a low intimate tone, "Yes but you have us and we have you right until the end, my son." Unused to such intimate affectionate remarks, there was an emotional pause. "Now that you are trying to get used to retirement, don't you miss your old job? After all those years of secrecy, maybe you can tell me about it, as if I didn't know that you were a spy for the CIA for almost thirty years. We missed you during all those years when you were away from home. We believed you were working for Shell Oil, traveling here and there. You should be publicly honored as an American hero. Nobody knows about your life of danger, risk and sacrifice."

Rico laughed, "So where was the money?" They both laughed. "You know, Padre, I have never thanked you enough for the encouragement you always gave me when I was growing up. Do you know what I'm talking about?"

"That I bullied you to get straight A's in school?"

"Yeah, of course, but there's also the Spanish. You insisted that I remained bilingual and keep improving the whole time we all lived together. That ability has served me very well, much more than you know." Another brief pause.

"The reason I called was to invite you to lunch tomorrow. One p.m. at the Rainier Club dining room."

"Sure, what's the occasion?"

"We're joining Nicky. It's confidential. He has some problems we are going to help him think through."

* * *

The three Brannon men indulged in their usual custom of affectionate hugs, chuckles and back slaps. Their table was located in the quietest part of the large dining room. The Rainier Club was an ancient fixture in downtown Seattle, a men's-only club for the rich influential business elite. Casey felt proud seated in this classy setting with his two accomplished sons.

"It's been a while, Nick, and you've come a long way." said Rico. "All your family and friends are proud of you, little brother."

"They're all proud of you, too, Rico, with all of your accomplishments in your secret life." Nick grinned, showing his perfect white teeth.

Casey said, "You sounded a bit worried on the phone, Nick. What's going on?"

Nick sipped his wine and rubbed his forehead, "It's about the Snark case. The two older boys, Adam and Jacob, did it for sure. We know the parents were accessories, so all four are guilty. The problem is that Adam and Jacob seem to be out to get the prosecutor."

"What about you?" asked Rico.

"Yeah, me too," Nick answered, "I'm concerned that those bastards might go after my family."

Casey said, "Nick, if you think that there is a serious threat aimed at you I want to know right now."

"Look, Daddy," said Nick, "we think the threats, as of now, are just a bluff." "The Snarks think they can scare us. They expect us to either give up or back out."

Casey pondered for a moment, "It looks like they may well have eliminated their siblings plus the two witnesses. If this is true, they are very dangerous."

"Dad," asked Nick, "if you were thinking of taking action against the Snarks, what would it be?"

Sitting silently Rico caught Casey's eye and winked.

"If they did what I think they are capable of," growled Casey, "I might have to take them out. I mean all four of them if necessary."

"Dad," said Nick, "you are talking like a character in one of your stories. You would certainly be caught and have to spend the rest of your life in prison. You are caught up in your own fantasy world."

Casey felt a dryness in his mouth. "Nick, you underestimate me. Don't you know that my research and the work that I do makes me nothing less than a master criminal? That is, if I chose to be one. I can virtually guarantee that they would never pin any crime on me. If I'm wrong and I am convicted of a capital crime, it would be okay. The death penalty has been suspended in the state of Washington just a few years ago by the Governor. If convicted, do you think any judge would sentence an eighty-four year old blind man to a hard-time prison like Walla Walla? A country club prison would be more likely, and anyway, so what? I'm at the end of the line anyway and only have very little time left on the planet."

"Okay Daddy, no more crazy talk," scolded Nick. "I'm thinking of sending Monica and Joy to stay with her sister in Vancouver, BC for a while until I know they will be safe. Do you and Mom approve? Do the two of you want to skip town for a while?"

"Hell no! Your mom and I are not worried one bit."

Nick finished his wine and declared, "There's something else, I'm being followed every place I go. There's always a car behind me when I drive anywhere and some guy always seems to be in back of me on the sidewalk or across the street trying his best not to look like he's watching me."

Casey intervened, "Nick, why haven't you asked the police for some security people or bodyguards? This has gone too far."

"I guess I just didn't quite know what to do," said Nick.

"Well, now we all know what to do," said Casey, grimly, "Get Monica and Joy to Vancouver today. They should be safe if they leave right away. Rico and I will do some fast research today and tomorrow. We'll pay a visit to the Snarks later. Hopefully, this problem will be resolved and nobody will be hurt. Nicky, there must be no contact between you and any of us or any other family member unless it's a drastic emergency. Now

191

let's get going!"

*   *   *

The doorbell sounded at seven p.m. as planned. Casey opened the door, "Come on in, Rico!"

To Casey's surprise, Rico was accompanied by two others – his sister Janet and her big handsome son, Leland. They all took time for the required greetings, handshakes and hugs. After all were comfortably seated and served with a glass of gleaming chardonnay, Janet asked, "Where's Mom?"

"Visiting her cousin Annie, the one who lives near Green Lake," said Casey. Looking sternly at Rico, he asked, "Why are Janet and Leland here?"

Looking directly into Casey's eyes, Rico, in a low raspy voice said, "The family is at risk. We need them to help. Their attitudes and capabilities are just right for what we need to do."

The others all nodded in agreement.

"I have thoroughly briefed them on the situation between Nicky and the Snarks. I'm sorry to surprise you like this, Daddy, but I felt this was the best way to deal with the problem we have."

Grandson Leland Keeler spoke up, "We can't just stand aside, Grandpa. We are ready to do anything you and Rico have planned."

Just as the group was preparing to leave , Janet's cell phone rang, "Yes," she said, "this is she. Who is this? What? What are you saying? Oh, dear God. Where was this exactly? Where are they now? Give me the number please, thank you."

She hung up and turned to face the others, "There's been a terrible accident. Monica and Joy were driving north when their car ran off the road, over a bank and into a ravine."

A flurry of questions interrupted her.

"It was about fifteen miles north of Marysville on Highway 99. The ambulances are headed for Providence hospital in Everett. They say they are critical."

"Okay, people," said Casey, "we need to stick together and keep our heads on straight. Think of it as being members of a team. Here's what I suggest. Make sure our cell phones are charged at all times. Janet, take Leland and hustle up to the hospital. Meet Nick there, and report back to me. Rico, do some surveillance on the Snark boys as best you can and keep me appraised. I will send for Norma. We will both be here waiting for your calls. Let's hope that Monica and Joy are all right."

*　　*　　*

Casey and Norma waited uneasily at the kitchen table, absentmindedly playing two-handed pinochle. Waiting for calls from Janet and Rico made them nervous and fearful for the fate of their loved ones after the disastrous car crash. Casey wondered to himself whether Monica had been headed for Canada to escape the threat from the Snarks. Did those murderers cause Monica's car to crash? If so, he thought, it would call for him to

193

avenge the family. He would have to kill them all.

The phone rattled, "Yes, Janet. Monica and Joy are badly hurt?" Casey repeated Janet's words aloud as he heard them over the phone so Norma could hear.

"They are both critical. The state patrol cops are pretty sure that they were run off the road by another vehicle. Nicky is here with us. He is a basket case." Janet, crying and sobbing said, "Leland and I are trying to calm him down. He says he is not going home yet. He is staying here until things improve."

Casey looked at Norma, "Janet says she is staying with Nick until tomorrow. Could we come up to the early tomorrow morning?"

"Tell her yes," said Norma, with a wavering voice and teary eyes.

Casey had barely put the phone down when it rang again, "Hey Rico, what can you tell me?"

"Considerable activity, Dad. The Snarks were in and out during the day. They made two trips, one to a suspicious warehouse on Leary Avenue. They brought back two big boxes. The second trip was to a drugstore on Queen Anne Avenue. I also observed a delivery to the house by a beat up Dodge pickup truck. One big box. It looks like they're building or putting something together in their house or basement. That's all I've got for now. We're coming to your house. What's up with Nicky and Monica?"

*   *   *

The next morning the family assembled at the Providence Hospital in Everett. The good news was that Monica and Joy both showed slight signs of improvement, but it was still touch-and-go. Nick was swarmed by the family members as they embraced him along with words of encouragement, sympathy and hope. Nick welcomed their attention with misty-eyed smiles and affectionate handshakes, hugs and kisses. Norma and Janet stayed at the hospital. Casey called for the men to meet that same afternoon at Rico's house to discuss the situation.

*   *   *

Janet's son Leland was the first to arrive at Rico's front door, closely followed by Casey. The men each found a chair at Rico's dining room table. Just as Rico was pouring the first cup of coffee, the telephone rang.

"Rico!" an excited voice said, "It's me, Nick. I'm still in Everett. My colleague in the office just called me. We think the Snarks' house just blew up! It's on TV and on all local stations. Turn it on right now!"

Rico hung up and ran to the living room for the TV, yelling for the others to follow him. The screen showed the gathering of fire trucks and police cars surrounded by a horde of onlookers and police attempting to control the mob of neighbors, all trying to peer into the enormous cloud of smoke covering what was left of the Snarks' three-bedroom house.

The TV reporter on the scene was shouting, "It appears that the house was completely blown to bits.

Since the family car was in the garage, itself blown to smithereens, the assumption is that the four members of the family known to live here have all lost their lives. The authorities believe it impossible that anyone could have survived such a horrendous blast from a very powerful bomb or explosive device."

"Somebody beat us to it!" yelled Casey. Leland had to choke back a laugh, but smothered it well. Rico remained deadly serious as he stared into the screen, but Casey seemed genuinely disappointed, at least for a few moments as they all continued to watch intently.

Two months later, an investigation had revealed the cause of the deadly Snark explosion. The Snark family was in the process of making some pipe bombs, presumably for use against the Brannons, when something went wrong in the process. Bomb-making is a risky business. Nick's wife Monica and their daughter Joy were completely recovered except for Monica's slight limp and Joy's occasional headache.

* * *

Four months after the big blast at the Snark's house, the Brannon family met for their annual Thanksgiving dinner at Casey and Norma's house. Preparing dinner for eleven was too big a job for Norma, but as usual, Janet and Monica joined in the fun of working together to create a turkey and stuffing masterpiece.

Casey, Nick and Leland drank beer, watched football on the television and teased each other in the living room as the ladies did their work. Rico was the last to arrive. As promised, he brought with him three other beautiful people. They were introduced all around as Isabella, Rico's friend, a stunningly beautiful black-haired, brown-eyed, lively middle-aged lady, her gorgeous twenty-two-year-old daughter, Carmella, and her thirteen-year-old-son, Phillip. All the guys winked or unobtrusively punched Rico as if to say, 'good work, man.' Polite curiosity was in order as the family members welcomed the attractive newcomers and enjoyed the new expression on Rico's face which matched the new spring in his step.

Janet's unmarried son Leland was obviously stunned by the appearance of the startlingly pretty Carmella. Twelve-year-old Joy couldn't help staring at thirteen-year-old Phillip, who was introduced as a boy with the ambition to become a doctor.

Casey proudly sat at the head of the big table. Norma sat to his left and Nick to his right.

Nick looked at his father and quietly said in a nostalgic moment, "Look at this great family of yours, Daddy. You deserve to be very proud. At your age, looking back, do you have any regrets?"

Casey looked thoughtfully into Nick's eyes as he sipped his chardonnay. With a faint smile he said quietly, "I wish I could have murdered the damned Snark family myself."

THE TONG

As they were every night, except Sunday, the dark International District streets were brightly lit only at the restaurant entrances. At seven-thirty p.m., Walter Myers found a parking place in the lot on near the popular Hong Kong Chinese restaurant. Walter, his wife Martha, both in their late-forties, along with their twelve-year-old son Jimmy, began walking toward the entrance of the restaurant.

"My, it's dark, Walt," murmured Martha.

"I'm ready to eat, Dad," squealed Jimmy cheerily.

Suddenly two men in dark clothing appeared, blocking the progress of the Myers family. "Jist where the hell do y'all think yer a goin?" The tall man in the broad brimmed hat and the five-day whiskers shouted directly into Walter Myer's face.

Walter felt a small shower of spit and smelled the booze on the man's breath. He tried not to show his fear and kept his composure as he drew Martha and Jimmy as close as he could, "We're, ah, we're going to the restaurant."

"Shut your mouth, you Yankee pig!" yelled the other

man with the turtleneck sweater and the stocking cap, at the same time, delivering a vicious slap to the side of Walter's face and knocking his glasses to the sidewalk where they broke into three pieces. The man with the big hat stepped even closer to Walter and smashed his knee into Walter's groin, sending him to his knees on the sidewalk trying his best not to scream in pain.

"Gimmie your wallet, creep," the man demanded.

Young Jimmy could stand it no longer, "Quit hurting my Dad!" he shouted. The turtleneck guy kicked the boy in the shins. Jimmy howled and he doubled up on the sidewalk. The man grabbed Martha's purse and both thugs abruptly turned and walked rapidly out of the parking lot and down the street.

Terrified, shaken and confused, Martha stooped to help Walter to his feet. Jimmy was also able to stand even though his right shin was so painful it took a great surge of willpower to contain expressions of real pain. It was all Martha could do to support both Walter and Jimmy as the three of them staggered into the restaurant.

Once inside, the greeter, Charley Wong, led them to comfortable surroundings in his private office and called the manager for an immediate meeting to evaluate the situation. The manager was Arthur Lew, owner of two restaurants including the Hong Kong, and a prominent leader in the Chinese community. Mr. Lew seemed genuinely empathetic and apologized profusely to the Myers' family. "We are in the process of calling the Seattle police this very minute," said Mr. Lew, politely. "I wonder if you would mind taking a few minutes to explain to our security people what just happened to you. Two officials from the international community happen to be in our restaurant at this moment. I will ask them to come into the office. I know them very well. They are very courteous and easy to talk to. After that, the city police will be here. Then I wish to offer you nice people a complimentary dinner. That's not all. I will give you some coupons for future dinners. Now Mr. Wong will fetch our two security men and bring them in here."

The security men were introduced as Mr. Pang and Mr. Chin. They were interested in every detail of the Myers' unfortunate experience when they were attacked and robbed outside the restaurant. During the interview the two men appeared earnest in their assurances to the family that everything possible would be done to bring the assailants to justice and create an environment of absolute safety for people in the International District. They promised that the appropriate letters and other paper work would be forwarded the following day to the proper authorities including the Harborview Hospital. They strongly urged the Myers family to visit the hospital that very evening for an exam and treatment. Under the circumstances, their medical costs would be covered by the Washington State Victim's Compensation Fund.

A few minutes later a contingent from the Seattle Police department arrived which included a uniformed patrolman named Brevik and two detectives named Brown and Slade. An intense questioning ensued in which the Myers family came fairly close to being assured that Walter's wallet and Martha's purse could possibly be found by police department searchers the next morning in a nearby dumpster, minus any cash. After that, their losses would just have to be borne. The Myers family skipped their free dinner and drove to the Harborview Hospital, five blocks away.

*   *   *

Two days later three well-dressed Chinese-American men entered the Hong Kong restaurant at lunchtime. Since they were regular customers, the staff knew them as the same Mr. Pang and Mr. Chin from two nights before when the Myers were robbed. Both Pang and Chin wore emotionless expressions. Both appeared physically fit and moved gracefully despite their fiftyish ages. The third man was thirtyish, physically impressive and could have passed as a Kung Fu martial arts athlete. His face, however wore an expression different from his two companions. Any movie casting director would probably cast Willy Fong as a darkly dangerous Asian enforcer for a Shanghai branch of Murder Incorporated. Insiders in the community, who knew the movers and shakers, could identify Pang, Chin and Fong as Tong members.

For centuries Chinese Tongs have played an important role in traditional Chinese culture. It would be no surprise to sociologists and historians that American-Chinese communities would feel the influence of Tong organizations. Tongs exert tight control in virtually all aspects of business, cultural issues, ethics and personal behavior by every person in the community. The Tongs, whether in China or Chinese-American communities, served as a means of keeping order. They also functioned in settling grievances and providing justice for various kinds of disputes. Where Tongs exist in America there is always a sensitive relationship between them and the local police authorities. The Tong membership is a closely guarded secret kept by all in the community regardless of location in the world.

The three Chinese-American gentlemen headed for another nearby restaurant called Nee How where they quietly, but quickly scanned the interior for a particular individual. Their next stop was Ginger Chow's where they spotted the Caucasian man they were looking for, enjoying his shrimp chow mein. Stepping close to the man dining at the table, the three leaned close. Morgan Pang spoke to the man in a low voice, "Excuse me sir, there is a very important matter that we need to discuss with you at this time outside the restaurant."

"At this time?" asked the man.

"Right this minute," hissed Morgan Pang.

Randy Chin spoke, "You have ten seconds. We can do it the easy way or the hard way, take your pick."

Sixty yards away in one of Chinatown's darkest alleys, the four men were gathered. The forty-something Caucasian man was forcibly seated on a wooden box with his wrists tied tightly behind his back. The man's normally self-assured manner was no longer apparent as he answered in a quavering voice, "My name is Caleb Wiggens, what do you..."

His voice was cut short by a lightning fast movement by Jerry Fong, who had rapidly applied the razor-sharp edge of his switch blade knife to Caleb Wiggen's throat and slurred, "Shut your mouth or I'll cut your head off!" By now, Caleb was totally intimidated and sat silently staring into the mask-like, cruel Asian faces. "We have seen you with the group of men who call themselves Tar Heels. What does that mean?" asked Morgan Pang.

In a hoarse voice, Wiggens mouthed his answer, "The volunteer soldiers from North Carolina were nicknamed Tar Heels when under attack by the Yankee army during the 'War Between the States.' They were proud of the fact that they rarely retreated as they stuck to their positions when in battle."

Jerry Fong eased the pressure of his razor sharp blade a bit from Caleb's throat and growled, "So a bunch of you Tar Heels have recently moved here. How many of you are there and where in Seattle do you live?"

"There are about three hundred of us who live in the neighborhood around the Marine hospital on north Beacon Hill, about a half mile from here." Caleb's eyes showed profound terror.

"Get your cell phone out," commanded Pang. "Dial your closest friend's number. What's his name?"

"Wilbur."

"Hello, Wilbur," said Pang, "I am a member of a special committee here in what you Tar Heels call Chinatown. We know that members of your community have been guilty of terrorizing and robbing our tourists and restaurant customers. I want you to spread the word that tomorrow morning you will find the first Tar Heels dead body in an alley on Third Avenue South. Each day after that, there will be one more dead Tar Heel who will be found somewhere in the neighborhood. This will end when your Tar Heel robberies stop, but it depends on how your people react to this. Do you have any questions or comments? No? Your answer is no? Very well, I assume you understand my message."

Pang handed Jerry Fong the cell phone and spoke in Mandarin, "Get his wallet." Chin handed Caleb's wallet to Pang, who removed the cash, glanced at the other contents and handed the wallet back. "I will turn this cash into the Tong office later today," he said. "Wipe the fingerprints off and put the wallet back into this slime ball's pocket."

In English, Pang said to Caleb, "Say your prayers, you low-life, big-nosed, stinking rat! Today you go to white man's hell!"

*   *   *

The next morning the same alley was crowded with police officers, detectives, photographers and other investigators, all trying to stay out of each other's way and preserve what evidence they might find in and around Caleb Wiggen's body.

A hard-faced veteran detective, spoke to a rookie cop standing next to him and said, "In case you didn't know, that .22 caliber bullet hole in this poor sap's forehead is the signature of a gang or crime organization. They are saying this is a deliberate assassination. It's intended to send a message."

The young cop stared at the bloody bullet hole in Caleb Wiggin's forehead and wondered to himself if he would ever get used to seeing such unnerving sights as part of his everyday job.

*   *   *

Virtually everyone in the local community was convinced that the old Chinatown grapevine was the fastest anywhere. Almost within minutes the murder of the Tar Heel was known by everyone including, Robert Soo, the leader of the Seattle District Dragon Tong and the eighty-year-old cleaning lady at the Hong Kong restaurant. The symbolic meaning of the murder of Caleb Wiggens was clearly understood and approved by the residents of the International District's rank and file. Restaurant customers and tourists were no longer harassed on the streets. The Tong operatives continued to maintain a watchful presence and the local residents were sensitive to any unusual behavior. The local police hoped there would be no acts of revenge on the part of the Tar Heel hillbillies and hoped they might pack up and go back to North Carolina or somewhere far from here.

*   *   *

The following Saturday morning, the entire city was outraged when the headline in the Seattle Times screamed, "Four Teenaged Girls Believed Kidnapped in the Central District". The subheading read, "Sixteen year-old Chinese-American girls disappear from Garfield High School." The text explained that the girls, besides being students at Garfield, were also members of the *Happy Dragon Chinese Girls' Drill Team.* The team was composed of Chinese-American high school students from the Central District and had been known for years as a popular marching group whose performances included manipulating a huge cloth dragon and a snappy drill routine while marching down the street in concert with the many other parade performers.

Police investigators concluded that the four girls had been captured right after a Friday afternoon practice session and were heading home. Upon learning of the girls' disappearance, residents of the International District went into a state of extreme distress and demanded action by the authorities to find the girls and arrest whoever was responsible for their disappearance.

It was suspected from the first that the kidnappers were probably from the Tar Heels' hillbilly community living in the north Beacon Hill neighborhood. Beginning Saturday morning, Police patrols slowly cruised back and forth on the streets and alleys on every block in the neighborhood. Saturday night the police were attracted to a neighborhood recreation hall where a party seemed to be in progress. Two patrolmen in a police car stopped to investigate and were invited inside to satisfy their curiosity. Their inspection revealed nothing suspicious. The cops were informed that the neighborhood men's club was having their monthly dinner party and nothing out of line would be taking place. They assured the officers that the gathering was simply a bunch of good-old-boys getting together to enjoy old-fashioned country food and have some laughs. What could be wrong with that?

*   *   *

Unbeknownst to the police, the servers at the men's club were to be the four sixteen-year-old Chinese girls. They had been safely confined in the basement of the North Hill Recreation Hall in preparation for the Saturday night party. The girls had not been abused except for being terrified as to what might happen to them at the hands of the crude men who went out of their way to keep them fearful so that they would do everything that was asked of them.

The huge bewhiskered potbellied man named Gilly was the main organizer of the upcoming party. He informed the girls that their chance of returning home was less than fifty-fifty. "You see, girls, you are worth real money to us. We know people who would pay us forty thousand dollars for the four of you. You would be sent out of the country and imprisoned in a house of prostitution forever. Pretty young girls like you are in demand as prostitutes. You may still have an outside chance that we might turn you loose, but it depends on how you do everything we tell you, and I mean everything, promptly and efficiently with no stalling or complaining. Your futures depend on it."

Prior to the time of the party another man named Johnny Mack had the girls rehearse their roles as waitresses serving drinks and food. His instructions also included clean-up procedures afterward. As distasteful to the girls as it was, they felt they had no choice but to do exactly as they were told. The big surprise to the girls was when the men brought out their waitress costumes, which were nothing more than black strips of cloth to be used as G-strings. Nothing was to be worn above the waist. The Hillbilly men's party got going at about eight-thirty and roared on into the night.

*   *   *

The Tong headquarters was located in a prominent three-story building on the east side of the International District. In the sub-basement several men were gathered in the so-called 'Green Room,' which was, except for the ceiling, faced with concrete painted a dull green. A drain was located in the center of the floor. Just outside a heavy door was a water hose connected to a faucet and coiled on a hose rack. Inside the fourteen foot-square room were ceiling lights, three powerful floor lamps, two cots resembling hospital operating room beds, a six-foot-long table, a large metal cabinet, a sink, a telephone, some assorted chairs and a large disposal container.

Of the six men gathered in the Green Room, two were captives from the self-described clan of Tar Heels. The biggest man was Gilly Perkins, a middle-aged, overweight, balding, wild-eyed, loud spoken leader in the Tar Heel community. His kidnappers had found that he was one of the organizers of the memorable men's club party of two nights before. Both Gilly Perkins and his wife Myrtle were rousted from their bed at three a.m., bound, gagged and still in their bathrobes, were then driven to the Tong Green Room. Myrtle was given a sedative and coffee and was provided with a comfortable lounge chair, a very low volume television program to watch, an adjacent lavatory to use and two polite Asian men to watch over her. Tar Heel organizer Johnny Mack Briggs was snatched at the same time from his bedroom and was now sitting next to his friend Gilly. Both had very frightened looks on their faces.

Tong members Charley Wong, Arthur Lew, Morgan Pang and Willie Fong were guarding the captives. Dressed in running suits covered by cheap white smocks, the Tong men were busy strapping the two nude Tar Heel men to the metal hospital beds and arranging various tools and other materials on the table top. As the four Asian men finished their preparations, they sat in their chairs in a neat arrangement closely facing Gilley and Johnny Mack. The two hillbillies felt themselves trembling with fear as the Tong men glared at them.

"We may let you live to see another day," said Charley Wong.

"And we may not," said Arthur Lew.

"It depends," said Morgan Pang.

"On how you answer our questions," said Willie Fong. "It depends on whether or not we can be sure you give us a truthful answer. If not, you will die just a few minutes from now."

"Here is the first question," said Charley Wong. "Where are your people keeping our girls? We assume they are alive." The gags were removed and the two captives enthusiastically confirmed the assumption.

"Now tell us," hissed Arthur Lew, "very slowly in precise detail, where they are kept, how they are being treated and all details of their confinement."

Information flowed and bubbled forth from the terrified mouths of the two captives until the questions and answers had run their course. At five-thirty a.m., Randy Chin and Arthur Lew arrived at the Seattle police precinct at First and Main streets with information about the kidnapped sixteen-year-olds. They were accompanied by their attorney, Wing Mar.

*   *   *

The unearthly screams could be heard even through the concrete walls of the Green Room. Upon hearing what she could identify as her husband's terrifying shrieks, Myrtle Briggs began to scream uncontrollably until passing out for a brief time. After waking, she began vomiting until the dry heaves took over.

The unidentified Tong men worked quickly, efficiently and were unemotional as they wrapped tourniquets to control blood flow near ankles and wrists. No anesthetic was to be used. The attackers cut, sliced and sawed the bones of their victims, ignoring the screams, moans, angry shrieks, bloody and desperate begging for mercy from the hapless hillbillies.

211

Severely traumatized, they were unable to understand what was actually happening to them. The unfortunate victims of unspeakable torture were to later learn the truth. Both of Gilly Perkin's feet had been amputated and Johnny Mack Brigg's two hands were gone forever.

*   *   *

The Chevy van slowly entered the Harborview county hospital emergency room parking lot. The van parked at the opposite side of the parking lot away from the receiving dock. Two men stepped out of the van and removed two semi-conscious bodies. After carefully laying them flat on the concrete surface, covered tightly with blankets where they could be easily seen, the two men reentered the van and it drove away.

On the drive back to the International District, one of the unidentified Tong men called the hospital emergency number to inform them about the location of the two unfortunate Tar Heel victims. The caller was concerned about the possibility that Perkins and Briggs might bleed to death in a short time because of the nature of their amputation wounds.

After a deadly warning to Myrtle Perkins about the consequences of ever speaking or testifying about her horrifying experience at the hands of the Tong operatives, she was swiftly transported back to her own house, tied to a chair and left.

*   *   *

In the meantime, the Seattle police were mobilizing for a huge raid on the north Beacon Hill community recreation center where they believed the four kidnapped girls were held in captivity. At nine a.m., an army of police vehicles invaded the neighborhood surrounding the recreation center. Police cars, prisoner vans and two half-tracks spewed out almost one hundred police officers including a tactical squad. Their weapons included pistols, rifles, shotguns, submachine guns, flashbang grenades and tear gas. The guards were quickly subdued and the girls brought out to safety much to the relief of just about everybody.

Before releasing the girls, Connie Lew, Grace Mar, Marcy Wong and Susan Pang, were videotaped and strongly encouraged to give testimony to the police. Afterward, the courageous girls were released to the custody of their families. That day and evening the entire city celebrated the safe release of the girls who had been the subject of so much worry.

*   *   *

Five weeks later, Seattle City Attorney Clyde Wikstrom sat in his office at his County City building headquarters in downtown Seattle. If everyone arrived as planned, those city officials attending would include Mayor James Hoyt and Chief of Police, William Swanberg. Others invited were Charley Wong, the unelected consensus Mayor, Arthur Lew, rumored to be head of the Chinese Tong, Morgan Pang, Community

213

activist, and their lawyer, Wing Mar, all residents of Seattle's International District.

With acknowledgements to all, including the assistants who accompanied the officials, Mr. Wikstrom briefly outlined the reason and purpose of the meeting. It was to disclose the latest information about the location of the departed Tar Heel community, now apparently located in northeastern Missouri. The other issue was the status of their lawsuit against the city of Seattle for the city's alleged responsibility concerning the amputation crimes against Gilley Perkins and Johnny Mack Briggs. Everyone knew about the lawsuit in which five million dollars was demanded for each victim. Their case might have been stronger if the crimes were ever solved and the criminals brought to justice.

Presently, after many bitter confrontations with their own lawyers, the complainants seemed to have been convinced of the fact that the case was extremely weak against the city of Seattle, the Mayor and the police department for failure to protect them from the criminals who had amputated their body parts. This had led them to the conclusion that their best chance for money was to settle out of court for whatever was possible. The Tar Heels seemed willing to accept three hundred thousand dollars for both Perkins and Briggs.

Based on months of investigative evidence the Seattle authorities were sure that the Tar Heel community would not return to the Seattle area. Chief Swanberg leaned across the table so he could clearly see the faces directly across from him and glared with his most intimidating and threatening ice-blue eyes at Wong, Lew and Pang. It was as if Swanberg could generate enough powerful physical energy to burn holes through steel, or better yet, intimidate a suspect with no evidence against him to confess all and throw himself upon the mercy of his accusers and beg for forgiveness. "You gentlemen can see how much money and trouble this case has caused us. What can we possibly say to the city council when we ask for approval of this settlement for three hundred thousand dollars of hard-working taxpayers' money? Now I want to know what you guys are going to do about this and I demand that you respond now!"

The three Chinese-American men along with their attorney sat impassively with blank expressions. Mr. Lew's expression changed not at all as he looked Chief Swanberg dead in the eyes and very respectfully spoke, "First Chief, we in the International District are very pleased to know that the hillbilly Tar Heels will never return. Second, we appreciate the convictions by the Federal Court of the Tar Heel kidnappers and their prison sentences. Third, we know that you believe some of our people have committed some sort of crime, but there is no evidence and never will be. Fourth, police are well known to have have acted on stereotypical perceptions. Fifth, we Chinese-Americans have also been victimized by many white Americans since the very first. This is our chance to verify the perception of us as phlegmatic, 'inscrutable Orientals.' We show no emotion, our faces are masks. We say no more."

OUR GAME WARDEN

The three big-city guys were getting wound up. I was one of them. All of us were in our forties. We sat in the American Legion Club in downtown Seattle. While enjoying drinks in the bar room we were excitedly planning a deer hunting trip for the third week in October, just three weeks away.

Bilbo Giles looked at me and took a sip of his scotch and water. With an obvious twinkle in his eye he asked, "How do we know that Vern here can see well enough to shoot a deer instead of one of us?"

"We'll be okay," I replied, "Vern is taking his new thick glasses and will keep his rifle unloaded, right Vern?"

"Of course," Vern chuckled, "unless one of you idiots happens to piss me off. Then my thirty-ought-six will be loaded, I promise you."

While my two friends sipped their drinks, I enlightened them with facts about the nice cabin we would be staying in on Decatur Island in the San Juan Island archipelago, about one hundred miles north of Seattle in the Rosario Straits, an inland sea offshoot from the Pacific ocean. Our goal was to each slay an island deer and proudly bring it home for our wives to cook.

From reading about pioneer days, we recalled that in the Wild West, eating venison was an important part of survival. Brave deer hunters in those days were considered manly, courageous, resourceful, legendary and heroic. It was part of the fun, keeping all of that in mind as we prepared for the trip during the next three weeks.

Taking Friday afternoon off from work, we drove two hours to Anacortes, a small town on a beautiful bay. The airport furnished our transportation to Decatur Island by means of a ten-minute flight, landing at the tiny airfield. We were about a mile from our cabin.

It was late Friday afternoon and we had just seen our first deer. The innocent little doe happened to be crossing the airstrip as our plane approached for a landing. At precisely the same moment, somebody was driving a car along the road adjacent to the landing strip. Since the runway was partially obscured by a bit of fog drifting across the airport, the car's lights were on. The deer paused in the beam of the car's lights, standing right in our way. The pilot could clearly see the deer, but suddenly swerving the airplane at that moment would have caused a disastrous accident. Our plane smashed into the deer, our propeller chopping its head completely off.

Fortunately Bones Willis was there to meet us with his beat-up twenty-year-old four-door Plymouth, as planned. Arriving at the cabin, we ate dinner and organized our gear. While we ate, I asked Bones Willis to tell the guys about himself. I got him started by describing him as an unmarried late thirties man living close to nature in a one acre patch on an island paradise.

"So you actually live off the land?" Vern Ackerman respectfully asked.

"Yeah, but every now and then I go visit Carl in Seattle so he can take me to a whorehouse."

The group broke up with laughter. "Bones goes in by himself," I said. "He actually believes it's a cardinal sin for me if I go in with him. When he goes to a house of ill-fame he hires three girls at a time! He's a physical wonder, a sexual superman!"

Bilbo asked, "It's none of my business, Bones, but you must have a secret income. How can you make it, 'living off the land'?"

Bones gulped some wine. "I have a small pension from an old injury when I worked for the shipyard. I have a still over at my house and I sell moonshine to many customers from these local islands. The authorities around here just mind their own business and nobody cares about that sort of thing. We have a lot of freedom in San Juan County."

I interrupted, "Hey, guys, be sure to keep looking out the windows. Every so often a deer will show up to eat the apples off the ground when they fall off those trees right outside in the yard."

"What a place," snickered Vern.

"It's starting to get dark," declared Bones. "Get your guns, ammo, flashlights, knives and rope. Bilbo, don't forget those gallon jugs of wine there on the table and the plastic drinking glasses. By the way, did Carl tell you fellers that I have been appointed acting deputy game warden for this part of San Juan County? Look, here's my badge. Okay, everybody in the car. The deer are waiting!"

Bilbo and Vern looked confused, "We thought it was illegal to hunt after sundown," protested Vern.

"Not if you're with the game warden," laughed Bones.

After piling into the car everyone provided himself with a full glass of muscatel wine from one of the gallon jugs kept aboard. This was part of the ritual when heading out for illegal nighttime hunting on Decatur Island.

"Okay guys, get your flashlights and rifles ready. We could spot a deer anytime. The darker it gets the brighter their eyes shine when you get them in the flashlight beam."

"Wait a minute," exclaimed Vern. "What happened to the hunting laws? I thought hunting from a car was illegal. And what about the law against drinking while hunting? Are you guys crazy?"

The car had been rattling down a deserted gravel road when Bones slammed on the brakes, causing everybody's drink to spill an ounce or two. Bones charged from the car into the road, sprinting at a rapid pace, chasing a fawn-sized deer that had jumped into a ravine by the side of the road. The headlights shone on the action as the guys in the car watched Bones leap on the back of the little creature while stabbing rapidly with his hunting knife again and again. The blood flowed and spattered. The execution was completed in less than a minute. The deer dropped from Bones' grasp and flopped to the ground as Bones turned around in the headlights facing the guys in the car and struck a pose with both arms raised like Sylvester Stallone in the movie *Rocky*. His clothes were covered with very red, shiny deer blood, a symbol perhaps of manly courage or a bloody warrior hero.

After gutting the deer, Bones placed what was left of him in the trunk of the car and we drove off to find another victim.

Ten minutes further on, Vern spotted some bright eyes on a hill at the side of the road. "Shoot!" yelled Bones. Both Vern and Bilbo fired several times, their rifle blasts magnifying the sounds inside the car to an unbearable degree, or at least I thought so.

After shooting from the car, we all jumped out and searched for a wounded or dead deer. We never recovered anything resembling a deer. At the end of the hunt that night we were tired and a bit swacked from drinking too much wine and firing our rifles, so we welcomed night-night time. Our sleeping bags were calling.

The next morning we set off on foot toward an area people referred to as "the spit." It was about a mile away. We intrepid hunters kept our guns ready as we negotiated a steep hill, a half mile of thick woods and a rocky cliff. The "spit" was a strip of land about thirty feet wide and three hundred feet long, connecting the very south end of Decatur Island to a four or five acre chunk of beautifully wooded land which would obviously become its own island as soon as the spit was eroded away by the winter tides and storms. In the meantime, perhaps for another one hundred years, the spit would be a picturesque island feature covered with very large pieces of intriguing driftwood lining the entire spit and adding to the curious uniqueness of this gorgeous location on Decatur Island.

"The best way to hunt this area," said Bones, "is to station the main shooter in the driftwood and the rest of us tramp around over there in the woods to scare out a deer or two. They sometimes run north on the spit to escape and our guy in the driftwood shoots them down. It works maybe half the time."

"Who gets the driftwood spot?" asked Bilbo.

Bones said, "I have some skinny little sticks, you three fellers will do a blind draw from my hand. The longest stick gets the driftwood hideout for one hour. The rest of us tramp around in the brush and woods on that peninsula at the south end of the spit and see if we can chase a deer out. Carl here drew the longest stick and will blast the deer when he comes across the spit. Right, Carl?"

"If I don't faint with excitement," I said.

Everyone trotted off to their assigned places, including me. Walking around on the spit, I examined the big driftwood pieces for the best concealment features and chose one. It was an old stump with ancient root appendages extending higher than my height and broad enough for a perfect hiding place. I arranged some wood pieces for a semi-satisfactory place to sit to ambush a deer, if lucky enough to get the chance.

Watching intently for about fifteen minutes, I saw two magnificent looking bucks, one two-point and a three-pointer come trotting onto the spit, heading straight toward my hiding place. To make the shot I had to step away from my driftwood a half-step to the side. Shooting off-hand, my cross-hairs on the chest, I squeezed off a round which dropped the two-point in his tracks, never to move again. The other bigger deer moved to his left and then to his right, trying to decide the best route for escape. My second shot struck him a little too far back of his shoulder for a killing shot, so he was still moving and dashed toward the water. My third shot got him where his neck met his front shoulder and as it turned out was a killing shot. Even so, his momentum carried him forward, about twenty or thirty feet from the beach into the water. The water itself was moving as the outgoing tide carried him out even further toward the even faster moving water in the straights. This meant that I had better retrieve the deer soon or it would disappear in the rapidly moving tide.

The best idea to get the deer, it seemed at the time, was to swim the icy water and float the dead creature back to the beach. The beautiful three-point buck was now about ninety feet away. I stripped off my clothes as fast as I could, reached into my pack for a length of rope which I stuck in between my teeth, splashed into the unimaginably cold forty-degree water and swam.

Reaching the deer I tied the short rope to the antlers

and thinking back to my first aid lifesaving class at Seward Park beach on Lake Washington from thirty years before, floated and dragged my prey to the beach and safety. Mine, not the deer's. After hearing my gun shots, the other hunters had returned from their deer-scaring job of tramping through the brush.

The brave band of city-boy week-end deer hunters all pitched in to dry off their luck-of-the-draw executioner (me) and help me get into my dry clothes as fast as possible. Pneumonia doesn't play favorites, so I'm told. Vern and I attached our deer tags to the antlers of the two beautiful dead animals. Leaving Vern to guard the corpses, the rest of us hiked back to the cabin. Bones, the game warden, pulled out a rowboat from under the cabin and instructed me to row back to the spit, pick up Vern and the two bucks and return. With four big bodies on board, the rowboat was overloaded and quite unstable, but Vern rowed back as per my instructions.

The deer were hung and the body cavities propped open with sticks for cooling. After lunch, the guys spread out and picked their spots to watch for deer with no luck. The Sunday morning hunt brought no luck either, and it was time to meet our plane at the airstrip. The pilot said that there was too much weight for our Beechcraft monoplane. I offered the two-point buck to Bones and he readily accepted, giving Vern's deer tag back to him to use again this season if he got lucky.

We bid goodbye to Bones Willis with many thanks and generous cash tips. The game warden seemed pleased and invited us to come again.

When we got back to Seattle and were about to get into our cars, I held out a quarter and said to Vern and Bilbo, "I am going to flip this coin to see which one of you wins the venison."

Bilbo won the toss and was delighted.

In thinking back on it, I fully realize that the moment when those two magnificent wild animals appeared in front of me at the same time was the ultimate dream of any hunter's lifetime. That accounts for the electrical vibration that ran up my spine at the moment. Even so, after the action was over, I was consumed with a profound sadness.

I guess that's why I never went hunting again.

SECRECY ASSIGNMENT

Professor Gilbert Addington cleared his throat and addressed the small group of students sitting at a large conference table in Rainbow Hall at the University of Washington. "Next Thursday, when we meet again, I will return the assignment that you all have turned in today. My comments and evaluations will be included, so quit worrying about that until next week.

"Our graduate classes are always difficult for students. To get through it takes discipline and all the persistence you can muster but we all know it's worth it. At the conclusion of your two-year graduate school commitment you will have earned a Master's Degree. Enough talk about what you already know. Your new assignment will require adequate research.

I have what I think will be a most challenging project. For this assignment you are all to function as fiction or science fiction writers, depending on what is called for. Your job is to complete your story containing about ten thousand words, in twenty pages. You are to assume that this is a paid story assignment from the editor of a short story fiction magazine. Each of you will be given a different topic or theme to extrapolate from in your imaginative fiction short story. The story should be based on the facts and believable rumors you can derive from your research. Thus you have plenty of latitude in creating a fascinating story which may unravel and reveal truths about these topics. Most people are unaware or confused about the topics I am about to assign you."

The murmurs from the class showed that the students were intrigued by this new assignment.

"Mr. Gables, here is the topic for your story: 'Artificial Intelligence.' Good luck, and write something good enough for the Pulitzer Prize." Philip Gables began to write furiously on a writing pad.

"Here is a challenging one for you, Miss Parsons: 'The Bermuda Triangle,' a real mystery. Let's see what you can do with it."

"Jordan Wright, here is a wonderful topic for a man like yourself, 'Big Foot,' as in 'The Abominable Snowman,' or 'Yeti,' as it is called in Nepal."

"Miss Carrie Zander, your topic is a very popular and controversial one. 'Unidentified Flying Objects,' go after it Carrie, and good luck."

"Last, but by no means the least, comes Andrew Harwood, our budding genius, 'The Jesus Myth,' the reincarnation of Buddha. Perhaps you are aware of the books that have been researched and written about Jesus' unknown history, about his travels to the Far East between the ages of twelve to thirty and the rumors that describe his life after surviving the crucifixion and travels with his wife, Mary Magdalene. We look forward to reading your story.

"I also look forward with great anticipation to hearing each of you read your outline to the rest of us at our session next week, same time, and same place. No excuses for not showing up and not being fully prepared. Do your job and enjoy every minute of it except for times of confusion, stress and sense of failure. If any of these psychological manifestations bother you too much then you should tell yourself to get used to it. It comes with the territory. Those feelings are a necessary part of becoming a professional writer. All that stress and unhappiness, along with extreme loneliness, comes with the job.

"On the other hand, upon achieving success as a professional writer will forever set you apart as a person of exceptional creative talent and intellectual ability that you rank among the top two per cent of all human beings in the world. When you work every day as a writer and turn out those marvelous essays, media reports or prize winning novels, you will experience an inner pride so phenomenal that there is nothing like it and you will thrive on it to the degree that you cannot imagine in your wildest dreams."

Each of the students felt a warm glow upon hearing such encouraging words from their leader.

Professor Addington paused and drew in his breath, "I have given this latest assignment a name. I call it the Secrecy Assignment. In conjuring up the task which faces you, a question was present in my mind. Each of the topics that you will be working on has been shrouded in secrecy. The question is, why? Maybe you can find an answer or invent one. You are writing fiction based on a mystery. Don't you think there is someone somewhere who knows the answer to each of these mysteries? Maybe all it takes is for a bright young writer with a fresh brain to think, read, explore and apply him or herself to an old, seemingly unsolvable secret."

*   *   *

After class the students met at the Hub for coffee and a discussion about the assignments. The five grads were generally pleased with their topics which they thought were sufficiently imaginative for plot possibilities and offered plenty of latitude for them to create their stories. Three of them questioned the appropriateness of Andrew's project about the Jesus Myths which they thought might be too close to the church-state controversy.

"I don't think there should be any controversy about a topic like this one," stated Andrew.

"Why do you say that?" asked Beth, "There's an ongoing controversy in the papers every day about school prayer."

"Yeah," said Carrie, "as well as all the support from the religionists for our tax money to be given to the charter schools and the private religious schools."

Philip spoke, "There never seems to be a controversy about the class they call *The Bible as Literature*. It is regarded by everyone as historical semi-fact and having important literary content."

"That's because the theology is taught with objectivity," declared Jordan.

Time was running out. As they all departed for their apartments with expectations for supper and at least a four-hour session of homework and study at the Suzallo Library or in their rooms.

*   *   *

Andrew Harwood's schedule was different. Feeling a need to visit his parents, he rode his motorcycle through the crowded traffic across town to the Alki Point area to his family home. Across the street from a beach on Elliott Bay, the two-bedroom bungalow was one of the few remaining houses in what used to be one of Seattle's quaint beach-front neighborhoods. The old houses were being systematically torn down and replaced by high-end apartments.

Loud affectionate yells, hugs and pats on the back greeted Andrew when he unexpectedly arrived. Andrew's father, Tom, smiled broadly as he drew his son close and said, "Andrew, you rascal, you need to keep in touch more often. You just don't know how much we miss you."

"I miss you and Mom too, Pop. At school they keep us too busy. I have to knock my brains out to keep up." His mother's greetings were even more affectionate and emotional. Mom will always be Mom, thought Andrew, and she will always love me with all her heart. She probably doesn't know how much I really love her and all that she means to me.

During dinner, most of the conversation was about changes in the neighborhood, the impossible traffic, a few crazy neighbors and the increased prices in the local restaurants. Andrew asked about church. "About the same," seemed to be the answer, which meant that Andrew's parents attended church every Sunday and loved everything about church and being with their friends who were all fellow true-believers.

"How's Uncle Bayne?" asked Andrew.

"He's the same as ever," said Tom, "he goes to church with me and your mother every Sunday."

"Does he still do religious preaching on weeknights?" Andrew tried not to sound disrespectful.

"Yes," said Andrew's mom, Gwyneth. "He is a lay preacher. He preaches to Christian organizations on meeting nights and sometimes substitutes for regular Pastors when needed. They tell us he is very good at it."

Tom spoke, "My brother is very conservative in his religious philosophy, a bit too much for me."

"Give him my best wishes," said Andrew.

While enjoying dessert and coffee, the parents insisted on hearing everything about Andrew's work at the university.

"They expect a lot more initiative than studying for a bachelor's degree. You need to work much more independently. The professors have no patience with anything less than perfect use of the English language. When turning in commentary, term papers, tests or anything in written form, they don't want to see misspelled words, incorrect grammar or anything but professional usage. They make us responsible for a much bigger workload than the undergrads. Often our required classes are small groups with one professor, teacher or a teaching assistant. I just got finished with a grad class today with only five of us and the prof really loaded us with a doozie."

Gwyneth was curious, "What do you mean by 'doozie,' dear?"

"That means that he gave the class a very challenging and time-consuming assignment. I got a challenging one, *The Jesus Myth*. It's about where some historians think Jesus spent his years from age twelve to age thirty."

"Tell 'em to read their Bible," laughed Mom.

"There's nothing in the Bible about it," declared Andrew. "That's why it's always been a mystery. There have been lots of scholars, historians and others who would love to get their hands on the descriptions and writings about Jesus when he spent some years in Tibet as some sort of well-respected holy presence. It has all been documented and safely stashed away in a well-guarded temple in one of Tibet's holiest places. He may have been considered a bodhisattva, which was a highly ranked Buddha-like spiritual leader. According to the myth, he spent eighteen years away from home. With his Asian guides, he visited Persia, Nepal, China, Tibet and India pursuing spiritual enlightenment when in contact with Asia's eminent scholars and religious leaders."

Andrew's Dad, Tom, looked surprised, in fact his eyebrows raised involuntarily and his lower lip dropped a bit. "I'm astounded," said Tom, "that you allow yourself to read stuff like that. It sounds like it comes straight from the dark side."

In a cracked and worried voice, Mom exclaimed, "Please stop work on that project, honey, if you go too far with it you could be in terrible danger! If the guardians of the Christian faith wanted us to know of a ridiculous story like that, they would have either published a true version of it or just banished the story so that no person of faith would ever have access to it."

"But Mom and Dad, nobody really thinks of it as the known truth. It's more like conjecture. Some think of it as a sort of fairy tale. The assignment is just used in this case as a challenge to see how well I can use my writer's imagination."

"Well, son," said Tom, "the story sounds like some sort of blasphemy. Knowing that, you may be able to write it in such a way that it will be acceptable as unfounded rumor to us Christian believers."

Andrew smiled and said, "I'll try my best, Dad."

*   *   *

"Well," said Professor Addington, "I see we all made it through the week. Let's get right down to business. Can we start with you, Carrie? Please tell us how far you have developed your outline."

Sitting at the large conference table with her notes spread before her, Carrie addressed the group. "My story is mainly about a young couple, both astrophysicists working for NASA who are embarking on a new investigation about unidentified flying objects. They are very effective investigators and enjoy working with each other as a team. As they get to know each other, they gradually realize they are falling head over heels in love. As the story progresses, they come to some startling conclusions about the nature and source of the UFOs which have so captured the imagination of people around the world. These discoveries have led the protagonist couple to seek information about metaphysical manifestations which affect everything in the universe. In their search for truth and objectivity, they suspect scientists have overlooked or ignored metaphysical *realities*. They are convinced that statement is not in any way a contradiction. This issue becomes the basis for their overriding objective to teach all they can to insure a happy, productive and fulfilling future. The startling conclusion by the two physicists up to this point is the following: UFOs are from an extra dimension of existence. We know nothing about this extra dimension but, like other scientific conclusions, it is assumed to exist because it has to. It is based on logical thinking and objective conjecture. We can imagine existences of other dimensions quite easily if we think of the traditional notions of heaven, purgatory and biblical hell, all invisible, unprovable, imaginative and extradimensional. These beliefs are not provable scientifically, so people hang their hopes on words written as far in the past as three thousand years. Belief in the supernatural is predominant in our culture. This is understandable because we have been taught to believe in such things.

To find the truth we are forced to ask ourselves, what else is there that we need to understand? Like other mysteries of existence we feel called upon to find the truth about them."

Professor Addington smiled and said, "Good job so far, Carrie. You have very cleverly teased the reader into being uncomfortable and frustrated by not being presented with a complete answer or unresolved theory about the UFO phenomenon. The story needs more character development with the two protagonists, but I am sure that will happen as the story moves along. Now we need thoughtful comments about Carrie's promising story and her creative theory about where UFOs come from and how it has strongly affected the two young scientists."

The four remaining students related their opinions, challenged a phrase or two and complemented Carrie Zander on her shocking conclusions.

It was Philip Gable's turn, "My topic is 'Artificial Intelligence.' The first part is factual information as told by a robot named Toby. Working on a factory assembly line, Toby is selected by his human master to submit to a program of educational information so he can function on a much higher level of responsibility. It turns out that at the present level of technology, our robots can memorize enormous amounts of information in a very short time. An example would be the case where a robot would be fed electronic information consisting of the entire text of the Bible, both the old and new testaments. This can all be learned in six seconds and never forgotten. The question is not so much how information can be stored in a robot's mechanical brain, or how the information can be effectively used, but whether or not our machines can be taught to make judgements and render intelligent decisions. The latest research indicates that computers and robots can not only develop the ability to think in such ways but also assume some abilities that are exactly like human beings. Displaying and acting out emotional feelings like sadness, disappointment, affection, anger and sympathy are examples. Two mid-twenties male scientists are the protagonists working on robot technology. Jonathan works with Garth but over time becomes jealous of the relationship between Toby, (the robot) and Garth. The reciprocal feelings and emotions become the thrust of the story. Dealing with relationships such as rivalry, jealousy and enmity between man and machine is the new technological dilemma."

At the finish of Philip Gables' presentation, Professor Addington chuckled a bit and said, "Philip, you have your hands full dealing with that problem which is bound to be an enormous one in the near future. I can't wait to see how you deal with it in your story." The other students bombarded Philip with questions and comments while wishing him luck in writing his story.

"Jordan Wright, your turn," said Addington.

Jordan spoke: "My topic is a challenging one, 'Bigfoot,' otherwise known in Nepal and Tibet as 'Yeti.' He is a giant man-like creature who rarely shows himself and lives in the deep forest and high mountains. There have been credible reports of Yeti sightings mostly in the

Himalaya Mountains of Nepal, Tibet and other Asian mountain areas. In mountainous Asian countries the creature is known as the 'Abominable Snowman.' They are reported to have been in the USA in mountain states like Alaska, Washington, Oregon, Idaho and California. Canadians also have reported encountering Bigfoot in the wilds of British Columbia.

"Photographs are supposed to have been taken of Bigfoot and castings made of the footprints. Some describe him as much bigger than a man, very smelly and ape-like in appearance. My fiction story is about two experienced American mountain climbers who encounter a small group of them high on the slopes of K2, the second highest peak in the Himalayas. When the Yeti walk into their camp one day, everyone tries communicating with no success. Later they eat a meal together. The Bigfoot creatures offer some chunks of raw meat (which they carried with them) to their hosts but Edmond and Doak, the American mountaineers declined the gift.

"Two days of very strong winds along with steady blizzard conditions keep everyone pinned down inside the tent and the Bigfoot men inside some nearby ice caves. When the storm breaks, the 'snowmen' have left Doak to fend for himself and taken Edmond with them. That was the last time anyone ever saw Doak Faber." Jordan paused and sipped some water.

"In my story, Edmond lives with an abominable snowman clan for two years, adapting as best he can to the lifestyle of the malodorous, brutish, primitive, half- naked repulsive creatures, more animal than man. Edmond tries to categorize his captors into an anthropological category. He believes they may be descendants of a Neanderthal species of some kind. Their diet consists of insects, worms, snakes, raw meat, nuts, berries, roots, rats, vermin, small animals and birds. As a result Edmond is sick to his stomach much of the time. He comes within a whisker of freezing to death, dying of exposure, starvation, dysentery and extreme fatigue at different times during captivity. As time passes, Edmond attempts to teach a few English words to the clan members, but finds that hand signals and body gesture work best.

"Attaching names to the clan individuals doesn't work very well either, except for the one Yeti that seems to be responsible for him. The closest he could get to hanging a name on him was 'Dog.' Their women live together in the deep woods at a lower altitude at least thirty miles away. Edmond recounts all this in the first person. During his two years with the Yeti, he traveled twice to where the women were camped. In my final story you will learn more about this experience.

"On his second visit to the females' camp, Edmond is able to take advantage of the fact that his captors are distracted because of their nearness to the women, and the men's powerful feelings of lustful attraction. A sight to behold.

"In the dark of night he creeps quietly away. When in cover of the deep woods he runs for hours in what he thinks is the direction to safety. After three days or so he comes to a village in Nepal where the villagers contact the authorities. From there he is transported to New Delhi, to Los Angeles and Seattle where his family and friends gave him a warm welcome.

"His two lost years as an Abominable snowman are over. It's been one year since his return to civilization. At this time, he has a good job and a girlfriend but admits to having some difficulty in adjusting, both emotionally and physically. His wonderful parents, relatives and friends all help to bring him back to an almost normal life. With a little help he has written a book about his adventure. It's not a bestseller but it attracts some movie producers who want to pay for the rights to the story. What do you think?"

Jordan's recitation of his story brought an enthusiastic response from his classmates accompanied by all manner of changes that were suggested. The four other classmates creative young minds were obviously stimulated by Jordan's story. It was an indication that each of the other writers had the urge to participate in some way with such an imaginative account of survival in a different world.

The professor shared the classes enthusiasm and commented that he, like the others, couldn't wait to see the final version. Phillip raised his hand and yelled, "I can't wait for the movie either!"

Addington looked across the table at Beth Parsons, "You're up, Beth. Tell us a story about the 'Bermuda Triangle.'"

Beth looked at the others as they hunkered down to listen, "My title so far," she announced, "is 'If It's Cloudy,

Stay Put.'" She perused her rough outline carefully as she read the words and spontaneously inserted words and phrases verbally, smoothly editing her written outline as she read to her classmates, "My protagonist is a brilliant and attractive twenty-five-year-old woman named Darma Lundvik. Since childhood, Darma has been very curious, adventurous and resourceful. She had a natural ability to understand what others are feeling emotionally. She earned a master's degree in Environmental Sciences at the University of Puget Sound and is now employed as an environmental research engineer for the State of Florida. The job was the realization of her childhood dreams to be involved in working for the best interests of the world community.

"Darma enjoys living in Miami, a city of mixed cultures, warm weather, quaint patches of green and blue water, sunny beaches, alligator swamps and enticing palm groves. Two years ago, when Darma was leaving her parent's home in Seattle, she assumed that she would return to her beloved snow covered peaks, rushing rivers, absence of insects, cool summers and friendly people. 'I'm sure that this is supposed to be my home country,' she thought, 'but how can I be sure if I haven't been any place else?' About that time she read a magazine article about the Bermuda Triangle, an area of great mystery in the mid- and southern Atlantic Ocean. The record number of disappearing ships, boats, airplanes and human vanishings has been the source of hundreds of speculations and theories by experts since the eighteenth century. The Bermuda Triangle is identified as being located between three geographical points on the map, Miami, Puerto Rico and the British Island of Bermuda, forming a rough triangular configuration.

"Darma thinks of her new job in Florida as the most thrilling thing ever. On her days off, she becomes an inveterate sightseer, explorer and researcher. Cutting to the chase, her travels lead her to the public swimming and sunning area at Miami Beach where she accidentally strikes up a conversation with a tall, blond and handsome thirty-year-old unshaven beach bum named Dirk Dahlquist, who coincidentally was born and raised in Seattle. From then on things change for both of them. Despite Dirk's shabby appearance, they connect in so many ways that they are together constantly. To Darma it's frightening that she feels love for this guy in such a short time. In only a few weeks their relationship has progressed from a state of mutual infatuation to feelings of profound caring for each other and an almost desperate need to be in each other's physical presence. Darma has no idea how they may succeed in marriage. She is ignorant of his financial position right up to the time, two months after their first meeting, when they both know that marriage is inevitable. At that point, Dirk receives notice that his father has passed away and he is needed at home in Seattle immediately. It is necessary for Darma to take time off work so that she and Dirk can fly home to Seattle to fulfill Dirk's family responsibilities.

"On the flight from Miami, Dirk feels the need to inform Darma about how he perceives things in the light of the new reality facing them.

"'First,' he says, as they sit very close to each other in their comfortable first class seats, 'I will introduce you as my fiancé. I can guarantee that everyone in my family will love you to pieces. Watch out for my mother. She will probably slobber all over you. Second, I have to tell you that my family is well-off financially.'

"'My Dad had a great talent for making money. We live in a four million dollar house on Lake Washington just a few blocks from Bill and Melinda Gates. My Dad's holdings include a shipping fleet of supply ships which sail to Alaska and other businesses. I have been told that his worth is between one and two billion. My Dad has turned over some of his investment properties to his only son, that's me. That means that you and I are independently wealthy with no financial worries. Third, I would like for us to get married while in Seattle. Fourth, if all this meets with your approval, after an appropriate mourning period, I think we should plan a tour of Europe very soon for a honeymoon. Maybe we could stay for about a month or so. Now Darma, could we talk about longer-term plans as we live a "happily ever after" life together?'

"Both giggled. Darma looks Dirk directly in the eyes, 'How many kids shall we have?'

"'Four,' answered Dirk, 'all PhDs.'"

Beth closed her notebook, smiled at her classmates, extended her forearms forward with her palms up, as if to say, "That's all, folks!" As she enjoyed the applause showered on her by the class.

Professor Addington spoke, "I liked your story very

much, Beth. I did not hear a whole lot about the Bermuda Triangle."

Beth responded, "I was not much interested in the Bermuda Triangle stories. However, after being assigned the topic, I wanted to fulfill my responsibility so I took the challenge to create a story that was connected to the topic, if only in a tangential way. I didn't want to write a story which was mostly full of possibly boring statistical information to the reader."

More applause emitted from the hands of the other grad students.

"Bravo!" said Addington. "Now it's your turn, Andrew. Go for it!"

"My Topic," said Andrew, addressing his classmates and Professor Addington, "is the so-called 'Jesus Myth.' I begin my fiction story with a non-fiction explanation of what it means. As follows: After this explanation, my story will begin.

"For two thousand years there has existed a perplexing mystery amongst the exponents of the New Testament. This includes advocates, scholars, historians and leadership figures in the worldwide Christian community. One puzzling aspect of this mysterious issue is why none of the world's scholars, historians or representatives from any of the world's great religions have ever seemed the least bit curious or interested in finding the truth of the matter. If the real truth was to be revealed, and found to be merely an unsubstantiated, groundless rumor, it would settle the question forever. If the rumor was found to be even partly true, it would change the foundation and basic tenets of the world's second most populous religion and change what we have always believed were historical facts. So what is the issue and what is the question?

"It is often called the 'Jesus Myth.' The underlying question is, where was Jesus between the ages of twelve and thirty? Searching the Bible reveals nothing. Where was the precocious, brilliant young boy who showed his amazing religious insight in discussions with the rabbis and religious leaders in Jerusalem itself? No record of any kind exists from his mother, any of his family in Nazareth, his friends, his acquaintances or his admirers from the Judaic community. As far as is known, there is no record of his existence whatsoever in Palestine, the Holy Land, during Jesus' teen years or during his twenties, thus, the greatest figure who ever lived, the 'Son of God' himself, was apparently incognito in his own country from age twelve to age thirty. Whether true or false, the 'Jesus Myth' offers an answer which is widely held as true by some who are not bound to the Christian faith. The comments or allegations about the Jesus-Buddha 'connections,' in truth, must be taken as conjecture, ergo subject to controversy.

"THE ENLIGHTENED ONE.

"At the time of Christ, the people of the Far Eastern countries knew nothing about the Christian religion since it did not yet exist. In China, Japan, India, Nepal, Persia, Tibet and other smaller countries, millions belonged to other religions such as Shintoism, Buddhism, Confucianism, Naturalism, Hinduism and others. Buddhists have always believed in reincarnation. They believe that Buddha returns as a man who has the reincarnated soul of Buddha himself and during his lifetime becomes aware of his identity so that he can assume his true purpose along with the responsibility that comes with it. This responsibility means serving his people as their Dalai Lama, the present (contemporary in reference to historical time) incarnation of Buddha, the Sacred One. Somehow, perhaps through a Buddhist priest or someone of significant authority in the Buddhist religion, a message is received and spread throughout the priesthood. The message comes from a spiritual source by means of a dream or a revelation. The message is a heads up to all those involved that a new enlightened Teacher had been born to a poor family thousands of miles to the west in a place called Bethlehem. This is the interpretation relative to the 'Jesus Myth' story. It is beholden to Buddhists to acknowledge and pay homage to the newest of the reincarnated Buddha wherever he should be discovered anywhere on earth as early as possible so that the new Dalai Lama may serve appropriately in his present life just as he has in past lifetimes since his physical 'death' about the year 477 BC.

"Meanwhile in Nazareth, life continued at its usual pace. On a day in the year twelve, three strangers appear in a carpentry shop asking to see Joseph, the owner. After polite greetings, the men ask if they can meet the boy, Jesus, Joseph's twelve-year-old son who is learning the carpentry trade as an apprentice to his father. Jesus and two of his four brothers, James and Simon, ages 15

246

and 10, stare. The three visitors each appear to be of a refined educated class. The men tell Jesus and Joseph that they are there for a profound spiritual purpose and were directed by God to take Jesus under their personal care. If Joseph approves, the three men will take responsibility for the boy and visit places where he will receive an education like no other, from the wisest men anywhere. When Jesus returns home at a future time, he will be the most enlightened and brilliant man in all of Judea and beyond. Jesus' brothers, James and Simon, look with admiration at the three men in their elegant Arab clothes. They then look at Jesus in a new way. "In addition," said the man named Krismar, "I intend to present to you, Joseph, this pouch of Roman coins, enough to support your family for a year. This is for lending us your son and giving him an incomparable gift which will ensure his own success in life and to help his family and his future followers through the ensuing years. At the same time the three of us will be fulfilling our duty and our commitment to God and to Buddha, the Enlightened One." Joseph looked seriously at his three sons, "What do you think, Jesus?"

"Father," said Jesus, "I love my family and my home more than anything I could imagine, but the offer these men have just made is astounding to me. If you feel you could let me go, then I will leave the decision up to you. If you are not inclined to approve of the offer by these men, then I will stay home and contribute to the family the best I can. This request by these learned men I think of as a great and wondrous opportunity to provide me with education and a greater experience of life."

"The very next day, young Jesus was provided with his own camel. He and the three holy men trot off to join the camel caravan which traveled the famous Silk Road. The ancient trade caravan connecting Europe to Asia, east to west covered about four thousand miles. Jesus' new mentors, Chang Li, Bhandi and Krismar were devoted to their new roles of protecting and caring for the boy they regarded as the Dalai Lama of their times, the true Buddha reincarnate. A respectful and caring relationship between the three Buddhist priests and the lad remained throughout their time together. The holy men saw to it that Jesus' every need was met, their tutoring was constant throughout their time together, their food was plentiful and the primary goal of educating their cooperative young charge was successful and comfortable in every way possible.

"During the course of their trip, Jesus was presented to religious leaders, scholars, philosophers and scientists who all seemed willing to share their knowledge and insight with the highly intelligent and enthusiastic young pupil. Some of these highly educated and wise men were aware of the secret of Jesus' true identity while others were not, it never seemed to matter. All seemed to sense that Jesus was, in some way or another, a young man with an important future. Some knew when first meeting the kid that he was a natural genius, bound for greatness. His three guides took the young Jesus of Nazareth first to Persia, then to Nepal, India, China and Japan. In each of the Eastern cultures, the opportunity for broad experiences and to gain profound insights into cultural differences and similarities was greatly enhanced by the instruction and guidance from Jesus' teachers. As Krismar had described to Joseph, 'the best education in the world.' Most professors, teachers, historians and philosophers at the time believed that Eastern intellectual accomplishments ran deeper than in Western cultures.

"When Jesus reached the age of twenty, his caretakers encouraged him to explore on his own, with their blessings. From then on, Jesus traveled mostly on his own, continuing to meet important individuals and soaking up information, opinions, theories, beliefs and philosophical interpretations of life, death and the meaning of it all. Jesus himself became a teacher with a wide following in Tibet. While there, a historian wrote of Jesus' presence, his notoriety and outstanding reputation. These documents are reported to be stored in a temple vault, somewhere in Tibet. Tibetans called Jesus by a special name and still acknowledge his holy presence after two thousand years.

"Jesus' return to Palestine, Judea, Galilee, Jerusalem, at age thirty has been recorded for history and pretty much accepted as historical fact. His next three years were documented in the New Testament. The Biblical account is generally believed by most Americans and fervently believed by all Christians.

"What of the account in the Bible about the crucifixion? That too needs correcting according to the Jesus Myth. It goes like this: After his confrontation with Pontius Pilate, Jesus was held by the Roman guards on the day of his crucifixion. Jesus' family and supporters did all they could to distract and delay the act of nailing him to the cross, by creating a ruckus to help stall the procedure. The intent was to stall it until the late afternoon which they hoped would shorten the time Jesus hung on the cross. His supporters meant to save Jesus by getting him down from the cross as soon as sunset when most of the guards would have left the area. After detaching him, they hid him in blankets and hustled him away to a secret place where, with good care, he might survive his deadly ordeal.

"After months in recovery, his family and friends arranged secret passage on a boat which took him and his wife, Mary Magdalene, to the southern coast of France which was considered to be the safest area in all of the surrounding countries.

"Jesus' wealthy friend, Nicodemus, paid for his care and voyage out of respect for Jesus' many messages of love and charity to the Israelites, to Romans and the rest of the Western world. Jesus and Mary made friends in their new home even though most of their neighbors had no idea who they were or where they came from. Jesus and Mary Magdalene produced a daughter, Sarah. It was through her that the bloodline of Jesus Christ continued for generations in the blood of French kings. The secret of Jesus' survival from crucifixion was never publicly released by the early Christians or any Christian sect thereafter. The secret of Jesus' survival and ultimate death at age eighty-four was never acknowledged or admitted by the Roman Catholic Church. There are a small number of people who knew the secret, indeed, secret societies have been organized to keep the secret and lives have been lost in defending it. Among the many organizations that have been part of the controversy include the Medieval Knights Templar."

Andrew raised his head and said, "With more details to come, that's as far as my outline takes us for now."

The enthusiasm by the class was a bit tentative. Andrew gave professor Addington a curious look.

The professor returned a look of sympathy, and said, "Good job, Andrew, but not all your classmates think you have avoided crossing into blasphemy. If published, your fascinating story will be openly attacked by the conservative church brethren. This will likely open a controversy and critics may demand that it be prohibited from further publication. The controversy will probably be good for book sales, however.

"Here's another one: Will the truth ultimately prevail in all these issues of secrecy?

"Now I must ask you grad students, embarking on professional careers as writers, reporters, essayists and editors, do you sincerely believe in freedom of speech?" The Professor paused and removed his glasses. His eyes met and locked briefly with each of the closely-grouped attentive students.

"Keep in mind: A writer writes, a writer reads everything, a writer is curious. A writer keeps an open mind. Hopefully we writers will always take the high road."

BLOOD BROTHERS

The letter was not expected and the brother was somewhat curious when he saw the return address. Just who the heck did he know in Seattle? Living in Mississippi, Bobby Lee Bland had barely even heard of the place and had no idea where it was located. Maybe somewhere around California? No, Alaska, that's probably where.

"Why don't you open the envelope and read the letter or whatever it is?" asked Sarah, his wife.

Bobby Lee read the letter. "I can't believe this," he exclaimed. "Here Sarah, you read it."

Twelve-year-old Lester, wearing his sweaty baseball uniform scrambled into the room and threw himself into an adjoining chair. "What's going on y'all?" he yelled at nobody in particular.

"Keep quiet," Sarah said sharply. "We're reading a letter we got from some Yankee. I'm not sure this could be true," Sarah commented, "but it says here your folks gave up their baby boy for adoption a year before you were born, Bobby Lee and you have a brother nobody in the family ever heard of."

"If it's true, my mother and daddy surely knew about it and kept it a secret," said Bobby Lee.

"Maybe something was wrong with the baby," offered Sarah. "Or maybe the folks were so poor at the time they thought they couldn't afford to keep the kid."

"Just guessin'," blurted her husband in his soft Southern accent.

Sarah studied the letter. "He thinks he is your blood brother. His name is Jack Santana and he wants you to come meet him up there in Seattle where he lives."

Lester spoke up as he looked at his mother. "Where's Seattle?"

"Far away," said his father. "Well, the timing couldn't be worse," grumbled Bobby Lee. "It's the damned recession. Losing my job at the furniture store two weeks ago was something I thought would never happen. I was always their best salesman. Ask anybody at the store. It was bad enough, Sarah, losing your part-time job at the drugstore last month. Lester, there's crackers and peanut butter on the sideboard. Get your skinny little butt in there and pour a glass of milk. This ain't any of your business, now go!" Bobby Lee continued, "There ain't enough in our savings account to last more than a few weeks even if we quit eating. To travel anywhere now is out of the question, especially to Timbuktu or Seattle. It's kinda interesting to think I have always had a secret brother, but I doubt that it's even true. Maybe it's one of those scams to try and get our money. Ain't that a laugh?"

The next day another letter, a registered letter this

time, with the same return address from Jack Santana arrived in the afternoon mail. "What does my long lost 'brother' want this time?" Bobby Lee snorted as he ripped open the envelope.

"This looks like a photo of the 'brother,'" exclaimed Sarah, as Bobby Lee dumped the contents of the envelope on the dining room table.

"Well lookie here," he shouted, "a check for six hundred bucks!" Laughter and giggling erupted as the two took turns examining the check as if receiving it was a fantasy of some kind. "Oh brother, or whoever you are," yelled Bobby Lee, "How could you know how bad we need this money?" Sarah excitedly grabbed the letter and began reading it aloud to Bobby Lee.

Dear Bobby,

Enclosed are copies of some documents of interest, a personal check, an invitation, a job application form and some photos. I hope you may find the time for a prompt response. About two months ago, I came across some old adoption papers which confirmed a relationship between you and me. Since then I have engaged a professional researcher to confirm the fact that you and I share the same birth parents which makes us blood brothers. Other facts regarding our parents include legal records about their ancestry and relatives, their wedding dates and our birth and adoption documents.

I hope you will excuse my probing, but I value my privacy and assure you that I treasure these documents as private and personal, shared only with you. I am very much inclined to see if you might be as interested in me as I am in you. As you can see, a photo of me, my wife and my adoptive parents are enclosed. Maybe our natural parents will remember my adoptive parents at the time of adoption forty-seven years ago. Take a close look at my picture. It would be most interesting to learn if you think we resemble each other or either of our birth parents.

Please pardon my snooping but I have also learned about the recent loss of your job at the Miller's furniture store. As it happens, I have a connection with the owner of a large furniture store here in Seattle. Business is perking along pretty well in these parts while the recession still restricts recovery in other places in the USA. As I understand it, business in the Jackson area remains slow. The Bernstein Furniture store is looking to hire an experienced, competent salesman at a good salary just now. If you might be interested in relocating permanently or temporarily, send the enclosed application form immediately as time is of the essence, as always in these cases.

While you're at it, send a picture of you and your wife. The check is to cover expenses for travel here and back. If you decide not to come, use the money to help tide you over the rough spot you are experiencing presently. I invite you, your wife and son Lester to visit me and my wife Molly for a few days. I am a school teacher and the end of the school year is just four days away. After that I will have no other commitments until the first of August. My family is very interested in hosting you, your wife and your son. You may stay at our place here in the University District in the north end of Seattle as our guests. It would be our pleasure to welcome your family as soon as you can make it. I will call you on Friday at six p.m., central time to discuss the above.

Jack

*   *   *

In the Bland family's attempt to deal with their economic problems, a family meeting was called. Buford,

75, regarded himself as the head of the family, along with his wife, Silvia. The small gathering at Buford's home included his son Bobby Lee, his wife Sarah and twelve-year-old Lester, Buford's only grandson. All were seated around the dining room table as Buford took a sip of coffee, cleared his throat and spoke, "More downtown stores and shops are going belly up every day. I've never seen anything like it." Facial expressions were grim.

Bobby Lee said, "Losing my job was bad enough but there don't seem to be any other jobs. I hate to think of applying for welfare."

"Have you tried to find something, Sarah?" asked Silvia.

"There's absolutely nothing around, Mom," said Sarah.

"Too bad we don't have any rich relatives," bleated Lester.

Buford thoughtfully blew cigarette smoke toward the ceiling, "There was a family rumor many years ago that my older brother Homer came into money. He was supposed to be in Texas. I say that because he sends me a Christmas card every four or five years, and that's what was on the postmark."

"Did he desert the family?" asked Bobby Lee.

"I guess you could call it that," Buford mused. "Homer was always kind of a restless kid. He left home in his early twenties and never came back to Mississippi as far as anyone ever knew. No point in thinking about help from relatives 'cause there ain't any left alive anyway."

"We don't have anything of value to sell," said Sarah.

Bobby Lee stirred sugar into his coffee. "We can consider the offer from that guy in Seattle who claims to be my brother. That may be all we have left. Daddy, is that story true about a baby before me that you and Mom gave up for adoption?"

Buford scratched his forehead as he answered. "We couldn't afford medical bills. The baby had spinal meningitis and a heart valve problem. He was also diagnosed as retarded. He was cuckoo. We had to give up on him, but then we had you. The story that guy from Seattle tells you sounds fishy to me. I'd lead him along just a bit more to see if there is a chance for some kind of job." Buford cleared his throat "Be careful, there are bad people out there. We still remember stories about the Yankee carpetbaggers."

Lester tucked his bubble gum into his left cheek with his tongue and asked wetly, "Do those pictures we got yesterday look like carpetbaggers?"

"We cain't always tell just by lookin'," chuckled Grandpa Buford.

"Does this Jack guy look like Daddy," asked Lester, "or you, Grandpa?"

"I think," said Sarah, "that Jack's adopted mother, or whatever she is, looks oriental or chynee or something."

"You cain't always tell much by pictures either," added Bobby Lee.

*   *   *

The Santana family sat comfortably in their

University District home, clustered around their huge teakwood dining room table, sipping coffee and munching on chocolate chip cookies, their dessert after the evening meal. Jack and his wife Molly sat across from Jack's father Antonio and mother Suling. Two other men sat comfortably at the table. Both in their early fifties, Marco Nosich and Rex Lang appeared relaxed almost as if part of the Santana family.

"Do you think he'll come?" asked Marco.

"He will come for sure," said Antonio. "He's in a squeeze. He'd be a fool not to come up here with a job offer and paid expenses. All our research indicates that he's a bit of a Southern ding dong, but he's up against it and he's not completely stupid."

"He sounds good," said Marco. "We can look him over more thoroughly when he gets here to see if he will work out."

*　　*　　*

The airport greetings were both cordial and a bit awkward, mostly on the part of the Bland family who were understandably anxious and a bit fearful of such a surprising turn in their lives. The warm handshakes and hugs imposed on them by Jack and Molly Santana were of great help in establishing a degree of trust. Along with the ritual small talk, a smiling Jack asked Bobby Lee a direct question. "Do you see a family resemblance when you look at me, your blood brother?"

Both looked intently at their faces. "There is a strong

259

resemblance," offered Sarah. "The shape of the head, the cheek bones and chin, especially." All agreed that there either was a strong or slight resemblance depending on the angle in which they studied Jack and Bobby Lee's faces, but there didn't seem to be a thorough consensus. Jack and Molly maintained an approving smile on their faces.

"I think there is a pretty strong resemblance," said Sarah.

*   *   *

The first morning after their arrival, the three Blands enjoyed a typical Santana breakfast consisting of orange juice, toast, bacon and eggs which were referred to by Antonio as "huevos rancheros."

"A lovely breakfast," exclaimed Sarah.

Jack Santana grinned, "Sorry, no grits."

"No Chitlins either," chuckled Antonio.

Sarah spoke with sincerity, "We cain't thank you enough for what y'all are doing for us."

"Ah cain't wait to see the furniture store," added Bobby Lee.

"Weekdays they don't open till ten a.m.," said Jack. "We'll drive you on a little tour first."

The morning tour included a drive around the University of Washington campus with Jack at the wheel, Molly beside him and the Bland family in the back seat of the year-old Oldsmobile La Cross.

"So this is where you work?" asked Lester. "Are you

a real college professor?"

"He's the real thing," smiled Molly.

"To your right," announced Jack, "are three lecture halls, to the left are classroom buildings and straight ahead is the campus quad, the fountain and the big Suzallo library. From this part of the campus we can see Mount Rainier and Lake Washington. A bit farther on are the dormitories and the UW football stadium. It seats about eighty thousand."

"How big is the University?" asked Bobby Lee.

"More than forty-five-thousand full-time and grad students," answered Jack. "Do you think you and I look alike, Bobby Lee?"

"Your nose is a bit wider than mine," said Bobby Lee.

"You have darker skin," said Lester.

"We may have similar hair," said Jack, "But right now I'm wearing a wig."

"He's recovering from chemo," said Molly, "but his hair will appear soon."

"We hope," chuckled Jack.

After driving around the campus, they drove slowly through the Arboretum, viewing the astonishing gardens where the spring and summer blossoming flowers and trees were at their yearly best. "I've never seen gardens and trees like this," exclaimed Sarah. "You even have plants that are native to Mississippi."

"Our weather is a lot different from what you are used to," said Molly, "as you probably know, especially in the summer months."

"I know," said Sarah, "it would take some getting

used to if we decide to stay."

The drive took them through some of the downtown streets revealing the atmosphere and bustle of the central city. "Seattle is as big as Memphis!" declared Lester.

"We thought it was just a small town way out West," chuckled Bobby Lee.

"Looks as big as New York," smiled Sarah.

Driving East, up one of Seattle's steep hills, Jack announced, "This is the Capitol Hill area. There are hospitals, clinics, apartments, colleges, restaurants and a diverse population."

"What do you mean by diverse?" asked Bobby Lee.

As Jack parked near a coffee shop, he answered, "Ethnic, religious, sexual and racial differences in the local population. Let's stop here for coffee."

As they occupied a booth and ordered coffee in Ginsberg's delicatessen, all listened as Jack spoke in a soft voice. "We saw just a bit of downtown. There is a lot more to see such as the colorful waterfront, the docks where the freighters and cruise ships tie up, the aquarium, the ferry terminals where residents from the local islands ride every day to and from their jobs in the city. Then there are the many seafood restaurants, the waterfront Great Wheel and the adjacent parks. Later, we'll tour the local lakes in the city and the canal. The Puget Sound is the big saltwater inlet from the Pacific Ocean. Later on we can introduce you to our nearby mountains including Mount Rainier, over fourteen thousand feet high, with over two dozen permanent glaciers and many ice caves, mountain trails, lakes and rivers."

"We don't have nothin' like that in Mississippi," yelled Lester.

"That's to look forward to," said Molly.

Jack gave the Blands a look which said, *listen to me.* "I would like to tell you a bit about Bernstein's furniture store." Everyone listened intently. "Al Bernstein, the owner, was a classmate of mine in college. He always was a man of genuine integrity. He is a great guy to have as a friend and is a leader in the community. Some people are urging him to run for Mayor."

"Now, Bobby Lee and Sarah," said Jack, giving them a serious stare, "I must tell you that the store will likely be offering a job to see you through this recession." Jack paused to wipe his glasses. "The store is located just inside a district made up of mostly African American families. The sales staff consists of mostly black men." Another pause as he looked at Bobby Lee who was face-to-face with Sarah and seemed to be very quietly saying, *Jiggaboos?* "The store manager is a very experienced and respected lady named Sherry Bernstein." Molly sucked in her breath as she read Sarah's lips which seemed to whisper something like *Jewess.* Jack said, "I can recommend this store as a well-managed efficient and profitable enterprise. "You," looking at Bobby Lee, "will, after a modest start, earn an average middle-class income, enough to provide well for your family and save as you go, and if Sarah decides to take a job, so much the better economically." Bobby Lee thought he could hide his eyes as he rolled them back in his head.

"Now," said Jack, "do you still want to visit the store,

one of the very best stores of its kind in the entire area? How about it?" Sarah and Bobby Lee looked silently at each other. Their previous enthusiasm seemed to have markedly diminished.

"I don't know what to say," murmured Bobby Lee. Tears appeared in Sarah's eyes.

"Let me put it to you this way," Jack growled. "Around here, the vast majority of people of different races work together. They play together, they cooperate, they intermarry and they all benefit. This is the real world and the future. My advice to you, Bobby Lee, is to face it, man-up and give it a try."

The visit to Bernstein's furniture store was a big surprise to Bobby Lee Bland because of the variety of furniture they offered. The stock varied from affordable choices on the basement level, to high-end furniture on the second floor, all on display in classy surroundings. If Bobby Lee accepted a sales job here, it would take lots of study to become familiar with the various lines carried by Bernstein's. Bobby Lee had to admit to himself that he was very impressed, even though still leery about possibly having to interact with Negroes, as he called African Americans.

Like many white Southerners, he had been raised with a sense of pride harkening back to the perceived glories of the Nineteenth Century antebellum plantation economy and the Confederate army. It was always easy to ignore the taint of racial hatred and feelings of white superiority which were slow to fade even many years after slavery had been abolished. Deep in the hearts of many, perhaps most, Southerners was an ever-present resentment toward the Yankee invaders during the Civil War. After all, Bobby Lee frequently reminded himself, he is the namesake of "the greatest figure in American history," Robert E. Lee, every white Southerner's hero. To perpetuate the image of the Confederacy's favorite general, one must put aside the criticism of Northern Patriots who, after the war, advocated hanging both Jefferson Davis and Robert E. Lee for treason. The Civil War resulted in the deaths of over 150,000 Americans from both sides.

After the tour, Bobby Lee was escorted to the office of the store manager. Sherry Bernstein shook hands warmly with the Mississippian and asked the anticipated questions, all the while eyeing him carefully. When she asked him questions she was aware he was hesitant, but she put it down as a natural response to his recent move and exposure to a different environment. "Mr. Bland," she said, "I get the feeling that you are not especially enthused about working here. Is that right?"

"I'm very impressed with the professionalism that I see here," retorted Bobby Lee. "I'm still nervous about the big changes in our lives lately, but I need the job very badly and if hired, I can assure you that I will give it everything I have. I feel good about the reputation that I have earned as an outstanding salesman. I can promise that I will not disappoint you."

Sherry Bernstein paused as she tried to visualize how this apparently sincere man would fit into her plan for the store's continued success. "I want you to start

Monday," said Ms. Bernstein. "You will have to learn our style before we turn you loose to sell. You will be on the floor observing and learning Mondays, Wednesdays and Fridays. Have you ever learned to drive a delivery truck? That will be your job on other days including Saturdays. Your salary, I can assure you, will be adequate for now."

*　*　*

"Our guest house on the back lot is available for your family at no rent for the first two months, Brother," smiled Jack, as all were gathered at the breakfast table. "It's furnished and there is space for a car next to the back alley."

"There is absolutely no way to thank you enough," squealed Sarah. The Blands all nodded and smiled.

After breakfast, Molly escorted Sarah and Lester to the local supermarket in preparation for their move into the tidy little cottage on the back lot. Antonio and Jack sat down at the dining room table with Bobby Lee for an informal meeting. "What do you teach at the University," asked Bobby Lee.

"I have a full professorship in the engineering program. I have taught there for nineteen years," said Jack. "I am a fully accredited and licensed engineer."

"Jack is also a famous inventor," bragged Antonio. "He's made a good deal of money on a product that has been in demand for the last ten years."

Bobby Lee seemed impressed, "What kind of product, Jack?"

With a modest smile, Jack replied, "I call it a 'safe

266

box.' It's about the size of a small foot locker, made of a special light-weight metal on which I have a patent. It's not only impenetrable, but also almost impossible to damage. It's also impossible," he chuckled, "to open. There is a secret procedure and code. We have done very well with it, especially with the military."

Maybe that's why he seems to be so damned rich, thought Bobby Lee.

"It's a separate business," confided Jack. "Tonight at dinner you'll meet some of my business friends."

Bobby Lee stared at his brother Jack. "After your birth to a poor Southern family and adoption at age one, you have really done well," said Bobby Lee.

Jack looked deeply into Bobby Lee's eyes and softly spoke, "Do you know why our parents gave me up for adoption?"

Bobby Lee sat upright, "I've heard something about it." The two men's eyes remained locked.

"It's time you knew," said Jack in a low-pitched quiet tone. "It was because as a tiny baby I had very dark skin, but it turned lighter as I grew up. My hair was black and nappy. I obviously had the genes of an African American ancestor. I looked like an African American baby. In Mississippi they no doubt would call me a 'pickaninny' or a 'mulatto.' That's why our parents got rid of me." The astonished look on Bobby Lee's face defied description.

The jaw fell, the eyes seemed to pop and the color drained from his face. After a moment of confused silence, Bobby Lee stared angrily at Jack and snapped, "Just what the hell are you telling me, that we are blood brothers except that I am white and you are black? That's just crazy! It's not possible! Are you joking or what! If so, it's not funny, Jack, so cut it out."

Jack's expression was grim as he maintained fierce eye contact with Bobby Lee. "It's entirely possible that a baby with African American characteristics could be born to Caucasian parents."

"I've never heard of that!" Bobby Lee asserted loudly.

"Caucasian children are sometimes born of black parents as well. Not often. It's rare but it happens that the genetics sometimes skip generations. It's scientific fact, Bobby Lee. Since the research is irrefutable, that is what happened to our parents back then."

"I can't believe this," said Bobby Lee holding his head in his hands.

"There is only one other possibility," said Jack.

"Like what?" moaned Bobby Lee.

"I don't want to tell you. You won't like it."

"Tell me anyway. It can't be any worse."

"Okay," said Jack. "If our white mother was impregnated a black man whether by mutual consent or rape."

Bobby Lee's eyes were moist and his voice trembled as he said, "Why are you telling me all this, maybe we ain't related at all!"

"I'm just sharing the truth with you. You really are my brother. I'm willing to pay for a DNA test to prove it to you once and for all. In the meantime, look at the bigger picture. Recently you were just about bankrupt with no place to turn. Now you have a place to live. Your family is in safe surroundings, you have a new job, and Antonio is lending you the use of his car. You also have affluent relatives who are looking out for you."

"Yeah, all that is true, Jack, but I wish you hadn't said those things about my mother and daddy. Then you say I have some kind of nigger grandparents or something. That really hurts me."

Jack's eyes flashed, "You need to discuss this with Sarah and digest all of the information I have just given you, like it or not. By the way, anyone who uses the 'N' word in this house is not welcome." Bobby Lee's expression was one of surprise, confusion and shock. Jack spoke softly, "That also goes for ethnic nicknames, which are forbidden. Wetbacks, beaners, greasers, chinks, slopies, gooks, Japs, red skins, coons, spades, jigs, spearchuckers, spooks, krauts, frogs, Pollocks, Orientals and all the rest." Bobby Lee stood and departed through the back door making a rapid beeline for the backyard cottage. Antonio remained seated quietly across the table. He looked across at Jack and smiled.

*　　*　　*

The Santana's dinner party that evening included the family, Antonio and Suling, Jack and Molly, Bobby Lee and Sarah and Lester. Also enjoying their pre-dinner drinks were the guests, Professor Conrad Goodrich and wife Janet, along with Marko Nosich and his partner Rex Lang. Drinks and dinner were being prepared by Luigi Fellino, caterers, a local favorite whose specialty was delectable Italian cuisine along with tasty wines and desserts to die for. The Blands were the center of attention and polite conversation ensued until all were seated at the elegantly decorated dinner table. Toasts to the Bland family were offered along with questions about Mississippi cultural traditions, the Southern economy and social mores, even including customary funeral and burial practices. Professor Goodrich, a close colleague of Jack Santana, seemed to be especially interested in how Bobby Lee and Sarah interpreted the history of slavery and the Civil War.

"We call it the 'War Between the States,'" said Bobby Lee.

Sarah spoke up, "We also refer to it as the 'War of Northern Aggression,'" after which everyone chuckled politely.

Bobby Lee eyed Professor Goodrich curiously. "What kinda classes do you teach at the University?" he asked.

"For many years I have specialized in evolutionary research."

"You mean that you teach the theory of evolution?" asked Sarah.

Lester brightened up and commented, "They don't teach evolution in our schools in Jackson. They tell you what it is and then tell you a lot of reasons why it isn't true. How do you get away with it?"

Doctor Goodrich smiled, "Those school authorities in Mississippi are doing what they believe is right. When you get to college, Lester, I am sure you will be taught the difference between a religious belief and a scientific fact."

Antonio quickly interceded, "Our old friend, Marco Nosich, can you tell us something about the latest technology you use to find a missing relative."

Marco swallowed a bit of cannoli. The dark brown iris in his eyes expanded a bit as he spoke of his lifelong passion with the electro-magnetic digitized powerhouse machine which has revolutionized almost everything in only a generation. "As you all no doubt know, the computer is the irreplaceable tool that we use to find out just about anything." Looking at his partner sitting at his right, he explained, "Our company is called Finders, Inc. Rex Lang here and I are partners. As good as I think I am on the computer, Rex is even better."

Rex politely interrupted, "I want you all to know the news. Marco and I have decided that we will be getting married soon, probably in about three weeks."

Applause erupted around the table. Everyone except the Blands clapped and cheered. "Congratulations!" shouted Antonio.

"You two are such a great couple," called Jack and Molly together.

Bobby Lee and Sarah sat in an uncomfortable silence. I can't believe what I just heard, thought Sarah. Do these people have no morality? Don't they believe the Bible?

Marco and Rex couldn't miss the horrified expressions on Bobby Lee and Sarah's faces. The two gay men were well aware of much cultural disapproval amounting to an estimated fifty percent of the American population. Confronted by such hardline attitudes, the two fiancés tried, as always, to maintain a calm demeanor.

"So Bobby Lee," said Marco, "with the technology we use every day we make our living seeking out legal documents, real estate transactions, tax policies and information, birth certificates, criminal records, marriages, divorces, lawsuit decisions and adoptions. Sometimes we are retained by law enforcement organizations to find people and track down missing persons and we can obtain evidence from dishonest people, criminals, crooks, rapists and murderers. We can also find truth about peoples' ancestors and ethnic history."

"Like tracing your family tree?" asked Janet Goodrich, who looked like an early middle-aged Scandinavian beauty queen.

"Family trees and ethnic ancestors are easy," muttered Rex Lang, with an engaging smile.

"Where did my ancestors come from," asked Lester Bland.

"I would guess," said Marco, "Scotch-Irish. If you want to find out for yourself, there is a place back east where you can send a cotton swab DNA sample from inside your cheek along with a hundred bucks and they will send you your ethnic history for as far back as about a million years."

"A million years?" gasped Sarah.

"Yeah, about the time primitive humans were migrating from Africa to Asia and Europe. You look a little shocked, Sarah. Maybe it's a topic for another time."

Antonio entered the conversation, "Next Sunday, Suling and I will be attending church at St. Margaret's.

Would any of the Bland family care to go along?"

"Is it a Catholic Church?" asked Bobby Lee.

"Yes, but maybe you would rather accompany Jack and Molly."

"We attend a Unitarian Church right here in the University District. You're welcome to come along. We may see Professor Goodrich and Janet there next Sunday."

These offers made Bobby Lee and Sarah feel uneasy and uncomfortable. "At home we are members of our neighborhood Southern Baptist church," said Sarah quietly.

"I'm not sure we have a Baptist church close by," said Jack.

"It has to be a Southern Baptist," answered Bobby Lee, "or a Pentecostal church."

"I think there is a Pentecostal church near the north end of the Aurora Bridge." Jack continued, "We'll drop you off at ten-thirty and pick you up at twelve- thirty next Sunday."

"Speaking of something really spiritual," roared Antonio, as Suling smiled, "let's have some more wine. This dinner is going to be out of this world."

That night in their own little cottage the Bland family prayed fervently, at first together and then individually. Far into the night, as Lester tried to get to sleep he heard his parents murmur prayerful words he didn't always understand, such as sodomy, blasphemy, atheism, demonism, monkey ancestry, Devil's advocacy, hellfire, damnation and Satanism.

*   *   *

Early Monday morning, Bobby Lee reported for work at Bernstein's. "I'm very pleased to see you Bobby Lee. You understand that you will be working in our warehouse storage building out in back. Work clothes will be in order today."

"In my bag right here," said Bernstein's latest employee.

"Report to our man, Jamal Jefferson," said Sherry Bernstein, "Now let's meet our bookkeeper, Tina Corio." As Bobby Lee shook hands, he attempted to hide his surprise at encountering a startlingly beautiful young woman in her early twenties.

Bobby Lee's first week on the job at Bernstein's was stressful and confusing. Sarah and Lester felt his restlessness and also felt on edge themselves as they attempted to adapt.

During supper on Saturday evening, at the end of the first week, Sarah spoke in a quiet voice, "I think it would be a good idea for each of us to express our feelings about what's going on."

"You first," suggested Bobby Lee.

Sarah responded, "Okay, I am doing all right here in Yankeetown. My main concern is how both of you are adapting. I think it's harder for y'all right now than it is for me."

"My first week at the store," said Bobby Lee, "was not too bad. It's kind of a struggle 'cause nothing so far is familiar. My boss in the warehouse is a Negro guy, about forty, who is teaching me how to drive our trucks. I also have to learn loading and unloading techniques. His name is Jamal Jefferson. Is Jamal a Muslim name? If so, he is a black Muslim. Ain't that a bugger?" The sarcasm was not acknowledged by Sarah and Lester. "The salesman job on Mondays, Wednesdays and Fridays is going to work out, but there's a lot to learn. Most of the other salesmen are mulatto or quadroon with dark or light brown complexions. Some use hair straightener and some have short nappy hair. They all wear suits and ties and their shoes are always shiny. They all seem to have outgoing, sort of pleasant personalities. They have all been friendly so far. The customers are mostly colored and are pretty well-dressed. They appear to understand English, or at least their version of it."

Lester could not restrain a slight giggle. Molly looked at Lester, "How is it going as the new kid in the Boy Scout troop?"

"It's been okay so far but I'm not sure if I really wanna join. For one thing, I'm supposed to wear a uniform with short pants, a scarf, knee socks and a funny hat."

"We'll find a way to pay for a uniform," said Bobby Lee. "Don't they go on hikes and camping trips in the summer? You might like that."

"Well," said Lester thoughtfully, "maybe, but I don't think I want to be cooped up in a little tent with a Negro or a Jew or whatever."

"Do they have a racial diversity in the troop?" asked his mother.

"Yeah," said Lester, "just like everywhere around here. What are you gonna do?"

"We didn't see many minorities at the Pentecostal Church last Sunday," said Bobby Lee.

"I don't think they fit in there," declared Sarah. "There is a lot of spiritual enthusiasm at that Pentecostal church."

"It's plenty loud alright," grinned Lester. "I was watching for people to start speaking in tongues."

"Those other churches, the Catholics, or the Lutherans are so quiet, they don't seem to feel the Holy Spirit," said Bobby Lee in an authoritative tone. "They just don't seem to get it."

At the supper table the Blands had already said grace and given thanks before eating, but now seemed to feel like another prayer was called for. They held hands as Bobby Lee delivered a prayer ending with the words, "and keep us separated from the Santana's friends who seem to accept homosexuality, gay marriage, sodomy, atheism, evolution and the rumor about the global warming myth, and protect us from all Satan's evil ways. Amen."

*   *   *

Bobby Lee's growing experience with trucks, pickups and deliveries to Bernstein's store was enhanced with each trip. He was most often assigned to load and deliver furniture from local manufacturers in Seattle and the adjoining cities such as Tacoma and Everett, but occasionally for a six-hundred-mile round trip drive to and from Spokane. Every so often, his assignment sent him to Vancouver, Canada, three hours north of Seattle. Crossing the border required him to use his US passport. After the first month, Bobby Lee was feeling comfortable about his newly acquired skills as a truck driver. His "swamper" duties requiring competency in loading and unloading furniture kept improving as well. Bobby Lee Bland was happiest when working at a pleasant job with a decent income and interesting challenges. He enjoyed his role as a conscientious, hard-working, tax paying, church going good ole boy. What more could a man ask for?

On a Friday during the second week on his new job as a sale trainee, Bobby Lee had just made his first sale, a medium priced bedroom set including chairs and a thirteen inch Sony television set. Tina Corio had come to his assistance when handling the transactional paper work. Finishing the details just after the eight p.m. closing time, Tina complimented him on his first sale at Bernstein's. "I thought," said Bobby Lee, "that you worked in the accounting department keepin' books."

Tina gave him a big smile, augmented by her sparkling white teeth, large irresistible brown eyes and perfect complexion. She quietly murmured, "I sometimes help the sales staff and at times I work as a greeter. I could see that you needed a bit of help just now so I stayed over to help you."

Bobby Lee could not stop himself from ogling her lovely body, shiny black hair and sexy short dress. This girl is such a knockout he thought. Hold it, what am I thinking? Get a hold of yourself. Think of Sarah and Lester, have you gone nuts?"

"You did well for yourself today, Bobby."

"It's Bobby Lee," he said.

"I think you are going to do well here, Bobby Lee, you have a nice manner with customers and you are very good looking." Another devastating smile. Bobby Lee tried not to show how completely charmed he was at that moment. "By the way," Tina cooed, "my brother was supposed to pick me up about this time but he hasn't shown up. Would you mind driving me home?"

The word 'temptation' was familiar to anyone who had been exposed to as many church sermons as Bobby Lee had been throughout his life. But somehow the word rang in his memory as if his conscience was issuing a warning. Thankfully it only lasted for a few seconds. He was pleased to drive Tina to her house in the nearby Montlake neighborhood. During the ride, Bobby Lee felt tongue tied and nervous along with a strange, imaginary, anticipation smoldering in his brain and his loins.

During the drive to Tina's house, Bobby Lee was almost overcome with a powerful sexual arousal he could barely control, even with maximum effort. His part of the conversation was clumsily terse. Tina overflowed with nervous small talk which evolved into comments about her makeup, her shoes and included babble about how and why she wore her intimate underthings. Bobby Lee was entranced and wondered if these topics were meant to excite his libido. When they reached the curb in front of her house he offered to walk her to her front door. Her key was barely in the keyhole with the door partly open when sky rockets seemed to pop. As they grasped each other in a desperate embrace, their lips fiercely locked together, their tongues probing ever deeply, their bodies pressed tightly together. When their lips relaxed and disengaged for a brief moment, Tina whispered, "There is nobody home. My brother won't be home until tomorrow." As they squeezed through the door it closed quietly behind them.

The next day, Bobby Lee was pretty much exhausted after a trip to and from Vancouver in which he had driven both ways accompanied by Jamal Jefferson. It turned out to be an especially big load of furniture from Canadian manufacturers mixed with goods from Asia and who knew where. Bobby Lee still depended on Jamal to handle the paperwork details. Jamal was turning out to be an important asset to Bobby Lee in his work at the repair shop and the warehouse. Jamal was also well versed in locating the transfer warehouses in Vancouver and the other points for pickup and delivery. Bobby Lee was not only dependent on Jamal Jefferson but he enjoyed their conversations when they traveled together on their assigned routes. Despite that, Bobby Lee believed they could never be social friends. He appreciated the fact that Jamal kept up on the news and local gossip and he seemed surprisingly intelligent about life in general.

After docking at the Bernstein's warehouse in Seattle about eight p.m., Bobby Lee was excused and told he could go home. After about ten minutes, while headed home in Antonio's car, he was suddenly forced to pull over by a car with a flashing rooftop light. Safely parked at the curb, two men emerged from the car with the lights. Both were well-dressed, wearing suits and narrow brimmed fedora hats. The biggest man approached the driver's window and asked for Bobby Lee's license and registration. "Are y'all cops?" he asked. The biggest man showed his badge. Bobby Lee could see no reason for being pulled over. His irritation showed as he exclaimed, "Why are you stopping me?"

"Don't worry, I'm not going to ticket you, but it's very important that we talk for a few minutes. You could be in a lot of trouble."

"How so?" asked Bobby Lee.

"I have reason to take you to jail right now, but doing that might turn out to be complicated."

Bobby Lee couldn't hide his fear and felt himself begin to sweat, "What is this about?" he demanded.

The big cop pointed to a sports bar just a few yards away and said, "Why don't you get out of your car and come with us inside that place where we can discuss all this for a few minutes. It might save us a trip downtown." Inside, the two cops chose a booth as far away from the patrons and the gigantic television screen as possible. The bartender couldn't miss the fact that the three new customers were not at all interested in the Mariner's game on the big screen. No surprise that the three ordered coffee.

Bobby Lee looked distressed, "I wish you would tell

me what this is about."

"Relax, Mr. Bland. I want to show you our identification so you know who we are and we'll take it from there."

Bobby Lee studied their identification cards very carefully. He scrutinized the faces of each of the two men closely. The big guy had the squinty eyes of a cop and black bushy eyebrows set into a square face, ears that flared out from the sides of his head and a strong jaw. The name on his identification card, tucked away in his wallet, was Stanley Tulley. His Federal agent identification card said his name was Howard Fisk. The smaller cop was a bit heavy-set with a lot of brown hair, round blue eyes and a broken nose, all part of a pale jowly countenance. His real name was Lenny Ross. The name on his ID card was Paul Byers. "Federal Agents?" asked Bobby Lee. "What could you possibly want with me?"

Agent Fisk aimed a threatening look, "The charge will probably be smuggling. If convicted it carries a sentence of at least twenty years in a Federal penitentiary, so let's get serious. As long as you have been smuggling contraband into the United States, you must have known we would catch up with you sooner or later."

"I don't know nothin about smuggling!" protested Bobby Lee. "Y'all have got the wrong guy."

"We want to talk to you about that load of furniture you brought from Canada tonight. You had to be aware that there were about six Chinese aliens aboard your truck hiding in the back under some canvas tarps."

"I can't believe this," wailed Bobby Lee.

"We have researched you thoroughly," said agent Fisk quietly, as he sipped his coffee. "There's nothing in your background to suggest that you could be a smuggler or a criminal."

"That doesn't mean you couldn't take to it," growled agent Byers. "If you are innocent of these crimes, it would be a breakdown of justice to convict you and send you away for twenty years in a Federal prison. Those prisons are very tough places. A guy like you wouldn't last long in any of those Hell holes. Not to mention the beatings and rapes in store for you in the meantime."

Agent Fisk glared intently at the terrified man, "There could be a way out for you, Mr. Bland."

"Tell me how," begged Bobby Lee, now in tears.

"By helping us," said Fisk, "If you play your cards right, Mr. Bland, you may beat the rap and go free."

"What do I have to do?" wailed Bobby Lee, distraught and trembling with fear.

"Keep your eyes open, remember all you hear and see and keep your mouth shut." said Fisk, "You will eventually have to testify. Then you will be helping us. Get a lawyer lined up and ready to stand up for you when we start arresting people. Here's my card. Call me if something really big occurs. Otherwise don't call me and don't bother me. Now go home."

An hour later Bobby Lee sat at the supper table with Sarah and Lester, who soon slipped away to the tiny living room for a TV program, almost certain to portray something about violence, car chases, murder or revenge. Bobby Lee was obviously stressed and needed to report his confrontation with the two Federal agents to Sarah.

The discussion lasted until the wee hours and included contemplation of strategies designed to keep Bobby Lee out of prison. Their decision was to swallow any resentment toward the Santanas and ask Jack for advice on what he could do to help then find a way out of this new crisis.

*   *   *

The meeting took place early the very next morning over coffee with Jack Santana. Lester was off to play a baseball game for his team the Rough Riders in the Babe Ruth league for boys age thirteen-to-fifteen. Lester's thirteenth birthday was imminent.

After Bobby Lee's best explanation of the smuggling accusation and the meeting with the two Federal agents, Jack Santana paused. "I have just the right attorney," said Jack, "his name is Nick Reamer. He's very experienced and a bull dog. He is not any more expensive than the rest."

"Jack, you know I can't afford to hire a lawyer. They charge an arm and a leg."

"Nick will want a retainer, probably about ten thousand. Then he'll bill for his time as we go along, maybe two or three hundred an hour."

"Oh my God," muttered Sarah.

Bobby Lee held his head in his hands and covered his eyes. "What have I gotten myself into? I didn't knowingly break any law for God's sake! Why is God doing this to me?" he cried.

"Calm down," said Jack. "I have some money set aside for emergencies. I'll take care of the expenses for now." Jack smiled. "What are brothers for?" There was unmistakable relief in the eyes of both of the Blands.

"I'll see how quickly we can get an appointment with Nicky. He owes me so I think he will meet with us very soon, so quit worrying. We are going to take care of it. Sometimes these cops, agents or whatever just exaggerate so they can bully people around a bit. Let's agree to put this aside for now. The issue is in good hands. Just trust me." Holding Bobby Lee and Sarah's gaze, Jack spoke in a firm confidential tone, "You both know about the background research I did on your families prior to contacting you?"

Both nodded, allowing their thoughts to turn away from threats of prison for the moment.

"Your father's older brother, Homer, has been identified by my researchers. He is eighty-nine, living as a widower after his fourth wife's death in Houston, Texas." Bobby Lee listened carefully, "He has amassed a fortune from his work among the big movers and shakers in the oil business. His assets, including oil stocks, securities, real estate and loads of cash, amount to almost sixty million. His brother Buford, your Dad, and you, Bobby Lee, are his only living blood relatives. Just a minute, I forgot myself, since I am a nephew just like you, of the same blood." Bobby Lee's eyes widened. "Uncle Homer," said Jack, "has terminal cancer. He will die in a few months. Does that suggest anything to you?"

Bobby Lee shook his head as if shaking off fleas, "We have to think about this," he said.

"Real hard," said Sarah.

"Think about it," said Jack. "There is more news from my research people. It's about your people, Sarah."

Sarah stiffened, "My people?" she asked.

"Have you ever heard of Isadore and Ruth Soloman?"

Sarah looked defiantly at Jack, "Who are they supposed to be?"

"They were your great grandparents on your Mother's side. They emigrated from Germany in 1902. Your great-grandparents on your Father's side emigrated from Poland in 1910. Their name was Goldman. Some years later they changed it to Coleman, your maiden name, Sarah. You should be proud of your ancestors who became citizens and made good in the American melting pot."

Bobby Lee gave Jack a steely stare, "Made good? What does that mean?"

"It means," said Jack quietly, "that those emigrants worked hard, paid their taxes, owned houses, cars, bank accounts, enjoyed their families and had money to spend. It means they achieved the American dream."

"Their names sound like they were all Jews!" Bobby Lee exclaimed.

"Maybe," said Jack, "with the same genes passed on from Jesus Christ, the greatest man who ever lived. Every Jewish person should swell with pride as should every Christian who worships His name and all He stood for."

Bobby Lee and Sarah abruptly turned and stomped

their way to the back door.

Together in the backyard cottage no words were spoken as Sarah prepared their pre-bedtime hot chocolate. Cups in hand, the two sat at the kitchen table and stared into each other's eyes. Bobby Lee's lips began to quiver. Soon tears appeared in both their eyes. Bobby Lee's voice trembled as he quietly spoke, "Sarah, you are a Jew."

"What counts," she whispered, "is that we love each other no matter what. You and I know that in our hearts we do."

He took her hands in his and looked up at the ceiling, his eyes glassy with tears, "You never told me about your real ancestry. Your parents were clever in covering it up."

"Didn't you ever suspect that my parents were Jewish?"

"When I think back," said Bobby Lee, "I may have suspected, but it was easy to put it aside because I was so taken with you back then."

A pause as they studied each other's faces. "Can you forgive me for being a secret Jew?" Sarah asked.

"You are a beautiful and loving Jewess," he said. "I will love you forever. Can you forgive me for being a stupid bigot?"

*   *   *

At breakfast on Sunday morning, Lester Bland seemed unusually animated. "Do you have a game today?" asked Sarah.

"Yes, Mom," Lester answered, unable to contain his glow.

"Do you like your new team?" inquired Bobby Lee.

Lester half-grinned and laughed. "Guess where I am in the batting order, Daddy?"

"Tell us," said Sarah.

"Third! Third, just like Babe Ruth, number three!"

Bobby Lee showed a broad smile, "That means you're their best hitter!"

Lester jumped out of his chair and demonstrated his batting stance. "I never had a good batting coach like Mr. Whitman. He got me to put more weight on my back foot, hold back my swing, use a lighter bat and shorten my stride. Now I am hitting line drives all over the field."

"Lester, that's great! We're so glad for you," smiled Sarah.

Lester demonstrated his new swing with an imaginary bat. "The game is at 2:00 p.m. today at lower Woodland Playfield!"

"Okay," said Bobby Lee, "after church and lunch, we'll watch the game. What position do you play on the team?"

"Short stop, Daddy, the coach tells me I am his best infielder."

* * *

At two a.m. Bobby Lee awoke and couldn't seem to get back to sleep. Thoughts swirled through his brain. *The one good thing is that Lester is happy playing baseball. Chances are he'll be just as happy when football and basketball start. Wait a minute, even better, Sarah and I have a deeper understanding. I wonder how long all that will last if I am about to be found guilty of smuggling and sent to some awful Yankee prison for twenty or thirty years. Those two Federal Agents are probably following me every place I go. In a short time we won't be able to use Antonio's car anymore so we have to borrow enough to buy an old beater just to get me to work and back. Now Jamal insists that we come to dinner at his house and meet his family. I'm starting to like the guy, but it makes me nervous. Imagine actually eating dinner at a colored guy's house. What would my mother and daddy say? Not only that, we can't allow ourselves to get closer to Brother Jack because of his disgusting friends, evolutionists, sodomists, blasphemists and who knows what else? The job at the store is going well but it will take forever to get ourselves out of debt even so. Then yesterday this phone call from hell. A guy named Vince Corio says he's the brother of Tina Corio from work. He says she's pregnant and traces it back to the night last month when I took her home from work and raped her in her own bedroom. This Vince guy says they are gonna file charges and have me sent to prison, this time for another fifteen or twenty years unless I pay them thirty thousand dollars to keep their mouths shut and get her a quick abortion. Abortion? I don't believe in abortion, but what the hell, even that would be better than having to support an illegitimate child for the rest of my life. Even if everyone else is lying, with my luck lately a jury would convict me for sure. I hate to ask him, but I think I have to get together with Jack. Maybe if I shared some of my problems with him he might be able to help. In spite of everything he's a pretty smart guy and very generous if I do say so. Maybe if I tried relaxing from the toes on up I could get back to sleep. Rape? God knows it was consensual. If anything, that Tina bitch raped me. What the hell more could happen to me?*

As usual, on Sunday morning, Jack Santana drove the Blands the two miles to the Aurora Pentecostal Church. Looking over at Bobby Lee sitting beside him in the front seat, Jack inquired, "How are things going for you at Bernstein's?"

"Very well, thanks to you, Jack, but there are some other matters I need to talk to you about."

"Yeah, it's about time we got together," said Jack. "How about tonight after dinner? Come over for dessert and we'll talk, okay?" Jack licked his spoon and smiled at Bobby Lee and Sarah. "Have you introduced yourself to the pastor?"

"Yes, his name is Otis Brunberg. We have met privately. We like him. He seems to have taken an interest in us."

"Do you mind if I contact him? I might want to ask him to write a letter on your behalf."

Sarah spoke up, "A letter to whom, Jack?"

Jack paused and gave the Blands a serious look, "You know that we have with all good intentions, probed into your family's ancestry and current social and economic status, right?" The Blands nodded with curious expressions. "Do you know anything about your Dad's older brother Homer?"

"Sorta," said Bobby Lee. "He's a dropout. He's a kind of a black sheep."

Jack blinked and scratched his chin as he spoke, "Uncle Homer lives in Houston, Texas. He is a multimillionaire in his eighties and he is dying of cancer. Also he has no living relatives either on his or his deceased former wives' side."

Sarah's eyes popped, "Are you suggesting that we ask him for money?"

Jack displayed another knowing smile, "We can discuss it can't we? What I want to find out, if I can do it in the proper way, is if Uncle Homer is intending to leave his fortune to his housekeeper or if he remembers his blood relatives upon his death."

"Which blood relatives are you referring to?" Bobby Lee looked accusingly at Jack, his blood brother.

"There are just three, our father Buford, you and me. You can take my word for it. It has been thoroughly researched. What we are unable to find out is what his will says. If, as we suspect, his family is not included, it may be because there has been no connection for so many years. If so, maybe he could be persuaded to demonstrate a proper family responsibility and cast an honorable aura on his soul at the time of his departure from this life. Bestowing his rightful heirs some of his millions would be of enormous assistance in their lives. He would be remembered forever with great gratitude and appreciation for a truly noble gesture. What do you think?"

Bobby Lee and Sarah sat transfixed, "You talk like a lawyer," said Sarah.

"Or like a college professor," murmured Bobby Lee. "I should call my Daddy today and see what he thinks."

As he stroked his chin, Jack Santana maintained his serious demeanor and spoke slowly, "I am suggesting that you and I and your father think seriously about contacting Uncle Homer and making our case. His money would serve a great purpose if he left some of it to you to provide security and a happy life for you and Lester into the future. Let's see if we can get Homer to meet with us and I will spring for the travel expenses."

"For Sarah, too?"

"We can decide as things move along," said Jack.

The next day at work, notwithstanding the emotional stress wearing him down, Bobby Lee consciously pushed his concentration to enhanced limits as he focused on his sales skills as never before. I have to lose myself in my work or I'll go nuts, he told himself. On two occasions he saw Tina Corio flash quickly by on the sales floor. She'll probably never look at me again, he thought. Even if she looks at me, her brother might just kill me. On the phone he sounded like the kind of guy who would do just that.

Two hours later while at lunch in a nearby pizzeria, his cell phone rang. "Hello, Brother," said Jack in an even tone, "Uncle Homer has responded to our email."

"What was his response?" asked Bobby Lee, between bites of cheese and pepperoni.

"I can hardly believe it. He wants to meet both of

us next Friday at his home in Houston. He has already talked to his brother Buford. They haven't seen each other in over fifty years. I'd sure like to know what they had to say to each other. Maybe Homer will include his brother, Buford, in his will after all. Maybe Homer's willingness to meet with us had something to do with the letter of recommendation I sent him from your Pastor. In any case, you need to take two days off work for personal business."

Bobby Lee felt his heart swell with hope. "I'll be ready to go on Friday morning, big brother," he chuckled.

The moment their taxi pulled up in front of the ostentatious Homer Bland mansion entrance, two black servants appeared. One of them opened the rear door and smiled brightly. "Welcome to Houston, gentlemen. May we help with your bags?"

"You bet," said Jack, "but I'll carry this package with me."

Decked out in dark suits, conservative ties and meticulously shined wing tip shoes, the blood brothers were led to what appeared to be a richly appointed den which could also be described as an office. Supporting himself by one hand clinging to his impressive desk, Homer Bland stood smiling, his right hand extended. "Ah'm very glad to see you both, gentlemen," he said in a warm Southern manner.

"It's a great pleasure, sir," they both responded. Appearing to the brothers as every bit as old as his eighty-nine years, he was obviously very ill as evidenced by a parchment complexion, sagging facial features and dark circles under the eyes. He stood about five-feet-nine and was a bit overweight at an estimated one-eighty. A few wisps of white hair were visible just above his ears, otherwise he was completely bald. His thick eyebrows were a mix of black and gray, while behind his round little eyeglasses, his eyes seemed to be very alert. They shone with intelligence and sharpness of perception.

"We brought a little something for you," said Jack, handing Homer a package neatly enveloped in gold wrapping paper. Homer quickly stripped away the wrapping revealing a cigar box on which large Spanish words identified the contents.

Homer peered closely and said, "Cuban cigarros. I'll be damned, genuine Cuban cigars! How did you know I have been yearning for some real Cubans? My favorite!"

"We can obtain them from Vancouver, British Columbia where they are legal," said Jack, flashing Bobby Lee a secretive look unnoticed by Uncle Homer.

"I'll start enjoying these later tonight. You fellers must have been researching me! Good work," he chuckled.

Homer tugged his left earlobe, "In order to get to know you better, I have studied the photos and letter from your pastor that I received yesterday. You both have very respectable looking families and you both are responsible appearing men. I have researched you both a little bit I will admit, so I am aware of your economic situations. Do you mind if I ask a few questions?"

"Of course not," they both assured their uncle.

"You are both sincere church-going Christians, are you not?" Both nodded enthusiastically. "Are you friendly with Negroes?" Both slowly nodded. "Do either of you have Jewish people as friends?" Both nodded cautiously. "What is your opinion about same sex marriage? I want to hear it."

"Despite the national trend to accept it," said Jack, "both Bobby Lee and I feel that a natural marriage must be between a man and a woman."

Homer gently rubbed the left side of his nose with his forefinger as his wide mouth turned up at the corners just a bit. "What about the abortion controversy, Bobby Lee?"

"It is against church teaching, sir, and I believe in scripture."

"Both of you, please call me Uncle Homer," the old man said with a smile. "Have you both learned a lot about the history of the 'War Between the States'?"

Both nephews responded, "Yes, of course, you bet, absolutely!"

"Then tell me how Yankee historians can justify Sherman's devastation of Southern civilian property in 1864 and '65."

Jack spoke, "No rational thinking person could justify Sherman's actions during the Civil War any more than any right thinking American could feel anything but shame over the Cherokee Trail of Tears in Andrew Jackson's time or the slaughter of Indians at Wounded Knee in the late 19th century."

Bobby Lee chimed in, "But that's past history, Uncle Homer. In hindsight it's much too easy to judge the actions of the military and the politicians from way back then when attitudes and beliefs were different."

Jack looked with some astonishment at Bobby Lee. How could those eloquent words come out of the mouth of his half-educated, good-ole-boy Mississippian brother? Then reflected: *Historians, especially Southern historians, have mostly ignored the abominably cruel conditions that existed at Andersonville Prison, Georgia during the war. Up to two-thirds of the Union prisoners died from neglect, disease and starvation. It was perhaps the worst scandal against the Confederacy during the entire Civil War.*

Uncle Homer shifted in his chair and spoke in a kind of low growl, "Here's my question Bobby Lee, if you received a financial windfall, exactly how would you spend it and how much would it take to fulfill your desires?"

His nephew gulped as he gathered his thoughts, "First I would put money in some safe investments so that there would be enough for my family no matter what might happen to me. Hopefully there would be money to cover college costs for my son Lester. If there was enough left over, I would start my own furniture store. I would buy a nice house in a good neighborhood. I would love to have a lifestyle that would allow time for me and the family to take part in some sort of charity like cancer or education for the poor or disabled."

Homer sat up a bit in his chair, "How much would it take?"

"I guess a million or two, I ain't real sure about that," replied Bobby Lee, softly.

Homer removed his eyeglasses and pointed them at Jack, "What about you, Jack?"

"I would adopt a similar procedure to protect my family. For the past few years I have had a dream of creating an organization that I believe would be of great benefit to millions of people. Starting such a program would require seed money of perhaps three or four million."

Homer's eyes narrowed as he stared at Jack, "What is your big idea?"

It was Jack's turn to swallow hard, "It would be a sustainable foundation for the purpose of ending homelessness in the USA. There are multiple problems when governments or community authorities, empty-headed politicians or unmotivated bureaucrats attempt to deal with those who have no homes and no place to turn. I am aware that there has been a good deal of money spent, with all good intentions, to solve the homeless problem. Mine is a startlingly new idea in how to deal with it. One, start with the biggest, widest perspective possible. Two, avoid bureaucracy by hiring well-paid, dedicated planners and administrators. Three, spend the money in the smartest way!"

Uncle Homer's expression hardened. Was he suffering great pain from the cancer racking his body at every moment, or was his face reflecting some kind of disapproval from the nephew's comments? "Okay," Uncle Homer said, as he seemed to choke down an unpleasant taste in his mouth, "Let's get down to business. The two long lost nephews never bothered to seek out their old uncle until they learned he is rich and about to die. Let's get in touch with him and see if we can get our hands on his money! So that's what this is all about, right? Bobby Lee Bland and black Jack Santana, a Latino name and a Roman Catholic to boot! It's apparent that you boys have rehearsed all your comments. Did you really think that you could fool the old uncle? You are dealing with a wise old Texas warrior, winner of many hard battles that the two of you can't even imagine. In my will I have designated some very worthwhile entities as my heirs. There are a number of them. Here are a couple I know you will approve of, The National Lodge of the Sons of the Confederacy, the Southern Baptist Church, and Princess, my favorite cat! Now, I think we are finished so you can suck up the snot in your noses and go back to no-man's land in the frozen north and play your con games."

*   *   *

The plane ride home was uneventful but provided a chance for a quiet conversation between the blood brothers. Throughout the flight, Bobby Lee continued to express disappointment about the unfortunate ending to their visit with Uncle Homer.

"We might look at it this way," said Jack, "for most of his life, Uncle Homer has been involved in the oil business, a risky high-powered, stressful competitive scramble for success. People in big business must continually look over their shoulder to avoid being outmaneuvered or cheated. He probably never had time for humanitarian interests or concern for the bigger problems of life outside of the exploitation and greed so typical in the world of Big Oil and everything connected with it. I think our lifestyle and ways of thinking made Homer kind of uncomfortable. It could be that now, at the end of his life, he has missed out on things that would have been of more importance. I suspect that, even aware of the fact that we are interested in an undeserved inheritance, he actually started to like us, but couldn't bear the thought of acceding to the wishes of two strangers."

Bobby Lee looked thoughtful, "I have to think about that. I do think that we aren't really a couple of scoundrels. We gave it a good honest try."

"Speaking of scoundrels," said Jack, "it's time for me to confess, but first I want to buy you a stiff drink." When the Southern Comfort whiskey arrived, Jack offered a toast to his brother as they both lifted their cocktail glasses.

Bobby Lee smacked his lips, enjoying the taste, and said, "I wonder if it's true that alcohol works faster at thirty thousand feet?"

"I'm counting on it." said Jack, "I don't think you realize that when I first got in touch with you a few months ago, I had an ulterior motive."

Bobby Lee sipped his drink, "An ulterior motive, such as?"

Jack's expression sharpened, "It was part of my plan to get some of Uncle Homer's money. My researchers had the Bland family thoroughly investigated, don't you know? I found out that Homer was stinking rich with no family and dying of cancer. I figured that getting together with you was the key. Then I learned about your difficulties and the timing seemed right for me to get in touch with you and put my plan into action. Helping you get settled and find a job was a pretty good thing all the way around. It was I who got those other people to put pressure on you so that you needed Homer's money as badly as I wanted it. I'm sure you won't soon forget our cast of characters: Marco Nosich and Rex Lang are the real thing but Stan Tulley and Lenny Ross were phony US Marshals. Then there were Tina Corio and her brother Vincent. I should include Nicky, the part-time bartender at the Edmond Meany hotel who was the fictitious lawyer on the telephone. I hired them all."

Bobby Lee choked a bit after a big gulp of his Southern Comfort, turned red and gasped, "I can't believe this. Is this your idea of a joke?"

Jack's face was grim, "It's not a joke and I want you to know that my motive was to acquire a large sum of money to start my Homeless Foundation. I'm telling you the truth from my inner heart. I can't blame you, Bobby Lee, if you never forgive me."

"I need another drink," sputtered Bobby Lee Bland.

"Let's look at some of the positives," soothed Jack. "You have a pretty good job at something you're great at, you've managed to rent a house in an adjacent neighborhood nearby in the 'U' district and your wife has a part-time job at a nearby drugstore. You have been able, in a short time, to buy a used car and things are looking up economically with better things to come."

Bobby Lee studied the whiskey in his glass, "Lester is happy playing sports," he whispered.

"And from now on," Jack declared, "whatever you decide to do, the pressure is off. No threats of prison or extortion."

"I was awfully worried," Bobby Lee mumbled.

*   *   *

The party at Jack and Molly Santana's house was scheduled for Saturday afternoon and evening. The usual supply of liquor and hors d'oeuvre supplemented the conversations between the talkative, thirsty and gregarious guests. Lester Bland found himself in a lively conversation about baseball with Rex Lang. Sarah was comparing opinions about the newest fashion trends with Tina Corio. Vincent Corio was involved in an all-important conversation about some recent mechanical recalls on certain Japanese cars with Lenny Ross, Marco Nosich and Stan Tulley. As everyone was enjoying cocktails, Jack and Molly made the rounds, making sure they all were acquainted enough to enjoy some jokes and gentle teasing, most frequently at Jack's expense. 'This is great,' thought Jack, 'everyone is laughing, telling stories and having a good time.'

"Dinner is served!" announced Molly. "It's a little early in the afternoon, but you have eaten all the snacks and half the booze," she said with a laugh, "so I think it's time to eat!" The catered dinner was wonderful as usual, as everyone ate a bit too much.

During the entrée course the phone rang and Molly answered, "It's for you, Jack," she called from the kitchen.

"I'll take it in there," he said, and headed for his study. The call kept him longer than he would have wished. He could not get away for almost ten minutes. Returning to the dinner table, Jack felt a little unsteady. Under his breath he asked himself, *Am I in shock?*

Molly looked closely at him and quietly asked, "Are you okay, Jack? You look kind of flushed."

"I'm alright, just a bit stunned." Jack stood and in his professor's voice, spoke, "While you enjoy your dessert, please let me have your attention. We have invited you here so that I may get something off my conscience and also offer you my profound thanks. I think most of you know about my scheme during the past few months. I was attempting, in a roundabout way, to acquire funding for my heartfelt plan to eliminate the homeless problem in the United States. In this attempt I did an unpardonable thing. I used the Bland family, without their knowledge, to try to gain access to the Bland family fortune. This is not only unethical, but should be illegal as well. I have discussed this with the Blands and have offered my abject apology. My profound thanks are due to the rest of you who submitted to my requests for each of you to act out the various actors' roles I assigned to you. You all turned out to be talented performers."

Laughter interrupted for a few moments. "You were pretty good yourself, Jack!" somebody shouted. More laughter.

"I must tell you now about my phone call of a few minutes ago from Homer's attorney, Wendell Dugan, calling from his office in Houston, Texas. Our Uncle Homer Bland passed away two days ago. It turns out that Bobby Lee and I were mentioned in Homer's most recent will. There was a hushed silence as everyone sat up and leaned forward. "Bobby Lee and I will be receiving checks within the next few days." Bobby Lee sat completely stunned. "Homer left five to Bobby Lee and ten to me."

"Five and ten what?" yelled Antonio.

Jack breathed one word, just loud enough for everyone to hear, "Million".

The applause was deafening, accompanied by a few whistles and screams of joy. "Wait!" one of the men yelled, "What happens next?"

Uncharacteristically, Jack was trembling with emotion and joy as he spoke. "Next, I begin communication with other prospective donors and start selecting my staff of administrators and organizers. There will be salaried positions for each of you if you are interested. By the way, have I paid everybody for your recent participation on our Homer Bland project?" Disregarding a few chuckles, Jack continued, "Also, starting now, I intend to stop using hair straightener and let my hair grow. Maybe I can hope for a modified afro." Jack couldn't restrain a laugh along with several others at the table. "As you might expect, my progress will be closely monitored by Homer's trust-administrator." Gesturing toward Bobby

Lee, Jack asked, "It may not be any of our business, Bobby Lee, but now that your wish is coming true, will you be headed back to Mississippi? What's next for you and your family?"

Bobby Lee stood and perused the group. Still dazed by the life changing revelations from the past few minutes, Bobby Lee spoke with sincerity, although in a shaky voice. "During the past few months some of you at this table succeeded in scaring the devil out of me and Sarah, but I think these past experiences have made me a better person. The closeness and support from the Santana family has been an education and inspiration for Sarah, Lester and me especially. I have to tell you, Brother Jack, that the very next thing we will do is accept a dinner invitation at Jamal Jefferson's home. I am also going to offer Jamal a partnership in my new furniture store business wherever I decide to get it started in the Seattle area. I'm growing up a bit, thanks to you, Antonio, Suling, Molly and Jack, my wonderful black brother. As for moving back to Mississippi, well, we've thought about it a lot and made comparisons."

At that point Sarah rose and stood beside her husband and joined in. "It's hard to leave your lifelong family, friends and old regional traditions, but you have to consider where your happiness seems to lie. We have admired the culture hereabouts and truly take to the remarkable people. They are, well," Bobby Lee interrupted, "so pleasantly diversified. We're staying here, right here, at home in Seattle."